Prodigal

Steve Malley

DEDICATION

This book is for Hazel, my moon and stars.

And for Charlotte, who started a whole new chapter.

FRIDAY NIGHT

THE DINER SAT abandoned on the county line. Lights glowed in the distance, but here the lot was dark. Weeds grew up through cracks in the asphalt. The old lighted sign was bullet-pocked and burned out. Scrawls of spray paint covered the weathered plywood nailed over the windows.

The Atlanta PD squad car rolled across the lot with a soft crunching sound. It stopped inches from the four wheel drive's front bumper. The two cops got out, circled around to the back. Both kept their hands on the butts of their guns.

One of the cops opened the rear door and pulled Kira out. The summer night was a soft kiss on her cheeks and throat. It felt good after the air-conditioned chill of disinfectant and vomit in the back of the squad car. The sights and smells of a Georgia summer night closed around her.

They unhooked her wrists, dropped a shapeless black bag at her feet. Their footsteps crunched on the broken asphalt behind her.

The cruiser's doors shut. The transmission thunked as the car dropped into reverse. The cops left the lot without another word.

"I hope they weren't too hard on you," the Sheriff said. Her accent was like the piney woods around them.

Kira rubbed at her wrists. Her hands burned as the blood came back into them. Homeland Security had pulled her out of line at Customs, left her chained to a rack of chairs for two hours. The cops who came for her were hard eyed men in thick soled shoes, buzzcuts and black Atlanta PD uniforms. They hooked Kira's hands behind her back, marched her through the airport and stuffed her into the squad car. The drive out had been another two hours.

"Didn't figure it was personal," Kira said. Four hours back, and she could already hear Southern vowels creeping back in.

"I knew you were coming, figured you might need a ride. Must have been some sort of mixup."

"Must have."

The Sheriff was a small hard-boned woman with a lined face and a bruise at the corner of her mouth. She stood straight and kept one thumb hooked over the butt of her nightstick.

Kira looked away from her and into the night sky. The woods at the edge of the lot were alive with crickets. Somewhere in the distance a whippoorwill gave voice to its lonesome call.

"You didn't mix it up with those city boys, did you?"

The Sheriff gestured at Kira left hand. The knuckles were scabbed and raw. Or she might have meant the split lip. Both were a couple days old and halfway healed.

"They didn't give me any trouble," Kira said. "When'd they close this place, anyway? Burgers were always pretty good here."

"Climb in. I'll give you a ride the rest of the way."

Kira hesitated.

"Up front."

The Sheriff drove a brown and white four wheel drive with a light rack and county decals on the side. After so many years outside The States the SUV seemed enormous, almost cartoonish.

Kira crossed to the passenger side and climbed in. The seat was soft and gave off a synthetic leather smell when she lowered her weight into it. A police scanner made soft sounds in the center of the dash. Taped above it, a frayed cardboard prayer card.

The Sheriff keyed the ignition and flipped on the headlights. The planes and lines of her face were green in the dashboard light.

"You have a good flight?"

Kira pushed dark hair out of her eyes and didn't answer. The older woman dropped the gear shift into Drive and rolled out of the lot.

"You know, I'm sorry they got wrong idea at the airport, but I'm not surprised."

"I'd heard security got tighter after 9/11."

"I mean, look at you. They probably thought you were a drug mule."

Kira looked across.

The Sheriff rubbed her thumb across the bruise on her mouth.

"That wasn't fair," she said. "You've had a hard couple days. We all have."

"Don't worry about it."

"You okay for money?"

"I'm fine."

The glare of the SUV's headlights showed two lane blacktop. A couple turns later, the road was a single lane of deep orange clay.

The Sheriff took the back ways, the old smugglers' roads. She drove with one hand on the wheel, guiding them through twisting country darkness.

"You know, lots of folks round here didn't figure they'd ever see you again," she said.

"Wasn't my plan either."

"Gotta be honest with you, Kira. Lot of em liked it that way."

"It's only a week."

"The Atlanta PD boys did mention you had a round trip ticket on you. They also said you were traveling under your mother's name."

Kira thumbed the switch to lower the window. Hot damp air flowed into the cab. She didn't mind. She'd had enough recycled and conditioned air.

The Sheriff looked over but said nothing.

After a time the 4x4 pulled into a rutted drive, mica-flecked gravel and pale orange soil. High-beam headlights splashed over peeling paint and grass gone to seed.

The house was dark and empty. But they both knew that.

The Sheriff stopped Kira before she hit the door handle. The woman's fingers on her arm were small and bony and blast furnace hot.

"Memory goes back a long ways around here," she said. "You need to keep that in mind."

"I'm here to bury my brother. That's all."

"Just try to stay out of trouble."

SATURDAY

KIRA WOKE CRAMPED and stiff. Curled up, her face stuck to the couch.

Alone in the dark, she felt disconnected from reality. Her body clock told her it was morning, but out the windows dawn was just a distant hope.

Her eyes were puffy and wet. The shirt in her arms still carried her brother's scent. Alone in the dark, it still seemed possible her brother might walk in from another part of the house.

The house itself was a hundred years old. Built by her great-grandfather, on the site of another, older place. Stones had lived here, generation after generation. Moving back, Jack was filling an old tradition.

She didn't know if he cared about traditions. Truth was, she didn't know much about him at all.

He'd never been much of a brother. Too many years between them. He went from older boy who never wanted his kid sister tagging along to rare visitor, a weekend here and there while he was stationed at Fort Benning. And then not even that. Total absence.

Still, Jack was the only brother she had. The last family she had left in this world.

Kira wiped her eyes with the back of one wrist. She put down her brother's shirt and straightened from the spot on the couch where she'd fallen asleep. Her feet made soft whispering pats on the smooth pine boards.

Her grandfather's Colt sat on the dining table. It was a long-barreled .45 revolver, the bluing worn from a lifetime riding on his hip. She touched the walnut grips, the tooled leather holster. A cardboard box of soft-nosed cartridges sat open on the table. She picked up one of the bullets, rolled it between finger and thumb. Jack must have had the gun out before he left. No way to know that drive would be his last.

She supposed she should be grateful. Jack was her last tie to this place.

These memories.

This life.

Once she laid him down in the family plot up the hill, there'd be no reason to ever return.

The pipes shuddered and groaned when she turned the taps. Water came, thick, opaque and pungent before it finally ran clear. The inside of the fridge was black and warm and smelled of mold, but there was coffee in the cupboard. The yellow and black can was a brand Kira hadn't seen in a decade.

She lit the gas ring on the stove and dropped a couple of scoops in the range top pot.

Just one week.

There didn't seem much point fighting the jet lag.

AN OLD HURRICANE lantern hung from a nail just inside the machine shed. The corners of the shed itself were a jumble of family history: the lantern's light fell on rusted farm implements from the days of horse and mule, parts for cars whose makers no longer existed and coils and coils of copper tubing gone green with verdigris.

The light from the lamp was dim, but Kira was able to find the spare filters buried on the dusty shelves, their cardboard containers faded and unreadable. As the first first red light streamed through the gaps where the wood had warped in the barn's eastern wall, the last drops of black sludge ran into a stained plastic tub.

Kira tightened the drain plug back on with a wrench and poured in fresh oil. She emptied what she insisted on thinking of as twenty liters of diesel into the fuel tank and hit the switch.

The generator rumbled into life on the third try. It wouldn't be long before the refrigerator started to cool and there would be enough power stored in the rack of car batteries to keep it running overnight.

She felt a flush of fierce pride. As a little girl she'd held these wrenches for her father. Now she'd done the job herself, something no one in her life right now— her real life— would have imagined.

Outside, with the generator and its noise behind a closed door, Kira cleaned her hands with an already oily rag. The sun was warm on her shoulders, her shadow a long dark arrow pointing at the house.

It was the first chance she'd had to actually see the old place. The front porch of the house sagged in the middle, and the barn's roofline had a dip in its spine. Not one part of either building stood at right angles to any other, like the only thing holding the timbers up was that they'd been leaning together so long.

The peach tree she remembered from her childhood was all but dead, and in the fields every growing thing was bleached the color of straw or burned yellow and brown. Last night's dew was already burning away, a fine halo of rising steam.

The place was a dump.

Back in the house she stripped and threw her clothes in a thirty year old Kenmore. There was power now to run the washing machine, and what she'd been wearing was filthy.

Something strangely naughty about walking naked through her childhood home. Her home now, she supposed. It didn't change that feeling, like her father or stepmother might pop out from behind a doorway and tell her to put on some clothes.

No hot water. It would be hours before the cylinder heated. An hour after dawn and the summer heat was already bad enough she didn't really mind.

Rummaging through her pack, she wished she'd had a chance to think about what she brought.

When she got the news she'd been staying with friends— friends of friends really— at a villa outside of Portofino. The clothes in her bag were bikinis and lingerie and cocktail dresses. Party clothes. The sort of thing you wore when you were going to stay drunk for a week or a month, not really wearing very much at all.

In truth, it was all she owned.

She finally settled on a wine-colored sundress. The skirt was too high and the neckline too low, but it was more modest than most of what she'd brought. The Italian Riviera was a world away from rural Georgia.

No car, of course. Jack had been driving their father's black Charger, and their grandfather's legendary pickup sat rusting in the barn on four flat tires.

When Kira lifted the hood, she saw that mice and squirrels had made nests in the engine bay. She left the nests undisturbed, shut the hood and started walking.

The landscape of her childhood was scorched and barren. Sky the color of curdled milk, sun as hot and bright as a naked flame. The air smelled of dry decay, and snakes of heat rose from the earth in front of her. Leaves hung wilted on trees, and the only cow she saw in the neighbor's pasture lay in what little shade there was, ribs showing through its hide, beset by flies.

Everything was covered in a fine and dusty grit.

The stream that ran west of the house was a wet patch in a twisting ribbon of mud. The water rang and jangled where it ran through a pipe under the road.

The road itself was rough red clay. A lane and a half wide at most. Humped in the center, rough ditches at the shoulder. Three centuries of one wheel or another following the curve of the earth.

Sweat gathered between her shoulder blades. Orange dust puffed around her feet as she walked.

Half a mile down, the road turned into a sharp curve. A ragged ugly hole in the brush and two tire-racked gouges in the embankment were the only marker.

The edges of Kira's sandals crumbled the clay as she stepped out onto the edge.

The track of torn and trampled undergrowth ended at the base of a lone beech, its trunk black and scarred.

A lone bobwhite called. Crickets chirped. Somewhere at the bottom of the gorge, tree frogs rose in winking chorus.

Kira stood with the sun on her shoulders and her face in shadow. By next spring, the land would heal.

But she'd still have this hole where she used to have a brother.

Kira blinked until her eye were clear. She wiped her cheeks with the back of one wrist and watched a lone turkey buzzard drifting on a thermal in the distance. As she stood, two more joined. And another pair. Circling, wheeling above the trees below.

Something out there was dead. Or dying.

In this place, it was hard to believe much had ever been alive.

Deep burble of engine, soft scrutch of tires. Kira turned.

A gleaming yellow Corvette rolled up alongside, chrome winking in the morning sun. The arm resting on the doorsill was hairless and smooth, tanned and muscular. The watch on the wrist was a TAG Hauer, chunky and gleaming.

The driver's face was boyish and merry, with eyes like bright glass and the first faint hints of lines creased pale in the soft browned flesh.

"Not exactly dressed for this place, are you," he said.

Kira pushed a tangle of hair out of her eyes and cocked her head to one side. The driver smiled, a quick wide flash of wolfish teeth.

"You don't recognize me, do you?"

"Any reason I should?"

"Aw now…" The man behind the wheel shook his head and chuckled. "You're breaking my heart, Kee."

Kira squinted. Memory snapped and bit: a wide-eyed little kid with dirty hair and holes in his jeans.

"Hap?"

"Got it in one." The smile flashed again. "What on earth are you doing up so early?"

"What're you doing here?"

"Looking for you, of course. You weren't back to the house, I figured you'd be headed into town."

He looked her up and down and the wolf's smile flashed again. Under its hood, the Corvette growled.

"Give all them church ladies heart attacks from the look of it. Hop in."

Kira took a step back and shook her head.

"Come on Kee, I won't bite. Not unless you ask."

"How'd you know I was here?"

Hap''s face stiffened. His brows lowered, and in the bright summer sunlight his skull pooled with shadow.

"It ain't like that," he said. "Daddy does want to see you, but just to offer his condolences."

Kira turned on one heel and started walking. The clay road was rough and cracked. The yellow sportscar idled alongside, soft top down.

"Come on now, Kira." Hap said. "All that's a long time ago. Daddy said it himself, forgive and forget."

Her silent look burned with contempt.

"Look, okay, we didn't even know for sure you were gonna be back by now, but everyone's been talking about it. I just figured, you did come back, I knew you wouldn't have a car or nothing."

Kira looked at his hands and his shoulders and felt a brief twist of speculation.

In Europe, men like him and cars like that were part of her life. More often than not, she had taken the rides they offered.

"Come on, you still got miles into town. At least let me buy you breakfast."

She stopped. The Corvette rumbled past her. Stopped. Rolled slowly backward. Hap leaned across the passenger seat and flashed those blinding teeth.

"What do you say, Kee?"

Kira looked up and down the length of the dirt road. The place where her brother had come off was no longer visible. The road ahead turned out of sight, following the curve of the hill.

The sun's heat was a slap against her skin.

"How is Bobby anyway? Nobody ever told me."

Blood rose in Hap's throat and darkened his face. His eyes glittered cold murder.

THE TOWN SQUARE was a battered version of Kira's memories. Dust obscured the sidewalks, and the leaves of the hundred year old magnolias were spotted with black mold.

There were seven of the trees, gnarled trunks and twisted limbs. There had been eight when she left. As a girl she remembered those trees thick with blooms all spring and summer, the air beneath them cool and fragrant.

Heat, drought and disease had taken their toll. The few flowers she saw were the color of corpses, and their perfume smelled like damp sponges and bad funerals.

The bronze statue in the center of the square was green with verdigris and white with bird droppings. Colonel Beauregard Harrow was supposed to be contemplating the sad waste of half a million war dead. To Kira, it had always looked like he was trying to get someone to pull his finger.

The courthouse was red brick and white limestone. A style she hadn't seen in over a decade.

The east wing had a wall rougher than the others. Its bricks were misshapen and weathered, obviously kilned by hand. That wall was part of the original structure, the only thing left standing after Sherman's March.

Behind that wall the Sheriff had her offices. The green and brown SUV was already parked out front.

The Bluebird was still going. Nothing like the crowds she remembered, but at least it was one of the few businesses around the square without plywood over the windows.

She stopped a moment. The magnolias blocked the sun, but their shade did not cool.

For some reason, being this close to the Bluebird brought it all home. It had been a favorite part of her childhood. For the whole of her adult life, cafes were places with bright awnings and tables out on the cobblestones. Places where waiters wore long aprons and the only English was spoken by tourists.

All that time, the Bluebird and places like it existed only in her memory. Being back like this, it was like being in some shabby amusement park, built to her memory but with all the details wrong.

It was unreal.

Bells jangled above the door as Kira entered. She stepped into stale air and the smell of grease. Staring eyes and a fall of silence.

Overhead fans thropped in slow circles. A single fly buzzed its own curving path through the silence.

The figure at the grill was big and blocky. Rolls of fat at the back of the neck, upper arm like a boiled ham.

He looked over his shoulder, set the long-bladed spatula down in the grease trough.

"Kira Stone…"

Another swim of memory: a face from the days when she ran with Bobby Taylor. One of those who laughed at his jokes, ran for his beer, and scraped what he could from whatever Bobby didn't want.

Matt, that was the name.

She wondered if her whole week would be names from her past. Hearing her own name spoken with that sense of presumed knowledge.

The years had not been kind. She remembered a bad drunk, a mean son of a bitch. A football player who used his size to get what he wanted. The man before her turned with a pained hitch and shuffle. His right arm was withered and skeletal, curled against his chest.

When he turned to face her, the eye on that side was a white marble nested in scar tissue, sightless and blind.

"We don't want trouble."

"Good to see you too." She shifted to take in the room. A handful of old men hunched over their plates and ignored her presence.

"Good to see all of you," she said. "A real warm welcome."

"I mean it now, Kira. No trouble."

"Just coffee."

Kira took a vacant stool at the counter. The vinyl was cool against the backs of her thighs. She felt a gummy seam where a strip of duct tape had folded at its edge. The fly buzzed past her head.

On either side of her, two men in gimme caps dropped worn dollar bills on the counter and left.

Matt picked a ceramic cup from a stack and set it in front of her. Filled it from a glass coffee pot and dropped packets of non-dairy creamer on the counter.

"Guess I ought to tell you, I'm real sorry about your loss. You know, Jack and all."

Kira flashed to that lone beech, the litter of broken glass around it like diamonds.

"Don't suppose you're back for good?" he said.

She looked up from under the tangle of her hair.

"Probably best." He wiped fluid from his injured eye with the back of one knuckle. "What'll you have?"

She looked down at the black liquid sloshing in the cup. The thin skin of rainbow color on its surface.

"I don't suppose you do a fruit cup?"

Now it was Matt's turn to answer her with a look.

"Know how to make an omelet?"

The last patron at the counter got up and left.

"Something I said?"

"Memories go back a long way around here, I guess." Matt's left hand was thick and wide. When he wiped it on his apron it left a sour sweaty smear. "Or maybe it's just two Stones, coming back so close together."

Kira's eyes moved over the room. A man in overalls and a woman in a housedress dropped their faces back to their plates.

"My brother wasn't dead, I'd still be back where I belong and he could have this whole damn town to himself, forever Amen."

The fly touched the back of Kira's hand and launched itself away.

A CHIPPED PLATE, greasy food steaming, had just clacked down on the counter in front of Kira when Hap Taylor came into the Bluebird.

A small crowd of rough types crowded through behind him. The last diners hustled out the door.

Kira didn't look up. She appeared to devote all her attention to using the bent and spotted cutlery in her hands.

"Daddy really wants to see you, Kee."

"The old man always get what he wants?"

One of Taylor's rough types, a dark and angular man with a beard and a bald spot, plunked down on the stool beside her. The other two stayed behind Hap.

Kira cut a bite-sized wedge from her eggs and added some bacon to the fork. As she chewed, Hap's reflection shifted uneasily in the chromed surface of the napkin dispenser. The men behind Hap didn't move.

"He just wants to talk a minute."

Kira's fork and knife clinked against the plate as she tried another bite. The eggs were rubbery but the bacon was just right. One thing Europeans just didn't seem to get, a good slice of bacon.

On the other side of the counter, Matt scraped down the grill, now apparently blind and deaf.

"I don't see what all the fuss is about," the man next to Kira said. A gold tooth flashed when he spoke. "She don't look that tough to me."

Kira stopped a moment, a forkful of the bacon halfway to her mouth. The stranger's eyes flicked from her scraped knuckles back to her face, hot and mocking.

"Ain't you just the cutest little bitty thing," he said. "Now why don't you come and walk out to the car before we have to drag you out?"

Kira pulled the meat from her fork with her teeth.

"I'm sorry, Kee," Hap said. "He's new."

"That was all a long time ago."

"You know, I do believe you got a little something on your chin."

One rough thumb touched the line of Kira's jaw. Her hands left vapor trails in the greasy air.

The stranger's face struck the counter with a loud and sudden crash of bone and meat.

Salt and pepper shakers jumped and rattled. Kira's food leapt on its plate. A jar of sugar fell and shattered.

She released the stranger's hair and wiped her hand on the back of his shirt. A fan-shaped spatter of blood lay bright on the countertop.

On the street outside, the Sheriff and two large deputies were moving fast across the street. Kira raised up on her palms until she could see down to the place on the floor where Matt crouched.

"You're done down there, do me a favor and wrap up my breakfast? I'm going to want it to go."

The Sheriff stopped just inside the doorway. She stood with her back stiff and her chin high. The pistol on her hip was a pearl-handled black Sig Sauer.

It had been a Christmas gift from Kira's father, long ago.

"Goddammit, Kira—"

"No trouble at all."

On the floor, the stranger tried to push to his feet and fell back with a clatter. Kira flashed Hap Taylor her sweetest smile.

"Hap and I were just on our way out to see his daddy." She took a step forward. The men around Hap took a step back.

"After that," she said, "Hap here is going to take me on out to the funeral home. I want to see my brother."

The Sheriff stood face to face with Kira in the doorway. A knot of muscle worked in the corner of the hard-boned skull. After a long beat, she narrowed her eyes and let the younger woman pass.

TAYLOR WAS AN ANCIENT spider in a white linen suit. He sat at the head of a once-beautiful table, in a room of dust and shadows and cobwebs.

The dining room lay at the center of the crumbling plantation house. It was a vast space, two stories tall. Along the railed walkway, dim figures stirred in the gloom.

Before him, ornate chafing dishes piled high with eggs, bacon, sausage, toast. The steam rising from the food was fragrant and appetizing. Two empty glasses sat on a tarnished silver tray, the pitcher of iced tea between them sweating in the heat.

His eyes sat deep in the shadows of his face. His skin was waxy and deeply lined. His smile when Kira entered the room was wet and red and wicked.

"My dear, so good to see you. Terrible shame about the circumstances, of course."

Kira said nothing. The room was the temperature of a morgue drawer, and a faint smell of rot hung in the air. She wished she'd worn something that left less of her skin bare.

"I'll have one of the boys set you a place." His fingers crawled toward a small bell.

"I'm not hungry."

His shrug was small and eloquent. Sophisticated. He reached once more for the bell.

Its sound was small and sweet. At odds with the house in which it rang. The last silvery note still faded in the air when a hard-muscled man with flat eyes and prison tattoos cleared the food onto a small cart. The tray and glasses remained. He looked a silent question at the old man.

"Go on, it's fine. Miss Stone and I have a lot of catching up to do, so I'm not to be disturbed."

He dismissed the convict with a casual flick of his bony fingers and slid his eyes to his youngest son.

"But—" Hap said.

"Just go, boy." The same dismissive flick, and Kira felt the young man stiffen beside her.

The father's eyes stayed on Kira's face. His gaze was hooded and glittering, and his mouth made a small amused shape as he listened to the muffled stomp of his son's retreating footsteps.

"Children these days," he said. "Sweet tea?"

"No thank you."

"Beer or wine perhaps?"

Kira shook her head no. The hunger in the old man's eyes threatened to devour her.

"You don't mind me pointing this out..." She swallowed before she spoke again. "This is all pretty different from the last time we talked."

"That was all so long ago. They say time heals all wounds, but that is not entirely correct."

Taylor sighed, the sound hollow and rattling.

"Time is a thief, Kira. It steals everything, even our anger. And at a certain point it has stolen enough, we cling to the little that remains."

"How is Bobby?"

The old man's dark and rubbery lips flattened. His eyes narrowed. Like a cloud passing over a hillside, the expression was there and gone.

"My sympathies for your own loss. I gather you and your brother were not altogether close."

"You brought me out here to tell me that?"

Taylor's mouth, wet and red, curled at the corners.

"I understand you lack transport. Feel free to pick up something from behind the barn."

"Have Sheriff Roberts catch me in a stolen car? No thanks."

"I'll have Hap sort something. A young woman needs her independence."

"Really, you don't—"

"You have sufficient money?"

"I'm fine."

"You'll allow me to pay the funeral expenses, of course."

"Why on earth would I do that?"

"At one time, Miss Stone, I was quite close to your parents. And to your older brother. Jack's passing, it's almost as though I lost my own son."

"Did you kill him?"

"I beg your pardon?"

"He left our grandfather's Colt out on the table. And there's an axe handle propped by the door. He was expecting trouble."

"And you suspect me."

Kira didn't answer this. She didn't have to.

"Miss Stone, your brother had nothing to fear from me." Subtle twist on the word brother. Letting her know. "His death was a tragedy, and an accident."

He gestured to the pitcher of tea on the silver tray.

"So much of your mother about you," he said,"but you have your father's eyes. Perhaps you'd be so kind as to pour me a glass?"

Kira hesitated, reached for the pitcher. Condensation beaded and ran down its sides and left a wet ring in the blackened scrollwork off the silver tray.

The empty glass cooled in her fingers as she poured. The iced tea held the room's muted light like liquid amber.

She set the tea in front of Taylor. Looked a moment at the crystalline depths of the pitcher's contents and licked her lips. The motion was involuntary, scarcely conscious. Cubes of ice cracked and shifted, rattled and banged against the sides of the glass.

Taylor drank noisily and dabbed his mouth with a square of folded handkerchief.

"Miss Stone… Kira, I thank you. Sometimes it seems as though a good glass of sweet tea is all that sustains me. The lifeblood of the South."

"I haven't had it in years," she said.

"No, you wouldn't."

Another drink, long and noisy. Color rose in his cheeks. For the first time, Kira saw that the high-backed chair he sat in had wheels at the sides.

"This house was once your grandfather's, did you know? Your grandfather Asa, on the Harrow side. I think he was rather sad to see it go."

Taylor raised his glass and peered into its amber depths.

"I still use the wall safe he concealed in the master bedroom. Every time I turn those dials, it gives me a warm feeling… Everything that man once valued is now mine."

The glass tipped again, and the old man drank it down. His lips trembled against the rim of the glass, and brown liquid ran down the sides of his mouth.

Kira was left to wonder: her mother's father had died almost thirty years ago. Taylor still carried the grudge.

"Well?" he said at length. "Aren't you the least bit curious as to why I wanted to see you?"

Kira shifted, uncomfortable She looked at the parquet floor between her feet.

"I can guess."

"I wonder."

She lifted her chin. Straightened her back.

"All due respect, I'm in the lion's den here. You're going to tell me what you want, or you won't. All I can say is, I'm only here a week. Once I bury Jack, I'm out of here."

The old man's eyes were sharp, and full of light. Among the dust and the shadows and the cobwebs, they were the jeweled eyes of some ancient and terrible idol.

The room around them, what had once been a ballroom, was cold and still. For a dozen heartbeats, the only sound was the tick-tick-tick of the old man's fingernails on the surface of the table.

"I'll speak to Hap about that car."

The long fingers enveloped the silver bell. Its bright tones rang in the dusty silence.

Taylor's tongue, small and pointed and colorless, pushed at his bottom lip. His upper lip pulled away from long brown teeth.

KIRA REELED FROM the door into daylight.

The day had built to a merciless heat. She stood in the full glare of that sun gulping lungful after lungful of blast furnace air. The great gray bulk of the old plantation house loomed behind her, ancient oaks and pecan trees shrouding its walls in perpetual shadow.

She breathed deep the smells of dust and earth and dead brown grass. She felt the sunlight on her face and chest and shoulders. She looked back at the house and shuddered.

"Daddy does have that effect on people." The voice from over Kira's shoulder gave her a start.

"State senators to stone killers," Hap Taylor said, "most folks come out of that house are pretty darn glad about it."

"Always the chance they won't."

Hap pushed off from the pecan tree he'd been leaning against and moved toward her. Brittle husks of nut shell crunched and cracked.

He stopped at the edge of the shade line. Sunlight glared on his legs and stomach, left his face bladed in shadow. The apple in his palm was a deep red.

White teeth crunched into the apple's flesh. The fruit made wet snapping sounds as he chewed.

"What'd he want to see you about, anyway?"

"I don't know." Kira thought about the strange meeting. "Look me over, maybe? Make sure I'm actually leaving."

"And are you?" He didn't meet her gaze when he spoke.

"I'm getting tired of saying it."

Down the long drive, an old car sat rusting in the high grass. Two men in white strap undershirts leaned against the rear bumper, assault rifles propped beside them. One bumped the other with his elbow and laughed.

Hap motioned to Kira. They followed a worn ribbon of bare earth that wound through the dead grass to the old plantation's barns and outbuildings.

The open air garage had been known far and wide as a chop shop. Grinders and welding torches and paint sprayers ran day and night. It was silent now, but a couple of vehicles still poked their noses around the corner of the barn, paintwork bright and shining and thoroughly out of place.

"Remember that one Christmas we went crawdadding in the creek out by your house?"

"They were worried I might lose a finger to frostbite," she said.

"And Daddy beat me til I couldn't sit down for a week."

His grin was bashful and subdued. He bumped his arm against her as they walked, and she remembered more of the shy child he'd been. The games they'd played.

"And this is you now?" she said. "Running the old man's errands?"

He looked down at the half-apple in his hand. Snapped it away from him into the grass. Something twisted the stalks into furious S-shapes away from the place where it landed.

"It's not like that, Kira. Not at all."

"I see."

Hap stood close. Staring into the hard planes of his chest, the shy child she remembered was once again a six foot man, broad shouldered and muscular.

"Truth is, I asked for this. Daddy and I hardly talk anymore, but I knew he wanted to see you."

His fingers reached, lingered above her bare arm. His aftershave smelled like ice and lemons. The tip of his thumb brushed her wrist and something tightened, low in her body.

She stepped back. Put distance between them before he noticed her reaction.

"I've got to get to the funeral home," she said. "Want to drive me?"

"Sure do, but I'm afraid I can't." His arm came forward. He caught himself, stuck his hands in his back pockets, shook his head.

"Hap…"

"Don't worry none. Daddy meant what he said about getting you a car."

He caught her look, tapped the phone in his jeans pocket.

"Last thing I need is to give Grace Roberts an excuse to lock my ass up," she said.

"Ah, she loves you, Kee. You know that."

"Sure. Especially if she catches me riding around in one of Old Man Taylor's back-of-the-barn specials."

"C'mon, I'll show you." His teeth were white and dazzling.

The barn had a strong lock, gleaming and oiled. He had the key, and the door rolled open wide enough to let the two of them inside. Wide enough to show the three humped shapes under cloth in the dusty golden light. Up in the shadowed rafters, wasps buzzed in their muddy nests.

He walked past the first two shapes and into the building's back corner. Kira trailed behind, intrigued.

He stopped in front of the rearmost shape. Took the dustcloth in both fists and whipped it away, proud as any magician unveiling a trick.

"You're kidding."

"Nope."

Sitting still, the Dodge still looked like it was going a hundred miles an hour. The body was black and gleaming, the color of midnight trapped under glass.

There in that barn, among the smells of sawdust and clay, the stifling heat and the drone of wasps, the Charger was a silent beast. Waiting.

"Daddy was real specific about you getting a car with a legal title." Hap's mouth was a wry twist. "Just so happens he didn't mention which one."

Kira touched the roof of the car. Her fingertips left small halos in the polish on the hardtop. She ran her palms along the curved length of one quarterpanel. Her pulse quickened in her throat, pushed back the threat of tears.

"I thought Jack was—"

"Jack was driving your daddy's. This here's *my* Daddy's."

"But it's—"

"The same, yeah. They bought them new together, back in the day. Only difference is your daddy got the 440 big block and mine paid extra for the 426 Hemi."

Kira didn't speak.

"Bet they don't have nothing like this back in Europe." Hap said. "That there's solid American muscle."

"It sure is."

The latch popped and Kira lifted the hood. The engine gleamed, showroom clean. She breathed deep, smelled coolant and dust, iron and oil.

"Kee, Something I been wanting to say…"

"Really, it's okay."

"Just, what with Jack and all…"

He stood close, that familiar male light in his eyes. Kira took her palms off the car, straightened to face him.

"You think this car will make me want to see you?"

"I think finding out you got this car will just about make the old man burst a blood vessel."

Laughter burst dark and smoky from Kira's throat. On impulse, she stood up on her toes and kissed the side of his jaw.

She kept it brief, broke away before he had a chance to get the wrong idea.

Or the right one. She wasn't sure how she felt.

The way he reached for her, the emotions that swam in his face, only made it all that much more complicated.

She put one palm up between their bodies. Hap stopped. His arms lowered, and that raw male need he buried behind that wide white smile.

"Papers are in the glovebox," he said. "Reckon I'll see you around."

"WHAT DO YOU THINK?"

"Think? I think it's too hot. *Know* I'd rather be fishing."

"Not that," Bix said. "John Lee's girl."

Deputy Graham leaned forward in his seat, squinted through the windshield. It gave him a better view of the house— some ways down the drive and a bitty corner of the second story was all. It also put him so the air conditioning vent blew directly into the collar of his shirt.

"I think all those damn trees, she could be getting killed in there and no way we'd ever know."

"She ain't gonna get killed." Deputy Bix lifted a stained Coke can to his lips and dribbled a thin stream of tobacco juice into it. "She's a goddamn Stone. If anything, they're on the same side."

"Usually how it happens."

The two men fell back into silence. There wasn't even much chatter on the radio, just the odd mike check here and there. This heat, it was too hot for folks to get up to much.

"Anyway, that ain't what I'm talking about," Bix said. "I was asking what you thought of the girl herself."

Graham considered a moment.

"She don't look all that much, just a little bitty thing. Course, so's the Sheriff."

"Sure did a number on Taylor's man this morning."

"Yup," Graham said. "Girl can handle herself."

"That's what I'm talking about, right there." Another pause. Another brown dribble. "All this time, all I ever heard is she's off partying, drinking her ass off—"

"Lying around those nude beaches they got there."

"Lying around those nude beaches. Hell's she doing going all Jackie Chan on Taylor's guy?"

"Didn't even break a sweat."

"Good moves for a party girl."

"She's still a Stone."

"Now you're picking nature over nurture here. That's just crazy." Again the Coke can rose to his lips.

Graham looked away out the window and made a face. That can was disgusting.

"Them beaches really nude?" Bix said.

Graham nodded.

"Like full buck naked?"

"Close enough. I was stationed in Germany, got down there a couple times. They'll wear a little something, like a g-string or bikini bottom type of thing, but that's about it."

"Tits everywhere…" Bix said it like some men might talk about Jesus.

"You get over it."

"*You* do, maybe."

"It's everybody. Little kids, old grandmas…"

"I'd be willing to look at a few grandmas if the Stone girl had hers out."

"I can't beli—"

They heard the car before they saw it. The low throaty roar built until it howled. The gleaming black muscle car practically flew past the end of Taylor's drive and hit the dirt road in a sideways drift. The rear tires scrabbled and bit. A rooster tail of orange dust threw high into the air, and the car was gone.

"Think that was her?"

"Shit."

THE CHARGER WAS A BEAST. The 426 Hemi under the hood growled and roared. The wheel in her hands throbbed and moved, a thing alive.

Kira smoothed through a turn, her blood singing. Europe had fast cars and mad roads: her life had been full of them. But no Ferrari or Lamborghini could touch the raw power of American muscle. No Alpine pass or Autobahn held the same thrill as these twisting ribbons of red clay.

For a moment she was a child again. In her father's car, his big hands on the wheel. His, or Jack's. Her own legs dangling at the edge of the seat.

She hit the gas. The Charger surged.

Her pain and grief were still there, a knot in her heart. But like past, future, and everything else, they were distant.

The course in front of her. Gas. Brakes. Steering. These were all that mattered right now.

She drove like a woman possessed.

The road dipped and rose. Kira's wheels left the earth, soaring and free.

She hit the ground running, laughter in her heart.

"IT IS WAY TOO HOT for this shit."

Deputy Graham slewed the cruiser through a turn. The road switched back fast enough that the car's back end threatened to swing out and spin them around.

Graham corrected out of the skid, powered into a straightaway fogged with a cloud of settling red dust.

"Hit the lights," he said. "We catch that bitch, I'm pulling her the hell over."

"Now I know you're kidding." Bix gripped the dash with one hand and the oh-shit bar with the other. "Boss told us point blank don't hassle her, just watch where she goes."

The road dipped and rose, a tight turn waiting at the top of the climb. For a single dizzying moment, sunlight and piny woods were the only things visible through the windshield before the tires found the road again.

The black Charger was a column of dust in the distance, growing further away every second.

"Besides," he said, "you know you're never gonna catch her."

Graham wrestled through another turn, eased his foot off the gas.

Cop shocks. Cop suspension. Goddamned cop engine. And none of it did a single bit of good.

He dragged one palm across the lower half of his face, wiped red dust and road grit from his mouth.

"Nobody drives like a Stone."

RHINELAND'S FUNERAL HOME didn't look like it had redecorated since sometime in the eighties. Kira wondered if that was because the senior citizens found it comforting, or if it had something to do with the fact that the nearest competition was over forty miles away.

The room was hushed. Dusty. It smelled of flowers, and some organ hymn played softly, just at the edge of hearing.

Kira wanted a drink so bad she could taste it.

That was the trouble with a drive like that. With adrenalin in general, really. Everything focused right down to the moment, it was perfect and free.

But reality always came crashing back.

She was wandering among the caskets in the showroom when Rhineland found her. He was ten or so years older than her, not the same man she remembered from her father's funeral but one of the family, all the same.

He came at her with a look of professional sorrow fixed on his face. She took in the pencil mustache and gel—spiked mullet and revised her ideas about the decor.

He stood beside her in muted anticipation, hands clasped in front of his body. Kira moved from one coffin to another. They ranged from godawful pastel metals piped to look like decorated birthday cakes to a cheap little box that might have been wood-grain veneer on fiberglass.

Finally, she stopped. The casket was dark wood. Brass handles and white satin inside.

She wanted that drink.

"How much?"

"Real good choice there. That's the Majestic Mahogany, two-inch thick handcrafted panels, solid bronze fittings and hand-sewn ivory white interior bedding. We have an optional upgrade package on that one, gives you real silk lining. Now, over here we have the Remembrance, eighteen-gauge steel with a hand-sewn and embroidered chalet crepe—"

"This one's fine."

"May I ask, who was your loved one?"

"My brother. You still haven't answered my question. How much is it?"

Rhineland squirmed in his dark suit.

"We keep those figures back in the office. You'll want a memorial service, of course."

He wore too much aftershave. The smell was something a teenage boy would pick.

"We have three memorial chapels to choose from. I know some people prefer a graveside service, but this time of year, the last thing you want is mourners out in the hot sun wearing black, fainting in the heat. Our chapels are all air-conditioned, plenty of room for floral displays, and microphones so your loved ones can hear every word of the eulogy. Or there's our Garden of Remembrance? All the amenities of an indoor chapel with the natural comfort of plants and real grass. Will you have an open casket?"

"My face is up here, Rhineland."

He had delivered this entire speech almost entirely to her tits. Now he lifted his gaze to her face.

"I'm sorry, what'd you say your name was?"

"Stone. Kira Stone. My brother's name was Jack."

Recognition dawned. The look that followed wasn't one that Kira expected. His face blanched. His mouth hung open, gulping for air.

"You okay there?"

"Jack Stone was a fine man. You'll never hear me say otherwise." Rhineland pulled his shirt collar away from his throat. "Tragic, his accident. Simply tragic."

"Did you know my brother?"

"Ah, sadly, no. But we were all looking forward to him moving back. Then to lose him this way… Perhaps a closed casket then. May I ask, what was Jack's denomination? So we can book the right minister and all."

"I…"

"Jeb Tucker. Real good, non-denominational. He even spoke at a Methodist service last month."

Kira thought of her brother inside that thick wood box. She looked down at the carpet and forced herself to breathe. The chilled perfumed air refused to fill her lungs.

Rhineland kept talking, but all Kira heard was the sound of dirt shoveled onto the coffin's lid.

THE SHERIFF'S OFFICE was in the county courthouse. From the front, the building looked just as it always had. A little sadder maybe, a little shabbier, but the same red brick and white granite style every government building and half the banks in the state seemed to share.

The marble foyer was dark and cool. Steps led up to the courtrooms above, and on the opposite wall a Depression-era WPA mural showed farmers and workers united. The powerful figures were now faded ghosts, their massive hands obscured by limp and breezeless state and national flags.

On either side of the foyer, tucked under the rise of the stairs, frosted glass doors waited. The gilt lettering, like something out of a black-and-white movie, read *TAX, TITLE AND LICENSE* on the one. On the other, simply *SHERIFF*.

The door opened onto a narrow hall paneled in 1970's plywood. Kira followed it to an open bullpen area, waist-high railing separating the hall from four desks. Three of the empty desks had elderly beige monitors and keyboards. The fourth still had a typewriter.

Signs and notices and random bits of paper seemed to be fixed to every vertical surface. The blinds along the far wall were closed against the sun, and the banks of low-hanging fluorescents lit the room in a bleached glare, harsh and merciless.

A woman with hair ten years out of date lifted her face from the TV Guide on her desk and looked Kira up and down. A teardrop of scar tissue sat just below her left eye.

"He'p you?"

This name she knew. Kira had given her the scar.

"Hey Cindy. I need a word with your boss."

The woman's mouth flattened into a thin line. Pink lipstick smudged past the edges of her lips.

"Can't do it. She's out on patrol."

"You're the dispatcher." Kira gestured to the mike stand and switchboard on the desk. "Get on your little rig and dispatch her."

Cindy's look was a study in flat-eyed contempt. Without another word, she slowly returned her attention to the magazine on her desk. The tips of her fingers shook where they touched the paper.

Kira looked at the door at the end of the hall. That one led to the small booking area and the handful of cells at the back of the building. A second door in that booking area led back into the bullpen. She wondered if those cells had changed at all.

Cindy stared hard at her TV Guide. A thin knot of veins stood out at her temple and dark color flushed from her collar to the points of her cheeks.

Kira pushed through the gate in the railing. An outraged screech behind her, she headed straight for the door she wanted.

The Sheriff stood to the side of her desk. Her back was straight, her uniform trim and tidy against her frame. She had an ungainly amount of equipment buckled around her hips and was in the act of adjusting a dark Stetson on the crown of her head.

"Kira. I was just on my way out to see you. Wanted to ask you round to supper tonight. I gotta check something out with an informant first, but after."

She took off the hat and dropped it on a wall peg. The auburn hair in its tight bun was undisturbed.

"It's fine, Cindy. Just shut the door on your way out."

Kira turned in time to see the receptionist's face as the door swung shut.

The Sheriff pulled her nightstick from its ring and laid it against the side of her desk. She lowered into the swivel chair with a creak and jingle of harness and equipment. The blinds were drawn in this room too. Thin blades of light and shadow fell across the hard planes of her face.

Kira sat at the other side of the desk, still shaking her head at the closed door.

"You know, I can't even remember why she hates me."

"Not much surprise, though."

"No. I guess not."

"You know how bad it was when you left," the Sheriff said. "And since then, all we've heard is wild stories, you partying it up all over Europe, jet sets and drugs and not even half the modesty the— my Lord, have you been drinking?"

"Can you blame me?"

"Kira, Jack was..."

She took a deep breath and started again.

"What is it you want, Kira?"

"I mean to put Jack in the family plot. Man at the funeral home says you're the one to give me the permit."

The Sheriff leaned in. Her forearms on the desk between the formed a muscular arrowhead, aimed at Kira's heart.

"Not that," she said. "I mean, what is it you want out of life? You're strong and you're tough and you're smart as a whip, but you spend your time making every bad decision possible. I'm worried about you. You and the company you keep."

"I don't know what you've heard, but—"

"This morning I came within five seconds of catching you in an act of assault. Maybe even attempted murder."

"Just a little misunderstanding is all," Kira said. "And he slipped."

"Look, Kira, I know. I understand. We're all grieving here, and a few uptight folks get their panties all wadded up in a bunch, that's not your problem. Nor should it be."

Kira ran the fingers of her right hand over the healing knuckles of her left.

"What the hell are you doing, running around with the Taylors anyway?"

"I don't see how it's any of your business."

"The man you assaulted this morning had a long record, most of it for violent crime. The Old Man's got a dozen more just like him, the worst bunch of rapists and murderers in three counties.

The man is a disease in this community and you're driving around town in his goddamned car."

"It's my life!"

"It's my town!"

The Sheriff slammed her palm down on the face of her desk. The sound echoed, loud as a shot. Both women threw themselves back in their chairs, arms folded tight across their bodies.

The silence stretched tight in the small room. In the end, the older woman spoke first.

"Try to see my side of it, Kee." Her fingertips found a strand of hair flown loose.

"You're here for your brother, and I respect that. There's bound to be problems, I know. But if that evil old man sucks you into his world, you know I'll have to put you away."

Kira wiped her palms on her thighs and swallowed.

"He just wanted to tell me there's no hard feelings," she said. "About Bobby."

"He didn't ask you to do anything? Isn't trying to mix you up in some criminal enterprise?"

"Far as I know, the old man just wants to clear his conscience before the Devil comes and takes him. What do you think I am, anyway?"

"What'd you tell him?"

Kira's eye narrowed. The blood rose in her face.

"You lost the right to pry into my business ten years ago." She pushed the chair away from her as she stood.

"Hey, I'm not done talking to you."

"Then have me arrested."

"Young lady, SIT BACK DOWN!"

"You're not my mother!"

The women stood, eyes locked, breathing hard.

"Go bury your brother. Get on back to your goddamn champagne and playboys. Leave the Taylors alone."

The Sheriff lowered her fists until the knuckles touched the top of her desk. Her head bowed.

"Now get the hell out of my office."

KIRA STOMPED ACROSS the square and kicked the statue of Beauregard Harrow. She cursed and kicked the statue again and felt like an idiot.

Not even two days back, and it was like the last ten years never happened. Was it always going to be like this?

Back at the car, she thumped her head against the steering wheel and forced back tears. No one in this town was going to see her cry. She keyed the ignition, left the town square in a cloud of burning rubber.

"HE SLEEPING?" the man in the doorway said. He was thick-built, looked like he had been slapped together from offcut slabs of beef.

The two at the kitchen table looked up from their cards. Their faces were stone, their eyes wary.

"What do you think?" the man in the feed cap said. "Pull up a chair and sit a hand."

The man in the cap had stringy hair and deep lines in his face. The one across the table from him was sunburned, with black tattoos creeping down his wrists onto his hands.

Play stopped while the thick-built man circled the other two. He moved slow and kept his hands in sight. The others edged away from the chair he pulled up, and from each other, until all three men were an equal distance apart.

The man in the cap and the tattooed man looked at each other, threw in their cards and dealt out a new hand.

The three played in near-silence for a time. The only sounds were muttered bets and raises, the tick of matchsticks on the kitchen table and the soft throp of the ceiling fan as it pushed the heat nowhere in particular.

"Anyone know how much longer?" the tattooed man asked.

"How the hell're we supposed to know?" the man in the cap said. "He takes as long as he takes."

"I didn't mean nothing, Verge. Just, I got places to be is all."

"Means he's got that titty dancer over in Griffin putting an itch in his pants," the thick-built man said to Virgil.

The lines deepened and twisted at the corners of Virgil's mouth, but the expression couldn't be called a smile.

"Tell you what," the thick-built man said, "you want, you go on down and see that girl of yours. We'll tell the old man he missed you, and you won't even need to get a shot for the clap."

The tattooed man threw his cards in and scratched his sunburn.

"Said I didn't mean nothing."

The bet was to the thick man. He threw three wooden matches into the pile in the center of the table and added three more. He slouched against the back of the kitchen chair, the cards in his hands almost resting on his chest.

"Old man sure does sleep a lot these days, though." His lips barely moved.

Virgil's fingers brushed the neat stack of matches in front of him. He matched the bet and, a moment later, dropped one more match into the pot.

"Sure does."

The thick-built man picked up a single match. He held it between thumb and forefinger, tapped it slowly, end over end against the top of the table.

"You ever think about it?"

Virgil's eyes slid sideways under the brim of his cap. The three men were alone in the room. Their own guards waited out on the porch. Elsewhere in the old plantation house, Taylor's own people moved, too quietly to be heard.

Still Virgil looked over both shoulders before he spoke.

"We've all thought about it."

"Goddammit Virge, Big Tom, this ain't funny."

"He's old.'

The thick-built man named Big Tom added the match between his fingers to the pot and raised three more. The slivers of wood ticked like fingernails against the table top.

"You know what he'd do if he heard you two?" the tattooed man tried again.

"He is old." Virgil scratched the stubble on his neck.

"You guys'd be dead before you knew it."

"He's still sharp," Tom said, "but not like he used to be. Lot of missed opportunities, lot of money going wanting."

Virgil looked at his cards and frowned.

All three sat in silence again.

"There's the son."

Three sets of shoulders shook. Quiet laughter scraped around the room.

The laughter died, and the players all looked from one to the other. The tattooed man lifted empty hands.

"Don't look at me," he said. "I got a good thing going, and I ain't looking for more."

That left Big Tom and Virgil facing each other over the tops of their cards. The silence stretched, grew brittle.

"Bet's to you," Tom said.

"Hey," the tattooed man said, a little too loud. "Y'all hear John Lee's girl is back?"

"Jack was bad enough."

"He was that."

"I hear the sister's worse."

Virgil looked at his cards and down at his stock of matches.

"Jack was smart, though. Same as his daddy," he said. "Wasn't for his accident, I reckon we'd all have ended up working for him."

Tom and Virgil locked eyes again. The tattooed man squirmed in his chair. The fan thropped slow circles overhead.

"You don't think the sister means to stay?"

"That could be a problem."

"Yeah, but for who?"

Virgil pushed three more matches to the center of the table.

"Call. Time to show what you got."

KIRA THRUST WITH the shovel. The blade bit, and she tamped it deeper with the sole of her shoe. She lifted and swung, and the hole grew imperceptibly deeper.

The soil was dark this far down. A deep iron red, it bore only the faintest resemblance to the hard-baked orange clay at the surface. When she started, she'd made good time with pickaxe and mattock. Now, the hole was up to her neck. Her work was slow.

A shadow fell across Kira's shoulders. A dark figure stood above her, sunlight dazzling at the edges of his body. Kira shielded her eyes with one hand and squinted.

"Hap?"

"The very same." He bent down, extended a hand to her in a cloud of citrus aftershave.

Kira braced both palms on the ground in front of her and lifted herself out. Hap watched her do it in a way that made her conscious of the dirt streaking her body, the sweat soaking through her tank top.

Hap blushed and dropped his eyes. He fidgeted with the buckle on his belt and jiggled the chunky steel watch on his wrist.

"I'd have come down," she said, "but I didn't hear your truck."

"Hell Kira, that's all right." A tiny puff of orange dust rose in the air when he scuffed the ground with his shoe.

"Can I ask, just what the heck are you up to?"

"What's it look like? I'm digging a grave."

"What I mean is, old Rhineland's got people for that, don't he?"

Kira looked down at the hole. The slanting light threw a blade of shadow across the bottom. It looked narrow and deep and final.

"No stranger's going to dig my brother's grave."

"Or put him in a proper cemetery either, I guess," he said.

Kira picked her way among the scattered headstones. Hap followed, hesitant.

Down the hill below them, her family home, the house and barns and outbuildings, all looked like a child's toys. The afternoon sun turned weathered shingles the color of hammered tin.

"See that?" Kira gestured at a nearby nub of stone. Its almost featureless surface was lightly grooved with what had once been letters and numbers. The name was all but lost, but the date of death was just deep enough to make out: 1841.

"Sheriff's setting up the permit." Kira pushed past Hap on the way back down to the house.

HAP BROUGHT BEER. Six cans in a small ice chest.

A fifth of Old Grand-Dad sat beside the chest, hidden in brown paper. The bag was crimped where he'd grabbed the bottle by the neck.

He peeled a can for each of them and they sat together on the steps at the bottom of the porch. Their fingers touched when she took her can.

They sat a moment in silence. The sunset sky was like something out of a painting, and its reflection glowed in the waxed finish of his Corvette, showed darker in the paint of the old Dodge.

"How's the car?" he said.

Kira looked out the corner of her eyes at him. Thick lashes, eyes shocking blue. Just like that, Hap felt thirteen and foolish all over again. He watched her throat work as she swallowed, felt the heat burn in his cheeks.

"I got Heineken," he said. "I know you'll be used to fine wines and champagnes and all, but this is about as close as we get around here to a fancy import."

"It's fine."

The sunset seemed to light her from within. Her skin glowed rose and gold, and the points of her breasts showed through the thin white cotton tank.

"What?"

"Just thinking," Hap said. "Daddy says you're the spitting image of your momma."

"That so."

"I was just thinking how your mom must have been beautiful."

She burned him with those eyes.

"I'm smelly and dirty and sore. And for what it's worth I never knew my mother. She killed herself when I was four."

"I didn't know." Hap looked down. The cold can seemed to burn his hands. "No one ever told me."

"No reason they should, I guess. Don't think they'd have told me, I hadn't found her."

"Jesus."

"It was a long time ago." She lifted the can to her mouth, thirsty. The sweat was drying on her skin, wet salt.

"Come out with me tonight," he said.

She lowered the can, an inch from her lips.

"We can go over to Macon, or up to Atlanta. Hell, let me just take you dancing at Junior's."

She set the can on the step beside her. Reached past him for the Old Grand-Dad. The movement pressed her body against the side of his leg. She seemed not to notice.

"I don't think that would be such a good idea," she said.

"Just dancing's all."

She pulled the bottle from its paper. The contents moved behind the glass, liquid gold. Traced one fingernail over the label, black and orange.

"I didn't know they still made this."

"How you holding up, Kee?"

"Back… back there it's all cocktails, stuff like that. Brandy sometimes."

"This can't be easy, I know."

"You know I used to love this when I was a kid? Fourteen, fifteen, made me feel all grown up."

"You can talk to me, you know."

She cracked the seal on the whiskey, raised the bottle to her lips. They were wide and soft and full around its neck.

Hap drank from the place where her mouth had been, tried not to cough as he swallowed liquid fire.

She followed with a pull from her beer. A tiny fleck of foam remained on her lower lip. Hap stared at that fleck, his blood pounding.

His heart crashed when she turned her face away.

"I still see Bobby."

The moment he blurted it out, he couldn't have said why. Black hair whipped across her face, she turned so fast.

"So he's—" Her voice hitched, caught. Hap knew how she felt.

"He's alive, yeah."

She took it, a fighter taking a body blow.

"Daddy's got him at the Medical Center over in Macon," he said. "I go over there sometimes and see him."

The whiskey bottle left his hand. This time she drank longer, harder.

When she lowered the bottle her eyes were bright and dangerous.

"Is he…." Her mouth twisted, and tears stood in her eyes. "Is he okay?"

"Bobby's a pretty damn far cry from okay. You fucked him up pretty bad."

Hap reached for his beer can. The hoarded cold of the ice chest had bled out into the day's heat. The liquid he swallowed was warm and bitter.

"You want, you could—"

"No way," she said. "Not a chance."

"It's not—"

"I said no."

Kira had curled away from him on the step, against the wall of the house. Her arms were folded over her knees, and her face was down in her arms. She made no sound as her shoulders shook.

"Kee…"

He reached for her, her skin golden in the sunlight.

Her hand never seemed to move. A sound like the snap of a leather belt, and his wrist went numb.

"I wasn't—"

Her head whipped up, and Hap jerked back. Tears stood in her eyes, and she was dangerously still. She was a doorway, and a cold wind blew through her.

Stones were like that. Unpredictable. Dangerous. Full of sudden violence.

It had made her brother Jack a terrifying presence.

With Kira, Hap's fear mingled with a desire so intense it made him ache.

THE SHERIFF PULLED a double armload of groceries and her gym bag out onto the tailgate of her vehicle. Down the road, the sound of Hap Taylor's engine shifted into high gear.

Kira came out of the house. She'd washed her face and rinsed her mouth, but the smell of liquor clung to her like a dirty secret.

"Wasn't interrupting anything, was I?"

Kira shook her head, hiding her face behind her hair the way she did when she didn't want to answer your questions.

"You know, it wasn't for his daddy, I'd say go for it."

That got her attention.

"Everybody knows he's no part of that life. Old man packed him off even before you left. Boarding schools Up North, holidays in Europe— figure ya'll'd have a fair bit to talk about."

"But the sins of the father?"

"Kira, you do not want that old man getting any kind of hook in you. He's just too dangerous."

Inside, they unpacked the groceries. Cold cuts. Bread. A bottle of lemonade and a bottle of Coke. Paper plates. Supper things.

The Sheriff ignored the open bottle of whiskey at the end of the counter, and how much of it was already missing.

"Store bought, I know," she said, "but I spent half my afternoon trying to chase down that informant. Guess he's decided now he don't want to talk to me."

"I'd forgotten you asked me to supper."

Way she said it, the Sheriff knew that wasn't what Kira meant.

"I care about you. That's all it was." She rubbed the corner of her mouth with one thumb. "All any of it ever was."

The child thought about some smart ass remark. Bit it back.

"Thanks," she said instead.

THEY USED A FLAT patch of earth that had once been a side yard. The Sheriff's gun belt hung over a half-rotted piece of fence rail. Otherwise, they stayed in the clothes they wore.

"No gloves?" Kira said.

"Didn't figure you were *that* drunk."

The two women paced the edges of the yard. Cracked red clay, sharp granite rocks. They faced each other, a couple of meters apart.

"Been awhile," Kira said.

"Too busy with your cocktails and your playboys."

"Something like that."

"Then this won't take long."

The Sheriff came out of natural stance with a side kick, crisp and clean. Caught air, the child twisting away. Came down into guard in time to protect her ribs.

They squared off properly then. Small shots, feints. Feeling each other out.

Kira came forward with a triple-kick-combo that came in at strange angles, some fancy foreign trick she'd picked up. Too fancy, too much focus to pull it off.

The Sheriff punished her inattention with a palm shot that stopped just short of the bridge of her nose.

They walked off to the edges of the yard. Dropped into guard and met in the center again.

This time the child kept it nice and simple, kept it tight. Nothing fancy, no showing off. Closest weapon to closest target. She had a good strong defense and all that decadent living hadn't put a dent in her speed.

In the end, the Sheriff used treachery.

Overcommitted to her punch, left herself open. Not too much, just enough. Kira went for the opening and the trap sprung, a throw that left the younger woman sprawled in the dust, knife hand poised over her throat.

"Not bad."

The Sheriff helped her back to her feet.

"Let's get you cleaned up so we can eat."

EVERYTHING WAS ready by the time Kira was out of the shower.

They sat across from each other, the seat at the head of the table empty. Kira remembered her father in that chair, big and shaggy and tired, a beer in his hand.

The Sheriff said a brief prayer. Head bowed, eyes closed, hands clasped over the paper plate before her. Her back was as straight as an iron bar.

Kira waited for 'amen' to lift her glass and drink.

"You weren't too bad out there," the Sheriff said. "Little rusty, but not too bad."

"Too busy with my champagne and playboys."

"Got anybody special? Back there, I mean."

"No. Not for awhile now."

Kira looked down at the sandwich in her hand. Watery ham. White bread with mayonnaise. A slice of processed cheese. Possibly the most American thing she'd ever eaten.

It was delicious.

"How about you?" she said.

"Not since John Lee. Never was any following that man."

The room seemed suddenly small and close. Both women realized they'd drifted into dangerous waters. The Sheriff steered them safely away with old stories about the legendary driver.

Last week Kira had been on a yacht off the coast of Malfi. Now she was surrounded by the sights and smells and sounds of her childhood. It was a little overwhelming.

She looked at her sandwich and longed for the bottle Hap left behind.

Listening to the old stories once again, she missed her father's voice. His hands. His way of speaking. The Sheriff had a different way of telling them, the later tales hinting at the eager young deputy never quite able to catch the old outlaw.

Except of course, that one day she did.

"So tell me, Kira, what's it like over there?"

"You sent me."

"To cousins I never met— furthest I've been was a school trip once to Washington DC." Her shoulders moved inside her uniform shirt, and her hands flexed on the glass of tea held between her palms. "So come on, you been up the Eiffel Tower, seen the Sistine Chapel?"

Kira could see what the other woman was trying to do, did her best to play along.

"Some," she said. "Not as much as I should, maybe. Mostly, me and my friends just kind of move from place to place, depending on who we meet, what's in season, like that."

"In season."

"Winters are usually the Alps. Some of us ski, some of the others stay in the lodges. One winter we all went to Morocco, that was pretty good, what I remember of it. Summers we head south, beaches and all that."

It was warm in the house, the day's heat trapped.

"One long party."

"One long party."

"And that's you? That's the right thing for you to be doing."

"It's a lot of fun."

"That isn't what I asked."

"It's a good life." Kira hated the way her own voice sounded.

Silence followed. Painful. Awkward. Sweat dampened Kira's upper lip. Small hairs plastered in curls at the Sheriff's temples. Ice cubes cracked and shifted as they melted in glasses.

SATURDAY NIGHT

AS NIGHT FELL, Kira wandered the house alone. Fatigue had its hooks sunk into her, right to the bone. Her body screamed she'd been awake at least a week: in reality it had been less than twenty hours.

She moved from room to room, touching surfaces, breathing scents. Evoking memories. She felt sheared away from herself. Disconnected.

Her life— whatever the Sheriff thought of it, her *real* life— was an endless pursuit of excitement and pleasure. She'd been a houseguest at mansions and estates and a squatter in an anarchist-punk commune. She'd crewed a yacht off the coast of Greece and rioted with protesters in Spain.

It was a life that made this place seem like a bad dream. The kind you only half-remember on waking. Now, alone in this house, it was hard to believe any of that had ever happened.

Kira felt like a ghost, haunting this place.

She stopped outside her father's bedroom. Her palms touched wood, warm and wavy and imperfect, hand-planed by her great-grandfather nearly a hundred years ago.

White linen showed gray in the darkness, and the air in that room was cool and still. She ran her hand once more over the door frame but did not enter.

Tears carved silent tracks down her face. She wiped her cheeks with the heel of one palm and turned away.

Jack's room was alien territory. As a little girl it had been off limits, forbidden. The penalties for trespass were the sort only an older brother could devise. Now, Kira was able to touch his baseball glove and high school trophies, his model airplanes and CD player, without fear.

This new freedom brought fresh tears to her eyes.

There were signs of recent occupation, too. An iPod docking station sat on the dresser. The closet was full of new and unfamiliar clothes. Much of Jack's civilian wardrobe looked like it had never been worn.

His old Playboys, half a dozen of them scavenged or pilfered across three decades, lay in a loose stack across the bed. The magazines' original hiding place remained a mystery.

She sat on the bed. The Playboys shifted and slid. Girls pouted up from faded covers, hair and makeup now hopelessly out of date. Beautiful once, now they just looked old-fashioned. Forever caught in a long-ago moment while the rest of the world moved on without them.

Kira swallowed around the knot in her throat. For those girls on the magazine covers, life had gone on. Even if that moment in front of the camera would never change, everything else had.

They could still look back on who they used to be. Her brother would never get that. He was trapped now, frozen forever. Like her father, Jack had become a collection of stories for people to tell sometimes.

Stories Kira mostly didn't know.

Grief and loss and pain overwhelmed her. Sobs wracked her body. She didn't know how long she cried.

HAP TAYLOR PULLED in at the side of the dirt road, among the other cars. Without the sound of the Corvette's engine, they could hear faint snatches of music and laughter coming through the trees.

"You sure about this?"

"I told you, I'm fine."

"Just, you didn't sound fine on the phone."

"You don't want to take me, I can go myself."

He looked over at her. She looked a lot better under the moon than she had in the porch light.

But that wasn't saying much.

She gave a big huff, said 'fine' under her breath and slammed the car door getting out. Hap ran to catch up.

He almost grabbed her arm, thought better of it at the last minute.

"It's over this way."

"I know that."

"Just, come on okay." He took her hand and led her through the woods. They could have followed the road, but this way was shorter.

When the lights and music were close, Hap stopped and turned. Kira swayed into him, the length of her body pressing against him a moment before she settled back onto her feet.

The smell of her skin reminded him of gunpowder.

"I was just thinking…" He risked his hands around her waist. "I know some spots we could go, places nicer, quieter, and a whole lot prettier than this."

"I want to drink."

"You been drinking."

"I want to dance."

"Then we'll dance, just us two. Let's go."

She broke away, stumbled through the trees. Her body was silhouetted against the Christmas lights strung around Junior's, a moment of hip-swaying black before she stepped out of the trees and into that multicolored world.

THE MEN STOOD in a rough circle of bare earth. An oil drum fire burned in the center, lighting their faces ruddy and hellish.

The heat from that fire was terrible,the black clouds rolling off of it stinging and noxious.

They were hard men, rough and merciless. All were armed. They muttered among themselves and told nervous jokes and kept looking over their own shoulders. More than one set of fingers shook lighting a smoke.

All around them, junked cars sat rusting. The cars lacked wheels or windows or headlights. The grass grew tall in the spaces between the junkers, but it wasn't snakes the men feared.

The van was old, its engine perfectly maintained. These days, when even the big engines made little more noise than a hiss and a hum, the sound of that van was distinctive.

All talking stopped. The men turned their heads and swayed their bodies, tracking the van's progress by the strange echoes it threw as it crawled through the litter of dead cars.

Finally, its ghost gray shape rolled past the entrance to the open space. Brake lights flared, and points of white light blazed. The men parted to make way as the van reversed into their circle.

It stopped a body's length from the oil drum fire. The front doors opened. Manny, head-shaved and scalp-tattooed, with eyes like ice. Ross, the enormous redhead with a bad streak a mile wide.

In the circle of faces, Virgil and Big Tom exchanged a wary look. Taylor had brought his enforcers.

Manny opened the back doors of the van. Ross stood scanning the crowd. His head moved inside a thick wedge of muscled neck, and the look on his face was hungry.

A motor whined. The iron plate unfolded and fell into place with a loud clank. Taylor wheeled himself out onto the plate and surveyed the assembled faces as he lowered to the ground.

The only sounds were the whine of the motor and the crackle of the fire.

The iron plate thumped to a stop. Taylor rolled on squeaking wheels until he sat in front of the oil drum. Hellish lights played over his upper body. The rest of him remained in shadow.

He looked from man to man. Firelight shadows danced in his wrinkles, and the lower half of his face twisted into something that might be called a smile.

FOR KIRA GROWING up, Junior's had been the stuff of myth.

As a little girl sitting in church, Junior's was the Devil's Snare, an unholy place where souls were forever lost. A little older, and the juke joint held a dark fascination. Efforts to warn her off only made her want more.

Her one attempt to sneak in had ended in a ride home in the back of Floyd Patterson's police car. Wasn't long after that, a night sneaking off to see Bobby had ended with her stepmother driving fast up the coast to a northern airport, putting her on a plane to a whole new life.

Junior's turned out to be a shabby little place. Not much more than a shack in the woods, strung with Christmas lights. The bar was an old door on two sawhorses, the tender scarred up and wearing a gun.

Her drink choices were simple. All were served in plastic cups.

It was a dive, but there were people here. It had music, and liquor. Laughter and dancing.

It beat the hell out of the silence at home.

TAYLOR LOOKED FROM man to man in the firelight. To a one, they flinched under his gaze.

"You all know why I called you out here tonight," he said. "We got business."

Shifting sideways looks crackled around the circle. The men shuffled and murmured and shied their eyes away from Taylor and his two enforcers.

The old man nodded. Manny and Ross stepped past the oil drum. The fire threw their shadows long and black over the men.

Ross moved to the far side of the circle, big, eager. Manny, smooth and cold, stopped closer.

When Ross came to the man with the white strip of bandage across his nose, those closest to that man faded off to the sides.

The bandaged man stared in disbelief a moment too long. By the time he tried to run it was already too late. Ross grabbed him by the legs and hauled him away from the junked car he was trying to crawl under.

The man in front of Manny had a pistol in his belt and another in his boot. He looked at Manny— and at the bandaged man struggling in Ross's grip— and dropped his head.

Manny gestured, and the man stepped forward on shaking knees.

He took his place in front of the oil drum. A moment later the bandaged man was dumped beside beside him.

Taylor sat forward in his wheelchair. He put his elbows on the armrests and steeled his fingertips. He looked from one man to the other, expectant.

The bandaged man spoke first.

"This is about the bitch, isn't it?" The broken nose and the gauze packing it made his voice flat, his consonants dull. His gold tooth winked in the firelight. "Look, thing is, she sucker punched me. It was a lucky shot."

"I see." Taylor's tone was mild. Dangerous.

"Tell you what, Boss, I'll show you. You just give me another shot at her and I'll tear that little whore—"

"You're lucky that 'little whore' as you called her didn't kill you."

"I told you, it was a sucker punch was all."

"Are you arguing with me?"

The bandaged man gulped.

"No sir. No, Boss."

Taylor's fingers smoothed over the blanket in his lap.

"I'm going to ask you two questions," he said and showed his teeth. "I hope you appreciate that much depends on your answers."

Every man in the circle saw the bandaged man tremble. Every man in that circle was glad it wasn't him.

"When you signed on, were you told about my wishes regarding acts of violence in the town center?"

"Yeah, but—"

"And did I at any time tell you to lay hands on the Stone woman?"

"No, but—"

"So as I understand it, you are either too stupid to follow orders or so full of yourself that you disobeyed me."

"I'm trying to tell you, it was a lucky shot. She didn't even—"

The shotgun blast tore through the man's argument. Blood and meat and bone exploded from his shoulder and he fell to his knees screaming. The man beside him started to move. The sound of Taylor cocking the second barrel stopped him.

"Ross..."

The big redhead hauled the wounded man to his feet. One hand held the man dangling in the air. The other curled into a fist, knuckles inches from the hard-packed earth.

The blow when it came threw blood and bits of tooth on the shoes of men twenty feet away.

The shotgun in Taylor's hand was just a small thing. Pistol-gripped, sawed off just ahead of the stock. Looking down its double barrels, the second man began to cry.

"Elton," the old man said. "It is Elton, isn't it? I believe you were the one who recommended this idiot into my service, did you not?"

"My wife's brother, Boss. I'm sorry."

Taylor's teeth flashed again. Light from the flames flickered across his face.

"Family. I understand," he said, "really I do."

The shotgun flicked, a fraction of an inch.

"And I understand too that blood has its obligations. Perhaps you feel I was too harsh on your brother in law? Perhaps you entertain thoughts of revenge?"

Elton struggled from words. Behind him, bone struck meat and a human voice shrieked.

"You're wearing a gun. Two, I believe." The sounds of the blows grew steady, quickened. "If you feel any need at all to avenge the family honor, you'd best do it now."

The circle of men had become a rough horseshoe. No one wanted to stand in Taylor's line of fire.

"I— I got kids to feed, Boss." The man held his hands up, palms out.

"Go on."

"I knew— I mean, I thought even if he wasn't none too bright, he'd be okay for you know, for errands and such."

"And yet on this one simple errand, your brother in law took it upon himself to provoke a dangerous foe. And to do so in defiance of my direct orders."

"I'm sorry, Boss."

Behind the man named Elton, the sounds of scuffed dirt. A heavy blow. A single hoarse cry.

"Ross, a minute please."

The redhead stood to his full height, blood-flecked and joyous. Taylor lifted his head and spoke out. His voice was as strong and clear as a lion's roar.

"I want you all to look at this man here, bleeding in front of you. He's where he is now because he defied me. He thought he knew better and he was wrong. The rest of you need to see what that means."

The crowd rippled, the men shuffling in place. Nobody wanted to look.. Nobody dared look away.

"Now this man over here," Taylor said, "he showed bad judgment. None of us can help who we get for kin. But all it takes is one damn fool to cost us our lives. Our money. Everything we've built."

The shotgun roared again. The man Elton collapsed over his ruined leg. Blood struck the earth with a sound like rain.

"Get on back with the others." As he spoke Taylor broke open the gun, plucked the two spent shells and inserted a fresh load. "Soon as we're done here you can get fixed up. You'll still be able to feed your kids."

He snapped the breech closed.

The others stood in silence as the man dragged himself up and hobbled back to his place in the circle. A distance of perhaps three yards. Slow and hitching. His progress marked by a wet red trail.

He almost made it. The closest thing he had to friends took his arms when he fell. They set him down in the dirt to hold his leg and weep.

Taylor lifted one hand.

"Ross…"

The big redhead went back to work. He took a long time.

HAP STUMBLED OUT of Junior's. Stood in the open air, trying to catch his breath. The night was warm, the way only Georgia in August can be. Back inside the tarpaper shack it was so hot the walls were dripping.

He wasn't the only one out here. A handful of folks stood scattered in their ones and twos, same as him. What sounded like a game of dice was going on around the corner. And a few of the cars in that lot and along the dirt road rocked on their springs, windows fogged.

Gravel scrutched behind him, and Hap jumped.

Kira laughed, none too sober.

"Speak of the devil," he said. Her hair hung in her eyes, wet and salty, and her dress— what there was of it— clung to her body.

"Say you were."

"I meant I was just thinking about you."

A woman moaned softly in one of the fogged-up cars nearby.

"I bet," Kira said. She lifted her plastic cup halfway to her mouth, saw that it was empty.

"You said you were gonna dance with me."

"I did dance with you."

"You said you'd dance."

She swayed to the music coming from inside. Turned away as she rubbed against him, spun out of his grasp, still moving to the beat.

"You always go like this?" he said. "How's a body supposed to keep up?"

"Too much for you there, son," a man called, and spit a stream of tobacco. "I'll take her off your hands."

"Excuse me?" Hap stepped further into the light.

"Mister Taylor." The man adjusted the cap on his head and ducked back inside.

"Mister… Taylor…" She said it with a giggle in her voice. "Mister…"

Hap's face burned. People acted like that, not because of him, but because they were afraid of an eighty year old man.

Kira's lips smashed into his. Their teeth cracked together and her tongue stabbed his mouth, a wet burst of secondhand whiskey.

"What was—"

"Shut up."

SUNDAY

THE HOUR WAS DAWN. Two men sat on the cracked asphalt behind the boarded-up diner. From the crumbling edge of the lot, the land fell away into scrub jungle. The air above the trees shimmered in the heat.

The two men dangled their legs over the edge and passed a bottle back and forth.

Both were red-eyed, their faces whiskery and drawn.

"You believe that shit?" the thick-built man named Big Tom said.

"Seem him do worse," said Virgil from under his cap. "We both have."

He took the brown glass bottle, tipped it to his lips.

Tom looked down at his knees, thick as country hams.

"We ain't never gonna do this, are we?"

Virgil wiped the lip of the bottle with his forearm and passed it back. The heat and the liquor made him feel sweaty and messy. The last twelve hours made him feel the stain on his soul.

"How you figure?" he said.

"Old man's got the rest of that bunch just about sewn up. Minute one of us tried to get a little support, that'd be us back there with Manny and Rolls."

Virgil stared at the unlit cigarette in his hand, lifted it slowly to his mouth.

"Those are two scary motherfuckers."

"Ain't just them either. Ever one of them assholes knows they catch us out with the old man, they'd be in prime position to take our spots. And that's even including our own guys. Our own guys."

"How I got mine."

"See what I mean? Hell, you'n me are about the only ones can even have this conversation."

"Both too big," Tom said. "The old man ain't gonna want to give either of us anything more than we already got. Taking one of us away'd just make the other one stronger."

"And anything he heard from you about me, he'd just figure you were trying to get me out of the way."

"And vice versa."

"And vice versa."

"Think Arn told him about us talking the other day?"

"We're still alive."

"Yeah, but we're valuable. What if last night was meant as a demonstration, like a message?"

"You think the old man's that subtle?"

"I think that old bastard's got more twists than a snake eating it's own asshole."

Big Tom jiggled the brown bottle in his hand, frowned and threw it into the bushes.

"Old man's got it sewn up pretty tight, all right," Virgil said.

"Sure does."

Virgil reached for his Marlboros, remembered the one already in his mouth. Heat flared against his cheeks as he fired it.

"Think the others'd be quite so afraid of the old man if he didn't have those damn enforcers?"

KIRA WOKE HARD, and only part of the way. Her brain was gummed with torn shreds of gauze. She struggled to pry her eyes open. Her bedsheets were a tangled mess.

The banging sound that woke her turned out to be the Sheriff opening and closing drawers.

"*Qu'est-ce que tu fais ici?* What're you doing here?"

"Good, you're awake. Now cover yourself up. It's indecent."

Kira lay where she was. Her mouth tasted terrible, and her body was sticky with sweat. There was no way to move that didn't hurt.

The Sheriff pushed one sandaled toe at Kira's pack and frowned at the contents.

"Don't you have a decent dress?"

"I have three," Kira said. "All quite good, actually."

"One that doesn't make you look like the goddamned Whore of Babylon?"

"That one in the closet. It's Givenchy."

"You can't wear that. It's black."

Kira stared, uncomprehending. Her thoughts were more than half back in that honky tonk out in the woods. Scraps and pieces, memory or dream, too few to cover the great blank spaces.

"To church,' the Sheriff said. "It's Sunday."

It made sense now. The other woman's floral print dress. Her sensible sandals and blue plastic handbag. The faint trace of perfume in the air.

"I—"

"Doesn't matter, I brought along a spare. Shoes too if you need them." She pulled a piece of polyester out of the handbag. "You and I are enough of a size."

"You're kidding."

"After your brother came back, hell, even before then any time he was home for just a few days, you better believe his butt was in a pew every Sunday."

Kira sat up. Held the top sheet against her breasts.

"I'm only here for a week."

"And folks round here can make that week easy or hard. Hell, Kira, why are you fighting me on this? Your mother's people built this town. They built that church."

"I'd rather you didn't talk about my mother."

The Sheriff threw the dress at Kira.

"Five minutes."

THE CLAPBOARD CHURCH was small and hot and stuffy. Kira and the Sheriff sat down in front, on a hardwood bench, sweating inside their polyester dresses. The whispers from behind them were a sound like a bucket of snakes twisting through dry grass.

The pastor raised his hands for silence. He looked down on Kira with a tight hard expression before launching into his speech.

Sermon was too strong a word for it. More like a tirade. The man spat a few sentences in favor of those who repented their sins and embraced Jesus. From there it was straight into every detail of the torments of Hell awaiting those who clung to their wicked ways.

The man up front was new, but the speech was much as she remembered. It had been over ten years since she'd set foot inside a church for anything but weddings or funerals. Sunday services hadn't been a part of her life over there, let alone this distinctly Southern variety. Video games and the internet had taken over for rap and heavy metal music, but there was still the same frequent use of words like 'agony', 'suffering' and 'torment'.

Not much had changed.

She squirmed against the hard wooden pew. At one point a fat man with a mustache sitting a few places down leaned forward and scowled in her direction. The Sheriff put a warning hand on Kira's wrist.

The pastor spoke as though God stopped by a couple times a week to hang out and discuss the state of Harrow, Georgia. From the sound of it, God didn't like outsiders or vipers in their midst, and He was pretty pissed off about strong liquor, fornication and fun of any sort.

Safe bet He didn't have a lot of nice things to say about Kira Stone.

"YOU WANTED TO see me, sir?"

Hap stood in what was once his father's study. Sometime while he had been away, a hospital bed had been moved in. Sickroom smells mingled with the rooms patina of dust and shadows, mildew and age.

The smells in that room weren't doing his stomach any favors. And the single line of sunlight where the curtains were drawn seemed to stab him in the eye. Only natural that he'd drop his gaze to the carpet underfoot.

Standing on that threadbare rug, in front of that big familiar desk, Hap unconsciously fell into the postures of childhood.

"You weren't there last night," the old man said.

"You didn't need me."

"I wanted you along, to observe."

"You beat a man to death over a little bit of nothing."

The old man smiled, slow and menacing. The nails at the ends of his fingers were long and yellowed.

"You think perhaps my methods are a little harsh?"

Hap caught himself digging one toe into the carpet and forced himself to stop.

"Your methods are always harsh, sir. I think you know that."

"So they are. And so they need to be— Hapworth, look at me when I talk to you. How many times have I told you, boy, that we are outlaws. Without recourse to the rule of law—"

" —the rules of our kind must be simple and few," Hap said right along with the old man. His head was killing him. "Punishment for breaking those rules must be vivid and severe."

"And the occasional object lesson?"

"Serves to reinforce the underlying order. You made an example of a pawn to keep your knights and bishops in line, I understand that."

"Then why weren't you there last night?"

Hap thought about telling the truth. But after that business with the diner and the car, he was forbidden from going anywhere near Kira Stone. And in the end, he was just another chess piece, kept in line.

"I didn't think you needed me. Sir."

The old man sighed. His yellowed nails scratched an idle pattern along the desktop.

"The Good Lord knows you weren't my first choice, son. Or my second. But at this point you may be all I have. I wanted you to be seen at my side, firm and resolute."

"You really think I could take over for you?"

The old man stared him down, pale eyes burning in the gloom.

"I never should have let your mother shelter you." He flicked his fingers. "Get out of my sight."

IT FELT LIKE FOREVER before the service finally ended.

Kira's first impulse was to push through the milling crowd and make for the door, but the Sheriff caught her elbow in an iron grip.

They held back while the rest of the room emptied out, back to front. And not without plenty of backwards looks and whispers behind hands.

"Jesus."

"Kira…"

"It's like high school all over again." She pulled at the neckline of the polyester dress. "How long do we have to do this?"

"Just shake hands with my bosses and play nice."

The fat man with the mustache turned out to be the mayor. He stood next to the pastor on the front steps, a handful of worn-looking busybodies beside him. The Sheriff shook hands down the line, murmured greetings Kira didn't quite catch.

The pastor's handshake was limp and wet. He didn't quite wipe his hand after Kira shook it, but he couldn't quit staring at it, either.

The mayor caught her in a two-handed grip, a real campaign special.

"Miss Stone," he said. "Seems like only yesterday you were just a baby."

He rubbed his index finger into her palm and she tore her hand away.

"Now I understand your visit with us is a brief one," he continued. "I can't imagine our small community has much to offer a young woman such as yourself."

The town council was a Greek chorus beside him, faces careful and without expression.

"I was quite close with your grandfather Ezra. Ezra Harrow, that was. Good friends." He lifted his gaze from Kira's breasts and she saw something in his eyes. Something gleaming and mean.

"Your mother just about broke that poor man's heart."

Kira looked from the fat man to the Sheriff and back again.

She kept her jaw clamped tight as she turned on one heel and walked away.

THAT SINGLE LINE OF sunlight in his father's study had been like a stab in Hap's eye. Out the front door the whole world was drenched in the stuff, worlds of pain unimagined.

On the front porch, half a dozen of his father's men lazed in the shade. Safe bet they weren't as hungover as he was.

A muttered word caught the edges of Hap's hearing, low enough to ignore. There was no ignoring the chorus of dirty laughter that followed.

Hap stopped. He looked from one man to the next. Tattoos and bad teeth and grime. The flat hard stares of a pack of junkyard dogs.

One man in particular leaned back and stretched his arms along the porch rail. The man's body was lean and muscled, his eyes bright and mocking.

The man had a tattoo of a scorpion, just under the corner of one eye. He met Hap's gaze and made a small kissing face.

Hap didn't say a word.

The guy snorted.

Hap punched him straight in the mouth.

FROM THE CHURCH, Kira and the Sheriff drove through the town center. The made a slow circuit around the statue of Beauregard Harrow. They rolled past dead storefronts— windows soaped or boarded, real estate signs faded by the sun.

Driving away from the center they passed the real estate office. There was no furniture behind its dust-streaked glass.

Town buildings gave way to rundown farms, fields gone to seed. Barns that were no more than piles of rotting wood.

"You embarrassed me back there," the Sheriff said.

"I didn't do anything."

"I have to work with these people, Kira."

"Why I held back."

The Sheriff shook her head. Kira crossed her arms. The two women leaned away in exasperated silence.

Eventually they left the dirt roads behind. The Sheriff turned onto the main road, headed north. They passed the diner where the Atlanta PD cops handed Kira over. At the top of the hill, they pulled over and rolled to a stop.

The Sheriff got out. She shut the door and walked away. A moment later, she heard Kira behind her.

"Look there."

Kira looked.

Down the hill, the sides of the highway were a dazzling glitter of glass and chrome. Walmart and McDonalds and Chick-Fil-A and Hooters and car lots flying flags without number all crowded at the edges of the asphalt.

"Why?" Kira said.

"Taylor. They got their share of corrupt sons of guns down there in Murtree County, but they're nothing compared to that evil old man."

The Sheriff turned her head and spat.

"Look at any map of this place," she said. "Harrow County's a goddamned maze of back roads, all twisting and looping in on each other. This place is a smuggler's paradise, has been since the

1700's. And that withered old son of a bitch spends money all the way up to the state legislature to make sure it stays that way."

"No," Kira said. "I meant, why are you showing me?"

"I want you to see what he's done to your home. How your people suffer while that man lines his pockets."

"My people."

"He's going to try to get you under his spell, Kira. The name Stone still carries weight in these parts—"

"Don't I know it."

"And you're a Harrow on your momma's side too. Plus, you're strong as hell. No way Taylor's going to be able to resist, so when he comes around with his fancy talk and his offers, I want you to think about this town dying while our neighbors prosper. I want you to make the right decision."

"I'm only here for a week."

"Europe's not your home, Kira, and I think deep down you know it. Your roots are here. This is where you belong."

"That's not what you said ten years ago."

The Sheriff's face reddened.

"Ten years ago you were a child. A reckless child who'd put herself in danger. Resent me all you want, but know this: if I hadn't sent you off, that old man would have killed you."

KIRA CAME HOME and stripped out of that awful blue dress. Without the cheap polyester against her skin, she felt like she could breathe again.

She kicked her duffel, sent clothes tumbling. She had cocktail dresses and dinner dresses, bikinis and strappy sandals, capri pants and short shorts and everything she needed for the summer season. Her soiled gravedigging outfit from Walmart was the ugliest thing in the room.

She swung a fist at the door frame, heard wood crack. The Sheriff was right, of course: Kira's wardrobe was all wrong for this place.

That was the point. That had always been the point.

Kira punched the door frame again. Her knuckle left a small bloody print, deep in the wood.

THREE STEPS. THREE wooden steps up to the porch. All it took to set Hap on the ground, looking up at the girl he'd wanted since he was four years old.

She looked down at him from that three-step height. Back straight. Eyes unreadable.

Hap's heart twisted, pain, longing, regret.

He covered, same way he always covered. With a smile and a wink.

"Thought you might want some company," he said. "Maybe get some lunch?"

She looked down at him in silence a moment longer. Pushed the hair away from her face. It fell right back in place.

"Got anything to drink?"

"Didn't figure you'd want any." He looked at the ground when he said it. "Not after last night."

He tried the smile again.

"Course, I do know a place."

MACON WAS ANOTHER world. Green lawns and cool shade. Laughing children. Hap said something about the drought not affecting them as badly, but it felt like something more.

Hap drove them into Macon, to a red-brick restaurant with cream-colored tablecloths. The waiter brought wine without being asked, a cheap red that tasted slightly of vinegar. Kira cupped her hands around the glass and lowered her head.

"I know how you feel," Hap said.

Kira looked at him without speaking.

"Hey, I might not have been jet-setting all around the Riviera and whatnot, but I do know what it's like to come back to this place, back to those people. To come back home and feel like a stranger."

He lifted the glass to his lips, set it back down again.

"And I know what it's like to lose a brother."

There was nothing to say to that. And her wine was empty.

"Look, Kira, I ain't pointing any fingers. I'm just saying, you got a lot on you right now, and I get it."

He gestured. The waiter refilled the wine and left the bottle. The label said it was Italian Chianti. It also said 'product of Arkansas'.

"Hap, about last night—"

"This wine sure is something."

"We didn't—?"

"Not what you're used to France, I bet."

"I just—"

"Course, I do reckon it's a step up from what you were knocking back last night."

"Forget it."

Kira let her hair fall in front of her eyes. Her face was burning.

"Look, I wasn't trying to…"

"You didn't want to sit around that lonely old house, with no one but ghosts for miles around, and nothing to think about but stuff that makes you sad. I told you, I get it."

"I guess you do."

"Sides," he said, "you're one hell of a dancer."

That brought a smile from her. It was a smile she didn't know she had.

The wine was working on her, settling her nerves. The smells from the kitchen were starting to seem like a good thing.

"How long you been back?" she said.

"Bout a year, little over."

"Long time."

'To be gone, or to be back?"

"Both, I guess."

"I was already off at boarding school when you and Bobby had your little see-to. Then college, a few little things out in California." He lifted his wine. "Daddy never did much want me underfoot."

A small silence. It was a truth too raw to be tossed out so casually.

"Why come back?" Kira said. "If it wasn't for… Just say I wouldn't."

"You've seen him, Kee. And you've seen that bunch around him. He's old."

Hap's glass was nearly full. He drained it, refilled. Knocked that back, left an inch in the bottom.

"He was always so strong, but now he's so old."

Kira looked away while he wiped his eyes on a napkin. She tried, and failed, to picture Bobby feeling that way. In truth, it was hard to imagine the Bobby she remembered loving anyone but himself. And it was impossible to imagine anyone at all loving Old Man Taylor.

"Sorry," Hap said after a minute. His wine was full again, and so was hers. The bottle was worse for wear. "Ain't really proper talk for a date, now is it?"

She raised one eyebrow, a silent challenge.

"It most certainly is a date," he said. "Last night you decided that being with me beat being home alone. And you decided again back on the porch this morning."

He gave her a wink and one of those dazzling too-white smiles.

"Besides, everyone knows a vacation fling'll perk up even the worst holiday."

"That what this is?"

"The worst holiday? Most certain."

"A vacation fling."

"Will be after lunch, when we check into one of those motels out yonder."

Kira eyed him over the rim of her glass. He did have a certain cocky boyish charm.

And a shadow fell over the table.

"It's never going to happen, is it?" Hap said.

"I'm sorry, it's—"

"Bobby. I know." His hands curled into fists on the table.

"This was a mistake."

It was an awkward drive back.

TAYLOR SHOWED UP that evening, just after sunset. Kira was surprised: he didn't come in any of the enormous cartoonish SUV's that seemed so popular on the roads. Nothing flash at all. He came in a boxy Ford panel van that had been old when Kira was born.

The front doors opened, and two men in white strap undershirts stood in the dust, facing the house. Muscles, jailhouse tattoos, flat-eyed stares.

A pair of bull-chested dogs, straining at the end of a chain.

Kira came down to meet them. The axe handle Jack had left next to the front door she held cocked on one shoulder.

The smaller man, dark and bald with tattoos to his chin, she remembered serving the old man's breakfast. The taller was a crewcut redhead with clouds of freckles mottling his ink. His knuckles were raw, his forearms scratched.

Kira's first thought was that someone had a lot of his DNA under their nails.

The bald man had cold eyes. The redhead's were hungry. She chose her distance and set her feet.

The van's side door opened. Taylor's white suit and Panama hat stood out in the gloom. His wheelchair was substantial, an antique that resembled a throne more than anything else.

"Miss Stone." He touched two long fingertips to the brim of his hat. "I hope the evening finds you well."

Kira said nothing. She watched his human dogs for any sign of movement.

"No need to fear," he said. "Manuel and Rolleston are here as attendants, only. This chair is heavy but, I regret to say, occasionally necessary."

No one moved. Taylor watched the standoff with a strange sort of approval.

"Manny. Rolls," he said at last. The guard dogs broke away, each man turning to take one side of Taylor's chair. Prison-yard muscle stood out on their arms as they lowered it to the ground.

"Boys, I do believe you're making Miss Stone uncomfortable. Wait in the van."

The two men, Manny and Rolls, hesitated. Taylor's face changed.

"Now."

They all but jumped inside.

"You won't need that." He gestured to the axe handle still in Kira's hand. "Or do you plan to strike an old man in a wheelchair?"

"Haven't ruled it out," she said, but tossed the stick up onto the porch just the same.

"And how is the Charger? Fast enough for your liking, I trust."

"Hap said that'd piss you off."

"I admit I was… surprised that he saw fit to bestow it on you."

The old man looked at Kira. His tongue worked at his bottom lip and his eyes were bright with strange and unreadable hungers.

"Been seeing a lot of him, have you?"

"I wouldn't say that."

"Rumor has it, you two are quite the item."

"Don't believe everything you hear."

But even as she said it, her mind was back in Macon that afternoon. It was the first time since she was a kid she could remember feeling ashamed.

And worse, she was sure Taylor knew it.

"Just as well," he said. "Hapworth lacks his older brother's constitution. I doubt he'd survive your affections."

"You're pretty hard on him."

"The world is hard, Miss Stone. And beneath all that 'beautiful waste', eurotrash persona, you know how very hard the world can be. Hapworth had it too easy, and it made him weak." He paused. The breath seemed to rattle in his chest. "Unfortunately, he is also the last of my blood. There is nothing to be done."

Taylor looked down at the blanket in his lap. The late light made him almost transparent, a tangle of blue veins under skin like parchment. When he looked back at her, she saw the bones in his skull.

"This town is dying, Miss Stone. If not for me, it would already be dead."

"You."

"Cotton moved overseas in the Seventies, and the last sawmill shut down the year you were born. Poultry is hanging on, but only just. I am the single largest remaining engine in the local economy. If you'd be so kind?"

It took Kira a moment to see what he meant. She stepped behind him, took the handles of his chair and began to wheel him forward.

"The Roberts girl refers to me as a 'cancer on the community'. It is one of her favorite phrases for me. I believe her childhood pastor was fond of decrying me in that fashion most Sunday mornings. What Sheriff Roberts never understood, of course, is that same pastor quietly spent his Saturday nights putting the collection plate money back into my pocket."

"I don't know that stealing from a church is something I'd brag about."

"Don't be naive. Men of the cloth are like everyone else, if not more so."

The chair had a high back and wooden arms. It had to be an antique, but the tires were modern, knobbly rubber tread, crisp enough to be brand new.

"I have many happy memories of this house, you know. Long years, before you you were born."

Kira said nothing. The late light filled the windows with its glow, even as shadows pooled around the foundations.

"Your father and I worked together, we drank together and whored together—"

"I'd rather you didn't talk about my father that way."

"At one time we both courted your mother."

"And don't talk about her at all."

Taylor made a small sound, pleased. His thin white hands smoothed the blanket in his lap. Ninety degrees in the shade, and this man was in a blanket.

"Is it too much to say that the single greatest regret of my life is that the luckier man won?"

"What is it you want, Taylor?"

"I wanted to look you over. To ask you, what do you think will happen to this place after I am gone?"

Kira looked down at the crown of the old man's hat and tightened her grip on the wheelchair.

THAT NIGHT, THE MOON streamed bright through the windows of Kira's old room. It lit the horse statue her father had given her for her ninth birthday, the posters of teen idols taped to the walls. The change on her dresser, a scattered mix of American coins, centimes and Euros, blazed like bright cold sparks.

It had been a strange day. The Sheriff seemed to think Taylor wanted her. The old man hadn't done any more than wheel around and talk about the past. Both seemed to think she cared about a town that had never much cared for her, when her only reason for ever coming back was laid up in a morgue drawer somewhere.

The shaft of moonlight didn't touch her bedside table. Her grandfather's gun lay in that darkness. Whatever was going on, she didn't want to end up in a drawer next to her brother.

Kira undressed. The clothes on her floor were getting muddled — high end from Europe mixing with cheap stuff from Walmart.

She crawled into bed. The sheets were stiff and cool and smelled faintly of dust.

She lay there a long time, unable to sleep. A bowl of ice cubes set in front of a fan did little to cool the room. The open window helped, but not enough.

It was late, but her body kept insisting it was early. Sheer exhaustion battled with the whispered lies of her disrupted rhythm.

She rolled over. The moonlight had shifted, raking the bedroom wall. The lead singer of a long-vanished boy band pouted at her. His pretty face was creased where the poster had been folded into the pages of Tiger Beat magazine.

Kira had actually met the singer, the previous year at Cannes. Or possibly Monaco, the season was one long haze. He had been bloated and fleshy, just out of rehab and trying to revive his career with his band's old songs and his new leather pants. Looking up at that poster now, it was hard to imagine that man as the first lust of her adolescence.

Bobby Taylor. Now, he was something else. Good looking. Rough. More than a little dangerous.

Papa always said, never trust a Taylor. By the time she found out her father was right, it was too late.

The sight of Bobby had been like a match lit under Kira's skin. Even now, the memory of his lips and hands warmed her. As long as she didn't think about the way it ended.

She tossed in her childhood bed, chasing sleep. Old memories of Bobby led to new thoughts of Hap. The plates of muscle under his shirt. The way he looked at her. She sat up and reached for her shirt.

There was no reception in the house. Kira stepped out the back and headed up the hill to the family plot.

Outside, the night was sultry. The merciless heat of the daylight hours was gone, but the air was still a warm hand along her flesh.

The gravestones were pale in the moonlight. The open grave for her brother showed black and bottomless. Kira touched one hand to her throat and moved away to the far side of the clearing.

At the top of the hill, her phone showed two bars. The carrier was unfamiliar, a company that hadn't existed when she left. She wondered what charges would show up on her bill.

Jean-Michele picked up on the second ring.

"Tiens!" His voice was sunshine, a lilting summer breeze. Behind him, Kira heard the clink of glasses, the shrill of scooters, the music of spoken Italian and a woman's voice raised in laughter.

"Jean-Michele, you old rogue!" It felt good to speak French again.

"Darling! So good to hear you! I thought you were this tiresome rental company." He spoke a quick *'grazie'* to someone there with him. "But how did you know to find me awake at this terrible hour."

"As if you've been to sleep."

"Ah, *cherie*, you know me too well."

For the first time in days, Kira smiled.

"Where are you?"

"This little place just outside Campari, terribly hot and terribly boring. I am glad you called, *ma cherie*. We were all so sad to lose you to *l'Amerique*."

"It's only a week."

"Ah. Next week we are in Spain. I know what you are thinking, Spain in August is the Devil's Testicles, but Marie has collected another of her little fat men and this one has his own small island off the coast. *Trés intimé,* and he assures us that with the beach and the breeze it is not the least beastly."

Kira closed her eyes to the graves around her. She could see Marie's little fat man, so like all the others, and his not-in-the-least-beastly island. Five more days and Kira would be able to lose herself once again in white sand and blue water and the summer season's gentle lecheries.

For a long time after she ended the call, Kira stood in the cemetery plot. The bright and tinkling, somewhat unreal world on the other side of that call was gone. Now she was alone, lit by a torch the color of bone shining through the trees.

MONDAY

DEPUTIES BIX AND Graham rolled past the Stone property at 8am sharp. The plan was to verify she was on the premises before setting up down the road apiece. Some spot where she'd have to drive past them, or they'd be able to see her leave.

"Excited for another day babysitting?" Bix said.

"Day she gave us Saturday, I'm kinda hoping she sleeps in."

"Then you sure ain't gonna like this."

Graham turned his head to follow his partner's line of vision. The black muscle car was nowhere to be seen.

"Might be in the barn or something?"

"You can see from here the barn's open, just got that old pickup inside. Our little girl's an early riser."

"Shit."

"Pretty much."

"What do you want to do?"

"What I want's to go fishing," Bix said. "What we're gonna do is go find that gal before the Sheriff knows we lost her."

"Shit…" Graham put the pedal down and the cruiser stormed away in a spray of gravel.

KIRA DROVE, THE steering wheel thrumming in her hands. The Charger responded like an extension of herself. It felt good, driving again.

She looped in wide circles, in and out of the county, on and off the highways. She used the old bootlegger roads, the back ways and hidden paths her family had used for over a hundred years. Behind the wheel, there was no need, no time, to think. Perhaps some down-deep part of her still dealt with questions and answers, problems and solutions, but for Kira herself there was only the car and the road, one smooth flow.

She'd forgotten how many churches there were. They seemed to pop up every few feet out on the main roads. Big signs out front, every one of them making Jesus sound like the sort of buddy who drops by for some barbecue and a few beers. More than a few seemed to imply that Heaven was assured, as long as you weren't liberal or a Democrat.

Even on the back roads, she found small meeting halls, backwoods chapels, an old Shaker church tucked back in the trees.

Religion was everywhere in Europe. There was always a church, a cathedral, the sound of bells. Somehow, it felt different.

She found herself heading around the turn back to the house. It was the same route she'd taken on foot her first morning, but in reverse. She stopped and got out.

The jet lag wasn't as bad now. Colors were not so sharp, so painfully bright. Sounds were not so muffled. Orange dust puffed around her shoes when she walked.

There'd been no rain here, not for a long time. Nothing to wash away the skid marks.

And there were no skid marks to wash away.

Brown grass, withered and burnt by the sun, flattened where Jack's car had gone off the road. Motor oil and radiator coolant stained the earth where her brother had died. Broken glass glittered like diamonds and shards of plastic melted in the sun.

Kira was still staring down at the crash site when her phone buzzed in her pocket.

"YES?"

"Miss Stone? This here's Tim Rhineland—"

"How did you get my number?"

"Your stepmom. I did try Hap Taylor first, on account of half the county saw y'all stepping out at Juniors on Saturday. He *said* he didn't have a number for you, not too polite about it neither truth be told, so I called up your stepmom. She was out on patrol or something, but they patched me through."

"*Merde*." Kira looked out at the orange dust hanging in the hot air. She had forgotten how small this town could be. "How can I help, Mr. Rhineland? I assume this is about Jack?"

"Yes'm. You see, I just came from the morgue— few of us little towns share space over in Barnesville? Anyway, I thought I'd get started on the embalming, see if there's any cosmetic work needs doing…"

Kira shut her eyes and pinched the bridge of her nose.

"We went over this," she said. "Closed casket, *no* cosmetics. How clear can I be?"

"Well, see, that ain't exactly a problem now." Rhineland made an indistinct sound, deep in his throat. "You see, your brother was cremated."

"You cremated my brother without asking?"

"No, no of course not. That was all done up at the morgue. I only just found out myself."

"I see."

She rolled her head on her neck to release the tension. At the bottom of the slope, the torn place where Jack hit the tree glowed white in the shade.

"I don't know what happened," Rhineland said. "Bureaucratic mix up, or maybe the nature of the accident…"

"I don't suppose it makes much difference," she said. "Just would've been nice to be asked."

"Sure would. Would have been nice to do a proper burial too." For the first time, the sadness in Rhineland's voice sounded genuine. "Not much call for caskets anymore. People are living longer than they used to, and when they go, more and more of them choose cremation. It's a sad state of affairs."

Kira mentally cursed the Sheriff for giving this man her number.

"Anyway," he said, "you see, the thing is…"

"Out with it."

"Miss Stone, I'm afraid I'm going to need you to come in and fill out some more paperwork."

THE 4X4 RUMBLED through the woods. The course the Sheriff drove was a sorry excuse, not worth calling a road. Two dirt ruts twisting up through the trees, it was barely worth calling it a trail.

Pine branches slapped the sides of the vehicle. Dried brown needles scrutched under the tires, and the light was cool and dim and green. As she steered between the trees, she cursed under her breath.

"What's that, ma'am?" said the man beside her. "Keer what?"

"I said, are you sure about this?"

"Sure I'm sure. Don't you believe me?"

The truck thumped and rumbled over a fallen limb. The Sheriff cut a look at the scruffy little man with the bad skin and the three day beard. He smiled, a ruined green mouthful. The Sheriff made a disgusted noise, deep in her throat.

Scooter Wilkes was a bad apple off a bad tree. The Wilkes clan were all through these hills, all the way up into the Carolinas, and not a one of them worth a damn. They were petty thieves and poachers, and hardscrabble farmers who never brought in a decent crop.

The little man across the seat from her now was the lowest of a no-account bunch. Greedy, dim, and sly.

And, this morning, eager to please.

"I seen it with my own eyes, Sheriff Roberts Ma'am. The Slocum boys been cooking, way back in the hills where their daddy used to grow, you know?"

"Their lab."

"Nah, you'll never get anywhere close to that. They got that hollow so wired up and boobytrapped, you couldn't get in there with a platoon of marines."

He spoke with a lot of tics and hand movement. His breath was terrible.

"No, this here place I'm showing you used to be an old house, shack, something like that. Had its own well, anyhow. Old as anything. Slocum boys come on out the hollow every now and then, chuck their stash down that old well. Taylor's boys come along pick it up the twelfth of every month, just like clockwork."

The Sheriff rolled her window down. The sharp smell of raw pine clashed with the odor of rotting teeth.

It was the same story he'd been telling her all morning. He was lying, junkies always lied. Hard part was figuring out how much.

But he was harmless, and he had proved useful before. Especially when it served his own agenda.

"You owe the Slocums money or something, Scoot?"

"I told you, I was out hunting when I came across that old house," he said. "Ain't nothing much of it but a little bit of root cellar and a couple pieces of chimney, and that old well. I saw the, uh, *substances in question* and come on back down and reported them to you."

"Bull," the Sheriff said. "You never hunted a day in your life. And I had to chase you over half this county before you said a word."

"It was the weekend. Don't you never, I don't know, let your hair down on the weekend?"

"What were you doing up here?"

He flashed his meth-ruined teeth.

"All due respect, Sheriff Ma'am, but ain't no way you're gonna get me to admit to doing anything illegal."

"You're a real piece of work, Scoot."

"Thank you, ma'am."

"It wasn't a compliment."

THE SECURITY CAMERAS showed that damn black muscle car as soon as it skidded into the lot. By the time the Stone woman made it to the front door, Rhineland was waiting.

Today she wore a bright blue top and little tiny white shorts. The top fit snug against her body, a tight and muscular package. Her legs were tanned, and she looked like she'd just stepped out of a resort somewhere. Rhineland never met women like her in his work.

It was a damn shame.

Rhineland fidgeted with the cuffs of his suit and pulled at his collar. He put on what he thought of as his funeral face and gave his best hushed and solemn greeting.

"The urn ready?" she said.

Bitch.

"If you'll just come this way, Miss Stone."

Rhineland turned gently. His footsteps crackled softly on the strip of yellowing plastic that kept mourners' dirty feet from messing up his carpets.

"You said you had it waiting."

"Just a little paperwork is all."

"I've got cash."

"Please, just follow me."

The Stone woman stopped.

"I already told you, I'm not renting one of your chapels, and I don't need any flowers or hired speakers to deliver a eulogy. Just a little copper box with my brother's ashes inside."

"You know, most folks lose a loved one are a lot more distraught. I ain't used to being treated like some kind of used car salesman."

She took one step forward. Her face was inches from Rhineland's chin, and her eyes were dangerous.

"My grief is my business. And if you want respect, my eyes are up here."

She spun on one heel, her steps crackling toward the door.

"Hey, you can't just leave. You haven't got your urn."

"Send it out to the house," she called out behind her.

"Wait!"

She stopped, stared at the place where Rhineland grabbed her arm. His hands left wet tracks on her skin when he pulled them away.

"Please, he said. "I ain't , I mean I'm *not*, trying to sell you nothing extra." He pulled at his collar. His suit felt suffocating. "It's just, I can't reuse the urn once it's had, once it's been used, and it's just a bitty piece of paper the state makes us sign. Transferring remains and like that. It's standard."

"I bet it is."

Distrust bristled in her voice. But she stood wiping Rhineland's sweat from her forearm. She didn't leave.

"Come on," he said. "It's right through here."

FOR A TIME THE only sounds were the engine's deep grumble, the click-click-click of Scoot's thumbnail against his bottom teeth and the slap and hiss of pine branches dragging along the truck's side.

"How much farther, Scoot?"

"I don't see why you gotta drag me out here anyway, Mizz Roberts. I already told you where to go— all you gotta do is bring your deputies out here later tonight and you'll get both the Slocums and Taylor's boys, easy as pie."

"Until I actually see those drugs, I'm not letting you out of my sight. If this is some wild goose chase to draw me away from the *real* drop, I'm gonna make you sorry, Scoot."

"What's the matter, Sheriff Ma'am?" Again the rotten teeth flashed. "Don't you trust me?"

The Sheriff kept her eyes on the path ahead, lifted her chin in the direction of the windshield.

"Wasn't two years ago you sold your own grandma's wheelchair to feed your habit. Only question in my mind is who thinks they bought you, and who you're really double-crossing."

"Just up ahead," he said. "It's all like I told you. You'll see."

Daylight blazed in the near distance. The Sheriff dropped the transmission into neutral and let the vehicle roll to a stop.

"Out."

A spark of defiance flickered across the junkie's face. It withered under the Sheriff's gaze. She waited until he was across the seat and outside the 4x4 before pulling his door shut and opening her own.

"You can't miss it," Scoot said as the Sheriff round the front grill. "That old well's just right over there. You don't need me to show you."

"Come stand over here by the bumper."

"It's hot out here, Sheriff. Can't I wait inside, in the air-conditioning?"

"Right arm, Scoot."

She pulled the cuffs from her belt, hooked one bracelet around his wrist and the other to the bull bars at the front of the vehicle.

"This ain't right." He danced from foot to foot, steel jangling on steel. "Sheriff Ma'am, this ain't right."

"Can't have you running off on me. Just you wait here a minute."

"Skeeters'll eat me alive…"

"I'll buy you some cream."

RHINELAND DIDN'T LEAD Kira back to the same office as before. She followed his mullet to a different door. This one led to a room of green tiles, steel cabinets and fluorescent lights. At least one bulb was about to die, lashing the room with flickering shadows. The air was flat and chemical, perfumed and chilled.

In the center of the room stood a stainless steel table with gutters down the sides. Two objects sat on the table's surface. One was a clipboard, complete with an official-looking form and ballpoint pen under the clip. The other was a small but handsome box of burnished copper. Square with beveled edges, reflections swimming in its depths.

And behind the copper box sat Taylor.

The old man looked up at Kira. Something bright and hungry swam in his eyes. His bodyguards, Manny and Rolls, surged forward behind him. A small gesture, a single hand lifted from the arm of the thronelike wheelchair, and they subsided.

In the uncertain light, Taylor's skin was that of a corpse.

"I do hope you'll forgive me," he said. "I lost quite a bit of sleep last night thinking about you."

Kira heard the door close behind her and mentally swore to make Rhineland pay.

"Don't be too harsh with the boy, my dear." Taylor smiled. His teeth were long and brown. "Death isn't quite the business it once was, and young Rhineland owes me a great deal. Of course, many of this town's leading citizens owe me more than they would care to admit."

Over the top of the old man's head, the bodyguards fixed Kira with hard and aggressive stares. The redhead's hands flexed open and closed.

On a concrete apron where the tile ended, the boxy Ford panel van sat with its rear door open this time. Some sort of machinery in back. A garage door of featureless gray metal was rolled down, sealing them in. No one outside would see or hear what happened.

The room itself offered nothing in the way of a weapon. Tile walls, floor and ceiling. Steel table, sink and cabinets. A machine like an industrial blender sat on a cart in the corner. There might be something in the cabinets, but the room itself was bare.

Taylor moved long white fingers through the air. They left colorless trails in the buzzing fluorescent light. He made a wet amused shape with his mouth.

"Forgive them," he said. "My attendants are… enthusiastic. But quite obedient, I assure you."

Kira straightened her back. The urge to crouch behind the table was strong, but she sensed the last thing to do with men like these was to show fear or weakness. She forced herself to stand tall.

Besides, Jack's urn was on the other side of the table.

"Have you given any thought to my question yesterday? What will happen to this place when I am gone?"

"A parade?"

"A facile answer. I had hoped for better."

"What do you want, Taylor?"

"What I want is your brother, still alive."

The disappointment in the old man's voice sounded genuine. The pads of his fingers closed gently on the urn and moved it six inches to his left. His fingertips made no smudge or mark on the polished copper.

"You are a powerful symbol to this community, you know."

"So I keep hearing. Last surviving Stone, Harrow on my mother's side. What none of you people seem to get is that I don't care."

"Whether you like it or not, Miss Stone, people are watching you. Your actions are important. As are your allies."

The form on the clipboard was titled Transfer and Release of Human Remains. Rhineland hadn't been a total liar.

"Silence is not an answer, Miss Stone."

The cheap black ballpoint clipped to the top had RHINELAND FUNERAL HOME and the address printed in gold. It didn't matter what she said. No one seemed to listen to her.

"For the last time, I don't care about you, or my stepmother, or this feud you've got going. End of this week, I'm putting an ocean between me and this place, and I will never set foot here again."

"If you are not seen to stand with me, you will be perceived to oppose me."

"Not my problem, Taylor. Now why don't you clear out so I can bury my brother, or scatter his ashes anyway, and live in peace."

The light in the old man's face faded. What remained looked almost like regret. He snatched the copper urn and wheeled backward with it in his lap. Kira took a half step around the table and Taylor's two human guard dogs fanned out to either side.

Rubber squeaked on tile. The old man pushed himself back to the mouth of the van. A small motor whined as a steel plate lifted his chair up into the belly of the van. Taylor's voice scraped from the darkness inside.

"If you can," he said, "leave her alive."

THE SHERIFF ADJUSTED the set of her Stetson and moved through the remaining trees.

Scoot's whining trailed behind her. Cuffing him to the bull bars had been the only way to keep him from running off. An impulse she didn't question told her she didn't want the meth addict loose at her back.

The crumbled remains of an old stone chimney lay near the center of the clearing. That pile of rocks told its own story: river rock, blackened by fire. The grass was sun-blasted straw, knee high and burnt brown by drought. More than once, that grass bent in rapid S-shapes, snakes fleeing before her.

The old well was right where he said it would be. The grass around it was trampled flat, and the boards showed signs they had been pried up and dropped back in place loose.

She knelt down, curled her fingers under one of the boards. If the drugs were down there, she might just have something. Maybe not enough to bring down Taylor himself, but a good chance to take one of his lieutenants and put a kick in his tail.

Scoot started screaming and banging his cuffs against the bull bars.

"Here! She's here!" he cried. "The Sheriff's here and she's alone!"

Pine trees whipped and waved on the far side of the clearing. Three men, ragtag hunters in tee shirts and camo pants, came scrambling out of the treeline. All carried assault rifles.

The Sheriff cleared leather. The pearl-handled Sig had been a present from John Lee Stone, years ago. One of the first the company made in America. It felt natural in her hand, part of her own body.

One hunter stopped and raised his weapon while the other two kept coming. The muzzle flashed. A three round burst stitched the ground in front of her.

A second man fired as he ran. His rifle was modified for full-auto. The rounds went wild, but they gave the third hunter time to aim.

Bullets sizzled the air around her head and thwocked into the earth around her feet. Chunks of stone flew from the ruined chimney.

The Sheriff went up on one knee and fired. The third hunter pitched backward in a red mist.

She was already moving, diving through the air as the other two returned fire. Grass shredded. Her hat flew. Hot winds plucked at her uniform. The Sheriff rolled to a crouch behind the safety of the chimney.

"Alright you two." Her voice was loud and strong. "This here's the only chance you're going to get. Throw down those guns, you're under arrest."

Both men emptied their clips into the ruined chimney. Bullets cracked against the charred stones or tumbled whining past. A chip of stone from a ricochet cut her cheek.

As soon as she heard the rattle and clatter of them reloading, the Sheriff stepped into the open.

The nearest man looked at her. Fear, anger and raw desperation mingled in his face.

She raised her hand, natural as pointing a finger, and pulled the trigger.

The third man was some distance away. The two had been moving away from each other, coming around that chimney from both sides.

He had a fresh magazine already slapped into the receiver. His hand hovered over the bolt.

"It's over," she said. The pistol hung in her hand, down next to her leg. "Throw down your weapon and get those hands right on top of your head."

The hunter's left hand shot the bolt. His right brought the weapon up, finger on the trigger.

The Sheriff blew his left eye out the back of his head.

THE HARD MEN came on slow. Kira worked her head on the column of her neck and watched them come.

They took their time stepping around the steel table. Two against one. Nowhere to run. No risk of interruption. They didn't see any need to hurry.

The bald one, Manny, was all business. The thick muscle banding his neck, chest and shoulders rippled with tension. His face had no expression.

Rolls, the buzz-cut redhead, was a different story. His knuckles were already torn and scabbed, his forearms covered in scratches. The light in his face was eager and disturbing.

"Just a beating, *chica*," Manny said. "Don't make trouble and we'll make it quick."

He didn't bother to hide the lie in his voice. Rolls snickered.

Kira let her gaze soften. Easier to track movement. She shifted to put more of the table between them. The two men sauntered closer.

They expected her to run. That much was clear. Maybe try the locked door behind her. Or simply freeze in fear. Maybe they even expected some token resistance, accepting sore shins or fingernails snapped off in their skin as part of the play.

Kira feinted right, darted left. It took her to the redhead's side of the table, and he moved to shut her down. She ducked under his big swiping grab and brought her knee up hard.

He covered his groin, quick and reflexive. Male fighters were usually prepared for a kick in the balls.

Which left him open for the nerve shot. Kira's knee struck the unprotected nerve bundle low on his thigh. The spasming leg refused to accept his weight, and Rolls started to topple. Kira hooked her arm around a shoulder thicker than her torso and pivoted her weight.

His face struck the tile wall with a meaty crunch. Whips of blood flew as she reversed the torque.

The man's head struck the steel table, a sound like a great bell. He tumbled to the floor in a boneless clatter.

Kira and Manny faced each other over the fallen redhead. The bald man's stance was wide and low, heavy on the front leg. He had one fist cocked near his shoulder, the other down and forward. He danced his weight from foot to foot. Whatever style he fought, safe bet it featured a lot of kicking.

Kira's lips pulled back in a tight private smile. Behind her, she heard the van's engine start. Wondered idly if Taylor meant to gas them both.

Manny backed away from where Rolls lay. Attacking over the top of that man's bulk would have been suicide, and he knew it. He kept his stance low and bouncy as he circled the table in the other direction.

Kira came around to meet him. The redhead was just as big a hazard to her, and the light in the room was growing brighter as the garage door clacked and rumbled to the ceiling. She had to shut this down quick if she wanted to keep the old man from escaping with her brother's ashes.

The bald fighter was a tricky bastard. Lots of feints and stomps and shoulder jumps, trying to draw her out. Kira kept her structure tight. Anything he threw, she'd be ready. All she had to do was wait for him to throw a real shot, and she'd take him apart.

But that damned garage door was rolling higher.

Daylight grew brighter in the room, and Kira's shadow darkened on Manny's face. She bent hard at the waist. Sunlight struck his eyes.

He was only blind for a moment. But he also knew that a moment was all it would take. Smart enough not to reel away, he rushed to tackle Kira. Grappling on the floor, sight wouldn't matter. Size and strength would.

Kira met his rush. She came up out of her crouch with a palm strike that knocked his head back and an elbow strike that broke his jaw entirely.

Arms closed around her, desperate, massive and strong. Kira wedged the top of her head into the man's sternum and drove fist after fist up under his ribs.

Her hips pumped with every shot, one after the other. The bald man was trapped on his feet, driven back until he crashed into the sink on the far wall. Glass broke as the thing that looked like a blender fell from its cart.

Daylight flooded the room. The garage door rattled to a stop. Kira took half a step back from her stunned and bloodied opponent and drove a hooking elbow deep into the center of his body. He struck the steel cabinets and fell in a clatter of ringing metal and rubber tubing.

The van dropped into gear. Blue smoke rose as tires spun on concrete. Kira turned as it shot forward, got all of two steps into her run when pain like a line of bright flame shot across her back.

She spun, took a second slash before she was able to deflect the blade.

There had been weapons in the cabinet after all. In the bald man's hand was a small hook, gleaming steel, razor sharp. He was a bloody wreck, but he wasn't fool enough to come swinging wild. He kept the wicked little blade in front of him, weaving deadly shapes in the air.

Kira moved back. Stayed out of range. Looked for her opening. Blood from her cuts made a warm apron across the tops of her breasts, a hot runnel down the small of her back.

Manny's face was a bloody mask. His mouth hung open from his broken jaw. Shards of tooth and bone had torn through the skin.

His eyes were murderous.

She was sure she'd broken ribs on his left side. That arm curled defensively against his body. He moved in small hitched steps, favoring his right leg. But there was nothing impaired about the hand that held the blade.

Step by shuffling step, he chased Kira down to kill her.

Running wasn't an option. She was just out of slashing range as it was. Turning to run might give him her throat.

She tried to get at his left. He moved to cut off her escape. They moved together, small shuffling steps, until Kira was boxed between the wall, the table and the redhead on the floor.

The enforcer's eyes changed. He had her trapped. This was to be his killing ground.

His fist tightened on the hook. A flash of light darted. Kira got an arm up to protect her face, felt a bright hot point of pain just below her wrist.

She threw herself herself to the floor. Tile smacked her palms and her heel smacked his right shin. Her kick scraped right up and through the resistance at the knee.

Cartilage snapped and tore. The bald man howled. Sheared loose from its moorings, the kneecap lodged in the skin of the upper thigh.

Kira was already rising back to her feet as Manny's leg bent backward and he clattered to the tiles. He struck on his left side and shrieked in pain.

The bright little blade was still tight in his fist. Kira planted a kick directly over his kidneys, and the blade flew.

Too late, she realized she'd been too focused on the bladed tool. A shadow fell across her vision as arms thicker than her waist engulfed her. A hot musky smell surrounded her. The redhead's arms were greasy and slick against her body. His breath panted ragged and hot against the top of her head.

He pulled her from her feet and slammed her into the table. The guttered edge dug at her hips, and the cold metal face was unyielding against her stomach.

One massive hand pressed her face into the steel. Black spots crowded her vision and she fought to breathe. His other hand snatched at the waist of her shorts.

Kira grabbed one big claw-hammered finger. She dug the point of her thumb into the nerve center just above the nail. That hand jerked and leapt, and Kira broke the finger.

The big man roared. Kira spun, the ballpoint pen from the mortuary clipboard tight in her fist. She caught a flash of bloodshot eye, one pupil a pinprick and the other a wide dark pool.

The pinprick vanished in a dark and sticky burst.

The bastard didn't let up. Broken finger, concussion, pen sticking out of his goddamned eye, Rolls was determined to tear her apart.

Kira drove the heel of her palm into the pen. A brief snap of bony resistance, and the redhead was no longer a problem.

For a long cold moment she lay on that table, trapped under the man's bulk. The black plastic tube in his eye read RHINELAND FUN.

Her panting breath slowed. Her racing heart subsided.

Kira wrestled out from under the redhead and staggered through the open garage doors. Out into the sun.

THE SHERIFF MOVED among the dead. Two head shots and a throat wound. Their bodies seemed shrunken.

She reckoned Jesus would know what to do with the part of them she hadn't killed.

They were a scruffy bunch. Five-day beards, sweat stains, body odor. Their weapons were cheap AK-47's done over with gun show conversion kits, and not one of them had taken the time to lace up their boots.

None were faces she knew.

In a way it made sense. The Slocums had been moonshiners once, and like a lot of local outlaws had moved into marijuana in the Seventies and later meth. She busted up their lab sites when she could, had sent a few of the clan off to Reidsville. Reason enough for hard feelings maybe, but they were cooks, not killers.

Made sense the old man would get shooters from out of town.

She took a second look. One of the head shots had caught a tumbling round, but the other two were recognizable enough. She didn't know these men, but she knew the family resemblance.

These weren't Slocums. They were Wilkeses.

That made its own kind of sense too.

An old deer camp lay back in the trees where they'd come out. It was little more than a bare patch of ground under a lean-to tin roof. Sleeping bags and ammo lockers, canned food and cases of beer.

The dirt floor was dark and wet. Three beer cans lay on their sides along with a half-finished tin of cocktail franks. The scattered sausages looked like severed fingers in the beer-soaked mud.

They'd been surprised to see her, sure enough.

Bad timing aside, someone had put a lot of thought into the ambush. There were night vision goggles still in their boxes. Three firing points were set up on the far side of the clearing. Sandbags would have protected a prone shooter, and had the men been in position, all would have had a good line on that old well.

She and her men would have been sitting ducks.

She holstered her weapon. Blood had run out of her shirtsleeve and down between her fingers. She hadn't realized she'd been wounded.

From their trash, this bunch hadn't been out here more than a day, if that. Maybe why Scoot hid out from her the last couple days: the trap wasn't ready yet.

If she hadn't found him this morning, would he have waited until sundown to come forward, ensure her slaughter?

This just didn't make sense for Taylor. The old man had every judge for miles around in his back pocket, but murdering an officer of the law would bring in the state CID, even the federal boys. The kind of attention he had always avoided.

What had changed?

The answers seemed obvious. Jack was back, then Jack was dead. Now Kira, last of the Stones, had returned.

What wasn't obvious was how that fit with this ambush. No matter how she looked at it, the Sheriff couldn't see what Taylor stood to gain. It was a hell of a risk, with no reward.

But if not Taylor, who?

One thing for sure, family connection or no, the junkie who led her here hadn't been the mastermind behind it.

She headed back to the 4x4, bounding her keys on her palm. "All right Scoot, you son of a bitch. Time to talk— who put you up to this?"

The Sheriff stopped.

Stray rounds had pocked her windshield, blown out a headlight and killed the little meth addict with the bad teeth. Beauregard 'Scoot' Wilkes lay in the dirt with his right arm stretched up over his head, still cuffed to the bull bars.

She curled her fist around her keys and spat in the dirt.

"Damn."

"KIRA?"

Hap Taylor stood at the front door and called inside the house. He waited, pulled open the screen door and leaned across the threshold.

"KIRA?"

Nothing. Didn't take but a minute to see she wasn't inside. One big living room/kitchen/everything and a short hall with the bedrooms. He called her names a couple times again as he stuck his head through.

He passed back out into daylight. Jumped when the screen door banged shut behind him. The Charger sat out front with the driver's door open and blood on the seat. It had him rattled.

His boots thumped on the wooden deck and the sound of crickets was loud in the woods around. He took a deep breath and put both hands up beside his mouth.

"KIIIIIIIIIIIIIRRRRRRRRRRRAAAAAAAA!"

He headed for the old barn. The way the sun hit it, only the front end of the Nash pickup was visible, that big round 40's hood like the prow of a ship sailing out of darkness. Kira's granddaddy, John Tucker Stone had outrun half the cops and revenuers in three different states in that truck, and now it sat rusting on blocks in a tumbledown barn.

Hap squinted through the gloom. Stepping from the sun into the shadows of the barn blinded him for a moment.

It was a bad moment.

He couldn't see, but the sound of a gun cocking was enough.

"Kira?" He stopped, raised his hands up slow. "What's going on, Kee?"

She was curled in the corner, on the far side of the old pickup. The gun in her hands was just short of a cannon, the barrel propped on her knees.

"Turn around," she said. "Real slow. Keep your hands where I can see them."

Hap turned, all the way around. Slow as you please. Hands up, sweat running down his flanks. The bright square of sunlight was painful to his eyes. Back in shadow, he was just able to make out plank walls and shelves. As he turned, he spoke.

"All due respect, Kee, but you called me, remember? Everything all right?"

He came full circle without getting shot. By then he could see everything was not all right.

Kira was covered in blood.

"God damn, Kee, what the hell'd you—"

"You come alone?"

"Course I came alone. Who was I supposed to bring?"

Kira darted a look past him. The barrel of the gun stayed pointed at Hap's chest.

"You mind?" he said. "Whatever's going on, we can talk about it, but that six-shooter's making me kind of nervous."

She stared at him for what felt like forever. Her hair was matted, her eyes wild and bright. Finally, she lowered the gun and Hap felt his sphincters unpucker.

"Wasn't sure I could trust you," she said.

"Then why call?"

Her eyes burned right into him.

"There was no one else."

"WHAT DO WE got?" the Sheriff said.

She was in one of her old uniforms, creases down the front where it'd been folded. A whole lot of white gauze was wrapped tight around her bicep— not neat like they'd do at a hospital but sort of awkward like you'd do to yourself.

If whatever was under that bandage hurt, she didn't let on.

"Gentlemen?"

The deputies shared a look. Bix shrugged. Graham stepped forward.

"Pretty darn big clusterf— uh, situation here, sure enough." He gestured back through the open garage doors to the green-tiled room. "Somebody took out *both* of Old Man Taylor's enforcers."

The Sheriff's head whipped up. Behind the sunglasses, her eyes were hard and bright.

"Dead?"

"No ma'am."

The Sheriff visibly relaxed.

Then, because Graham's day wasn't already bad enough, he had to add, "Leastways, not yet."

She hitched her thumbs in her gunbelt and stepped past. Graham and Bix shared a look.

Taylor's enforcer lay curled on his side. His hands were cuffed behind him and his right leg trailed, bent and twisted at awful angles. The Sheriff stopped with her shoes inches from the man's nose.

"Ambulance is coming down from Griffin," Bix said. "Shouldn't be too much longer."

She tilted her head to one side. A trail of blood led all the way back to the big guy on the steel table.

"Crawled all the way down here," Graham said. "Tough little bastard was still crawling when we showed up."

"Rhineland call it in?"

The deputy leaned out to one side and spat.

"No, this one right here. Rhineland's playing *'Who me?'* on this. Gave me a story stinks like something you'd find under the porch."

"That so."

Graham took a cautious step backward, fell in beside Bix. Boss used that tone, it was best to have your partner close by.

Behind her back, the two deputies shared another look.

"You all frisk this one?"

"Both clean."

She walked a careful circle around the man handcuffed at her feet and disappeared into the tiled room.

"Think she knows?" Bix, whispering out the side of his mouth.

Graham lifted one shoulder, fraction of an inch.

"She's gotta at least suspect. I mean, under the circumstances and all."

The Sheriff came back out. She had a green and white piece of paper wadded up in one hand. The corner of her jaw was working, and she was flexing her fist hard enough to start her arm bleeding again under her bandage.

"Sure wasn't these two's day, was it."

"You want we should bring her in, Boss?"

Graham saw his own image, reflected in her lenses. Bix came to his partner's aid.

"Just for questioning," he said. "You gotta admit, ma'am, the Stone girl's back less than three days and Taylor's best men go down, it don't look good."

"You two were tailing her. What'd you see?"

Deputy Graham felt his face burning. He didn't dare look at his partner.

"What I thought," she said. "You don't know where she was."

The Sheriff's fist tightened. Paper rustled. Knuckles cracked. The red stain widened on the white cotton bandage.

"Rhineland."

HAP BROUGHT THE medical kit back from his Vette. The metal case banged against the side of his leg as he walked, and the shadows inside the barn once again blinded him. Bright flecks of sawdust swirled up in the air when he set the case down.

Kira sat back against the wall. That big old Colt lay on some paint cans beside her, and her face was stiff with pain.

Hap's fingertips hovered over the bloody rag that had been her top. Finally Kira grabbed the hem in both hands and pulled the damn thing up over her head.

Her bra had been a lacy piece of nothing. Definitely not from any store this side of Atlanta, or even New York. The back of it had been slashed in half. It clung to the front of her body by the tops of the cups, dark and sticky with blood.

"Jesus, girl..." Hap said it soft, practically a whisper.

"No. Your father." Kira dropped what was left of the bra with the remains of the top. "Two of his men actually. Manny and Rolls?"

"You're kidding." Hap tried not to stare at her breasts. Even with her covering them with one arm, he didn't do a very good job. This wasn't the time or the place, but it was hard not to.

He got busy with the latches on the medical kit. A ziploc bag in bottom tray held latex gloves.

"Manny and Rolls are Daddy's main enforcers," he said. "Hard men from Charleston to Biloxi are afraid of those two."

"Not any more."

"Damn."

Hap skinned on the gloves. It was close in that barn, and hot. He was more than a little aware of all that naked skin. The way her forearm pressed against her breasts. Her small white shorts and bare legs.

The gunpowder scent that rose from her body mixed with the stench of blood.

"Did you kill them?" he asked.

She shrugged. Offhand, not caring if two men were alive or dead. Hap fumbled with gauze pads and peroxide, used them to wash the blood away from her body.

Most of it turned out not to be her own. She had a wide slash on her back, a smaller one on chest. A deep wound on her wrist. Everything else was minor, just scrapes and bruises.

She hissed through her teeth once, when the peroxide-soaked pad touched the cut across her shoulders. Otherwise, Kira was silent.

The way she knelt beside him, the tops of her buttocks were just visible above her shorts. He looked into that clefted darkness and wondered if she wore underwear.

He shook his head and cleared his throat.

"I think I got something in here ought to patch you up." His voice shook when he spoke. "I took this kit out of the kitchen in the staff quarters. There's stuff in here for everything from stabbings to bullet wounds. Yup, this here's the stuff."

He crunched the vial of Dermabond and turned it upside down. Kira hissed when he lined up the edges of the wound, and again when he brushed the adhesive over the cut.

"You want to tell me what brought this on?"

"I was hoping you'd tell me."

"Like he'd tell me anything." Hap worked the Dermabond down the entire length of the slash. There were fine hairs, nearly invisible, on the skin between her shoulder blades.

"I do need to thank you for something, though."

"Hm?"

"When Rhineland wanted my number, you wouldn't give it to him."

"The funeral guy? He's part of this?" Kira winced as Hap pinched another piece of skin together. He was almost at the end of the long cut. "I thought he was just being a creep."

"I just don't get it. Old Ma— your father stole Jack's ashes."

"That's weird."

Hap pressed the edges of the slash wound together, counting in his head. Kira twisted her face around, trying to get a look at his face.

"This whole thing's been weird, right from the start. First, my brother dies on a turn he probably could have taken in his sleep. Then his body is cremated without asking, and your father steals the ashes."

Hap let go of her skin. The cut stayed closed. He started the second layer.

"I don't know what to tell you," he said. "Daddy only cares about two things in this world— money, and power. I flat-out can't see how messing you up like this figures."

He placed his gloved fingers on Kira's bare skin. He brushed on a third and final coat of the liquid stitches. The smell of gunpowder was in the air.

She turned without speaking to face him. Her breasts were small and perfect, a hand's width away. He tried not to stare at her nipples. The cut on her chest still oozed above her heart. Blood collected at the bottom edge of the wound, threatened to spill onto the curve of her flesh.

Hap swallowed. He had no idea how he was going to get through this.

"I'll tell you something else, too," he said. "Rolls and Manny are dangerous. Stone killers. I'd say you're lucky to be alive."

"I had an excellent teacher."

THE FUNERAL DIRECTOR sat on the front step to his own business. It was about as far as a body could be from that abattoir inside and still stay on the property.

Rhineland looked up when the Sheriff's shadow fell across him. His skin was waxy and green and covered in sweat.

"On in back," she said and stepped past him.

The man's office was a wreck. Filing cabinets tipped open. Fistfuls of paper jammed into a shredder. A nest of loose wires and cords where monitor, mouse and keyboard should have hooked into a computer hard drive.

She stood in the room, tapping her fingers on her gunbelt. She stepped into the private washroom and glanced in the bowl. Rhineland dropped himself into his chair, looking nervous and miserable.

The Sheriff stared at him for a long moment. What little color he had drained out of him.

His Adam's apple was big in his skinny neck. It bobbed when he swallowed.

"They burgled your office too?"

"Beg pardon, Sheriff Ma'am?"

"Those two thieves out back. The ones broke in looking for cash or chemicals or the Good Lord knows what, then fell out fighting among themselves. Looks like they might have burgled this office along with that room in back."

"I—"

Deputy Bix'll take your statement. About how you came on back here after lunch and found this place broken into."

A cellphone clattered on the desk in front of him. Rhineland recoiled as though bit.

"You probably used that there phone to call 911. I reckon in all the excitement and such, you forgot you even had a landline. That sound about right?"

"You want me to swear against Taylor's boys?"

The Sheriff leaned in, knuckles on the desk. Blood welled under her bandage and beaded down her arm.

"Way I see it," she said "you got a choice. You can swear out a complaint, tell me everything happened here the way I figured. Or I can take a closer look. Might start with those papers in that shredder there, or the powder residue on the side of your toilet bowl. Reckon I'd hunt up that computer too— I'm thinking the trunk of your car— look and see what those security cameras recorded."

Rhineland stared at the bead of blood tracing a thin dark line down the Sheriff's arm.

"I wonder, if I started looking at that security feed, who-all I'd see and what-all they'd be doing. I wonder too, what else might be on that computer of yours."

The bead of blood ran past her knuckles. A small red puddle grew on Rhineland's desk.

"It's your choice."

LATE AFTERNOON, the world held its breath. Or simply quit breathing altogether. The sky was bright metal. The day's trapped heat rose from the earth. Every living thing in that burning world was caught between hammer and anvil, the air itself a thick and suffocating presence.

It was a bad time to be a sentry.

Inside the plantation house, the air was different. Cool and dark, crawling with the smells of damp plaster, mold and fresh earth.

Kira crouched at the edge of a faded Turkish carpet. Watching. Listening. Alert.

A hospital bed dominated the room. One side rail was down, the sheets rumpled. Beside it, an old time safe sat on four squat legs, like something out of a black and white movie. Around her, the old house creaked and knocked and ticked, but nothing like a footstep sounded upstairs or out in the hall.

Cautiously, she straightened.

When she was a kid, running around with Bobby, the old man had a suite of rooms upstairs. Back then, he still got around with a cane.

Beside the bed, a dresser. Its age-browned mirror reflected Kira's movements through a dark and smoky veil.

Photos sat on the dresser, framed and arranged facing the bed. Bobby Taylor on the day of his last yearbook photo. A sepia-toned man and woman stood in front of an old Model-T. The man had a shiftless look about him, the woman hard and cheerless. Kira shuddered.

A single photograph in a heavy silver frame showed her parents. Whatever they sat on was white and chrome, and behind them was a lot of blue water. The man sitting between them wore Old Man Taylor's white suit and Panama hat, but his shoulders were broad, his hands wide and powerful. He had one arm draped across her mother's shoulders, the other clinking beer bottles with her father. Smiles all around. Her mother's legs were long and bare, stretched out to rest on her father's knee. Black hair whipped around her face, and her fingers seemed to stroke the back of the hand held so close to her breast.

The sky in the window beyond seemed to deepen as Kira stood staring at her parents. They seemed so young, so happy. She shook herself and backed away.

Moving through that house was like being underground. Damp earth, dry rot. Subtle currents moved in the air, damp hands brushed along the skin.

The room Kira sought was dark and high, gathered in shadows. A few burning candles gave movement and life to the darkness. Impossible to imagine a dinner party in that room. Or that long oak table pushed back for dancing. Or laughter, echoing off the walls.

It was impossible to imagine anything in that room but Taylor.

The old man sat at the head of the table, alone among the dust and shadows and cobwebs. His suit stood out in the gloom like something poisonous growing on a forest floor.

The square copper urn caught and held the light in a dull glow. It threw jaundiced reflections on the bottom of his chin and the loose folds of his neck. At his left hand stood a dusty bottle and a half full glass.

Kira thumbed back the hammer on her grandfather's .45 revolver.

"Miss Stone." Taylor's voice was soft, his eyes hooded. "I was beginning to wonder if I would see you tonight."

The Colt had a long iron barrel. She sighted it on the old man's heart.

"Reach for that bell and you'll be dead before it rings."

Taylor raised his glass in silent salute. Blood colored liquid moved against its sides. He did not so much as glance at the bell.

"For what it's worth," he said, "I am pleased to see you here. Are Manuel and Rolleston alive?"

Kira shrugged. The weight of the gun, and the movement, put strain on the liquid stitches.

"Do you not care?"

"About as much as they would, if things had gone the other way."

Taylor smiled in the dark. Red wine stained the edges of his lips.

"Ruthless."

The way he said it was tender. Almost loving.

"Your grandfather's revolver must be getting heavy."

The old man shifted in his chair. The shotgun had been cut down to a pistol grip, the double barrels sawed off at the stock. Those twin dark mouths came up over the lip of the table and rested on its edge.

Both hammers were cocked, and Taylor's finger was on the triggers.

THE SUN WAS A red smear on the horizon. Nat Graham sat out on his porch watching the last of the blue fade to the first of the purple. Budweiser in one hand and a Marlboro in the other, just as God intended.

His hair was wet and his cheeks were bright with a fresh shave. The skin around his eyes tightened when the Ram pickup turned down his drive.

John Jack Bixby stepped down from the truck and up to the porch steps. Like his partner his hair was wet, but the day's stubble darkened his chin. He stopped with one boot up on the second step.

"Beer if you want it." Graham gestured with his own can at the empty rocker and the full ice chest.

Bix nodded. He came up the steps, fished a cold beer out of the ice chest and perched one hip on the porch railing. The can cracked, and foam trailed down over his fingers.

Graham leaned back in his rocker and took a sip.

For a time, the two men drank in silence. The sun disappeared over the rim of the earth.

"I keep thinking," Bix said at last, "about that clusterfuck down to Rhineland's today."

"We've seen worse."

"That ain't what I'm thinking about. Not *what* happened, but *who*."

"Taylor's boys, you mean."

"Not just any of Taylor's boys. Two of the old man's most genuine, scary, wet-your-pants badasses."

"You know what they say about them Stones." Graham sipped his beer, ashed his cigarette. "Never saw much of it in Jack, but the sister's got it in spades."

"Except of course, the sister had nothing to do with it. Boss said so herself."

The Bud in Graham's hand was getting light. He drained it down and cracked a fresh one.

"Ever known her to do something like that before?" he said.

Bix swigged beer and wiped foam from his lips.

"That ain't why I came out here."

"PLEASE, SIT." Taylor's shotgun did not move. "At this range, you'll be torn to ribbons."

"Maybe we both die together." She kept the old man's face lined up over iron sights.

That face, ancient and wicked, seemed faintly amused.

"For what it's worth, Kira, I bear you no ill will."

"You got a funny way of showing it."

"I'm actually rather proud of you." Again he raised his glass to her. If he was in any way disturbed by the guns they pointed at each other, he didn't show it.

"Do you play chess?"

"Pardon?"

"Sometimes, one must sacrifice a valuable piece to secure a greater victory. It is the nature of the game."

"Manny and Rolls," she said.

"Two rooks for a queen."

Kira's grip tightened on her weapon.

"And Bobby didn't figure into it anywhere."

"Think of it as a form of test. I needed to know if time and the... excesses of you recent lifestyle had blunted your edge."

"Whatever trick you're playing..."

"My rooks were beginning to develop ambition, but I could have dealt with that myself. This way," the shotgun barrels tapped the table's edge, "you have proven your mettle and grown your legend."

"My legend..."

"Of course, you did leave them alive, but such is youth."

"Just give me the urn and I'm out of here."

"I'm afraid in our line of work, you'll find the quality of mercy overrated."

"Our line…"

He pushed the urn across the table toward her.

Kira accepted in silence. Her brother's ashes were heavier than she would have thought, and her skin left oily streaks on the polished copper.

"I thought it was obvious," Taylor said. "I want you to take the reins of my organization. To be my heir."

"YOU HEARD?"

"I heard."

"Hell of a thing."

The two men were back in the lot behind the abandoned diner. Their pickups sat nose to nose. They stood shoulder to shoulder, their backs to the weathered brick.

"We'd still be ratted out, minute either of us moved."

The man named Big Tom rolled his head on the thick column of his neck.

"No Manny and Rolls, though. The Stone girl sure did us a favor there."

Virgil leaned over and spat in the dirt. Under the bill of his cap, his eyes were unreadable.

"You reckon that girl pulled all the old snake's fangs?"

A truck rattled past. Both men jumped. Big Tom wiped his palms on his jeans. He licked his lips before he spoke.

"Just a matter of time before somebody tries it."

The two men stood in silence. The first stars pricked the sky overhead, diamonds glittering in a soft purple shroud.

"Fifty-fifty?"

"Fifty-fifty."

The two men shook on it. The gathering dark hid both their faces.

"I'M AN OLD man, Kira." Taylor was becoming a soft shape in a darkening house. "I've lived far longer than anyone expected, but nothing lasts forever. I had hoped to pass my organization on to one of my sons, but the last of those hopes is now dead."

He nodded to himself, lifted his glass. Garters of blood-colored liquid streaked the sides.

"Hapworth is all I have left, and the boy is simply unsuitable. He's soft and gentle, too much like his mother."

"It's that important to you, put one of your men in charge."

"It's the Darwinism of Subordinates, my dear. Those truly capable of running things without me had to be ruthlessly culled. Those remaining are weak and endlessly set one against the other. You will understand better, once you sit at the head of this table."

"Yeah, that's not going to happen."

"This town needs you, Kira. If it didn't, I'd have had you killed the moment you came back."

"As opposed to this morning."

"A gambit. One that worked, might I add. Yesterday, you were the wild child who ran away. Today, you're a force to be reckoned with."

"You're crazy."

"I'm out of options."

"I should kill you right now."

She realized she no longer held her grandfather's Colt high. Taylor's eyes were on her, swimming with wine red lights.

"So very like your mother," he said. "She was... a beautiful woman."

It was the first time she had seen anything like softness in the old spider. In its own way, that was even more frightening.

"This town bears her name, Kira. Help me to honor it by continuing my work here."

"Your work…"

"It's what Jack was doing when he died."

NIGHT HAD FALLEN. Still hot, but not as bad. And in Graham's opinion, any relief from that burning sun was an act of divine charity. At the edge of the treeline, fireflies carved bright brief tracks in the wooded darkness.

The two deputies still sat out on Graham's front porch. Their rockers creaked, and the bug light hanging under the rafters lit their faces in sharp blue flashes.

Graham reached into the ice chest, clawed his fingers through icy water and came up empty.

"We agreed, then?" Bix said. His voice was blurry, an out of tune radio station.

Graham shook water from ice-aching fingers. The bug light overhead let out a loud sizzling crack.

"I don't know. Seems a hell of thing."

"LAPD did the same thing in the 50's. There was a movie about it, with Russel Crowe."

"This ain't the movies."

Bix crunched the empty can in his fist. Aluminum crackled and hit the melted ice with a splash.

"I'm telling you," he said, "we can do this."

THE SHERIFF CRUISED past Junior's at the end of her night. She was bone tired: every little bit of the adrenalin that had got her through that crime scene was long since used up. She was running on fumes.

The bar wasn't much. Just a tar paper shack strung with Christmas lights on a dirt-and-gravel lot. But at night— even on a Monday night— when decent folks were in bed, Junior's was the place for everybody else.

When trouble was on the wind, it stirred through Junior's.

To her surprise, the lot was all but empty. The few trucks parked there were all ones she knew, the type of drinkers fond of dim light.

Inside, Patsy Cline played softly on the iPod dock behind the bar. The music choice was Junior's, and Junior's alone. The old jukebox had caused too much bloodshed.

"Bit quiet for you, isn't it?" she said.

Junior gestured with his chin. Half a dozen quiet drunks, no point getting loud and raucous.

"What's going on?"

"Think you know." Junior's voice was a deep bass rumble.

"So tell me anyhow."

Junior spread his big hands on top of the bar and flexed his shoulders. The cast of his face was mulish, and he wouldn't meet her eyes.

She was tired, and it had been a long day. Her temper wasn't what it should have been. Her fists seemed to open and close all on their own, until Matt Johnson spoke up.

"Things're changing," the Bluebird's owner said. He hunched his shoulders and curled his good hand around the glass of whiskey in front of him. "Stones've come back, the old man's enforcers are gone… Everything's shifting, and folks are hunkered down until they see which way the wind blows."

The Sheriff rubbed one thumb along the corner of her jaw. Easy to forget sometimes how fast word got around.

"Jack came, everyone knew the old man was gonna hand things over. Now he's gone." Matt's bad eye, a white marble set in scar-textured plastic, leaked a clear milky fluid. He didn't seem to notice.

"Don't recall you sitting no vigil before," she said.

"That was before his baby sister took down two of Taylor's best. Who's gonna run things now?"

"First off, I'm the law around these parts. You might want to remember that before you start talking in front of me about that old spider 'running things'."

She was conscious of other faces in the room. Every eye was on her.

"And you might want to get your story straight before you go shooting your mouth off. Those two thugs of Taylor's injured each other in a fight, and that's the way of it. You don't really believe that little bitty girl beat up those two big ex-cons?"

Matt dropped his eyes to the glass in front of him. He scratched his withered arm and stared down like he could make himself small enough to hide in the bottom of the glass.

She turned back on Junior, one thumb hooked over the ring of her baton.

"And what's your problem, anyway? You're not like this with me."

Junior looked down at the spot behind the bar where he kept a nickel-plated .357. His mouth was a flat line. He closed his eyes and shook his head.

Again, it was Matt who spoke. His voice was a bare mumble.

"Junior's part Wilkes, on his momma's side. Scooter and them back in the woods, they were his cousins."

The Sheriff rocked back on her heels. Four men had tried to kill her, and she'd left their bodies cooking in the August sun.

Hard to believe it had only been that morning. And not the only time that day she had perverted the course of justice.

She wondered what all else she'd have to do before the dust settled.

To Junior she said, "Sorry for you loss. But you need to remember, those boys backed the wrong horse."

KIRA LEFT THE plantation house by the front door. Her grandfather's long-barrelled Colt was stuck down the waist of her shorts, and she held her brother's ashes close to her heart. Her steps were those of a sailor on the deck of a ship at sea.

The moon was bright in the night sky. The trees, pecans and oaks, were shadowed pools of ink. Everything else was bleached the color of ash and bone.

The eyes of strangers tracked her as she moved. Her footsteps made soft sounds on the gravel drive. The crushed rock curved pale in the moonlight to the twin pillars that marked the entrance to the old plantation. Freedom was two pale splinters in a vast darkness.

Behind her, the house had the shape of a blocky and crumbling skull. The flaking columns were a row of fangs, the ground floor behind them a wide black maw.

Twice now, that house had swallowed her. And twice allowed her to escape.

A single light burned in a window. Left hand corner, upper story. A figure stood in that window, features lost in silhouette.

It didn't matter. Kira knew the set of those shoulders. The tilt of that head.

The man looking out at her was Hap Taylor.

She stared up at him, wondering what he saw. After a moment, he turned away and let the curtain fall.

She had come tonight to kill his father. Strange payment for tending her wounds that afternoon. Instead, she left with her brother's remains and her head full of questions.

Taylor's guards stood sentry under the trees. As she walked she saw them. Twos and threes, each man with a shotgun or assault rifle at his side.

Their eyes gleamed in the dark— the eyeshine of wild animals.

Had this really been what her brother wanted? She and Jack had never been close, but he was her blood. Now, she was forced to wonder if she ever really knew him at all.

The men's eyes followed Kira down the drive. No one moved or spoke. They watched her passage in silence.

TUESDAY

ANOTHER RESTLESS NIGHT. Or early morning. It was hard to tell . Kira lay tangled in her bedsheets. The thoughts in her mind were more knotted still.

Old Man Taylor. Her stepmother. Her brother.

Her mother and father.

There were the obvious questions. Taylor and his agenda. What Jack had really been doing when he died. How much her stepmother knew.

Those thoughts were big and immediate, a ball of snakes twisting around on each other, banging against the surface of her mind.

They were also questions that wouldn't matter in five more days— four now, she corrected. It was that late.

No, the thoughts that truly tormented her, that bit deep and wouldn't let go, were thoughts of her parents. Smaller snakes in that writhing ball, but all the more venomous.

Kira rolled over and punched her pillow. A wave of childhood smells rose up to meet her. She rolled onto her other side, crashed her head down into those scents.

She didn't remember her mother. Not really.

There were photos, of course. When she was little she had spent hour after hour pouring over them, touching their faded colors, making up stories about the woman staring out at the camera. Her mother was beautiful, that kind of beauty that haunted you, made you ache just to look at her, but in no picture had she ever seen the woman smile.

Until tonight. At Taylor's.

When she tried, really tried to remember her mother for real— not the magical figure from the stories she told herself as a child— Kira could summon nothing more than a few sense impressions. Humming. Lipstick spiraling out of its tube. The feel of dark blue silk against tiny fingers. The smells of perfume and powder.

It was all she had. When her mother went to live with the angels, Kira had simply been too young.

Her stepmother's words: went to live with the angels. She never had anything else to say, claimed they never knew each other.

Possibly true. It was a small town, but the two women were from different worlds.

Kira went up one elbow, punched the pillow again, this time pulled it up over her head. Even with the window open the heat was terrible.

Fading photos of a woman, beautiful and serious, who went to live with the angels. That was all she had of a mother.

The one person who had known her mother best hadn't been known for talking.

Where her stepmother answered her questions with vague platitudes, her father would simply grunt and turn away.

For John Lee Stone, silence was a way of life.

Kira sat up in bed. The cut on her back was stiff and immobile. Her body ached from the fight. It had been awhile, but the feeling was familiar.

The posters on her wall, the horse statue beside her bed seemed to mock her. She grabbed her pillow and top sheet and left that little girl's room, looking for another place to lay her head.

The copper urn stood in the center of the dining table. Its flat planes caught the moonlight in a strange luster.

Her mother and father were in the family plot up the hill. Beside them, an open grave waited for this small box, all that was left of her brother.

She was still staring at the urn when headlights swept across the front windows.

ONCE THE PHONE went off, it didn't take Virgil more than a few seconds to fish it out of his pants. His wife snorted and rolled over, threw one meaty arm against him. He pushed her back over, the phone muffled in against his chest.

He slid into the living room and answered the call in a hush. Back in the bedroom, his wife kept on snoring.

"Big Tom? What the hell you doing up this late?"

"Maybe I'm up early," the man said at the other end of the line. "All depends on how ya look at it."

Virgil kept on moving through the house until he was out on the front porch, easing the screen door shut so it didn't slap or slam.

"I got to thinking," Big Tom said, "the old man had something, getting everyone to mind him on account of Manny and Rolls. Figured we could use something like that."

"I thought we were gonna—"

"Just at first. Get everyone in line, get em all to mind."

Virgil stood on the porch in his underwear, scratching at the place where the elastic drooped. His yard was bare clay and patches of halfhearted grass. Mostly it was a litter of high-priced boats and trucks, his kids' trikes and big wheels, and here and there, one or two unmarked graves.

He pressed the phone closer to his ear.

"Reckon I can see it. Might save us some trouble, we get everything locked down right away."

"Exactly."

"Have to be somebody out of town." Virgil heard his own voice and dropped back into that hush again. "The old man always brought them in for outside." Back in the house, nothing stirred.

"Way ahead of you, partner. I already made the call."

"Who'd you get?"

He didn't like the idea of Big Tom moving without him. Especially when Big Tom had to be thinking the same as he was.

"I got us the best."

"Who?"

"I got us Temple."

HAP STOOD FRAMED in the doorway. Moonlight and darkness.

He stood peering into the main room. Small points of light gleamed in his eyes.

Kira had grabbed the nearest piece of cloth— an old shirt of Jack's she'd left on the couch. There hadn't been time to put it on.

She felt self-conscious and foolish. It was only Hap, and nudity wasn't that big a deal anyway. Still she clutched the shirt against her body, a veil of thick blue cloth robbed of all color in the dark.

He launched himself from the doorway, three reeling steps into the room. Homing in on the rustle of cloth perhaps. Or maybe seeking her by scent and body heat alone.

"What are y—"

Hap tore the shirt from her hands. Dangerous, and he had to know it. She had a brief flash of cigarettes, whiskey and expensive aftershave, and his mouth was on hers. Rough. Bruising.

Kira met his kiss, matched it. Stubble like small steel wire rasped and burned her lips.

She tore at his clothes. They fell back against the couch, landed on the floor beside it.

Stubble burned her jaw, her throat. The hollows of her collarbones. He bit down on her nipple and a raw sound rose from her throat.

Sound of buckle and zipper, and his body lifted. His erection thumped against her pubic mound. Kira groped blind, pulled at couch cushions, clawed at the floor.

He entered her. Hard. Deep. She wasn't ready, but that was okay: she wanted it to hurt.

He stayed there a moment, buried inside her. His eyes went wide and unseeing, as though gazing at distant wonders.

She bit his chest, and he began to fuck.

Her bare feet found the floorboards and she pushed, her hips rising to meet his thrusts. Soon she was wet, a ball of heat like a fistful of coals growing in her womb.

His hips slammed into hers, slap of meat and bone, a battering ram hammering a door already breached. She tucked her feet into the backs of his knees. Textures of denim against her heels, sweat-slick flesh against her knees.

Hap took her. Rough. Angry. Hard. He pulled her hair and bruised her lips with his mouth. Every thrust was driven by frustration and desperation and raw animal lust. Every thrust stoked that fistful of coals inside her, forcing it hotter and hotter.

Kira fucked back against him, gave him her own anger, grief and lust. That hot fist inside her swelled, became impossible.

Orgasm ripped through her body and blotted out the world.

KIRA FELT LIKE THAT robot in the second Terminator movie. Blown into a million pieces, specks and flecks and puddles of shiny liquid.

And piece by piece, the droplets flowed back together. Found each other. Slowly reformed.

By the time Kira was able to sit up, someone was pressing a glass of water into her hand.

Someone.

Hap.

"Damn."

"Told you it'd be worth it," he said.

"I think I tore my stitches."

He dropped onto the couch. His knees were next to her head and the room was like an oven. The water was cold, and too soon gone.

"You must have a death wish," she said, and pressed the cool glass against her forehead.

"Coming after you like that?"

"Or at all."

His hand found her shoulder. Caressed it. One thumb worked the hollow between knots.

"Way you got me," he said, "it seemed worth the risk."

Her only answer was a soft moan. He really was good with his hands.

They sat like that for a time, Kira on the floor, Hap on the couch behind her rubbing her neck and shoulders. It felt good and, in the dark, somehow okay.

"Hap?" she said, because a moment like that just couldn't last.

His hands froze.

"Was Jack really taking over for your father?"

The massage resumed.

"He was out to the house a lot. Those two'd shut themselves up in a room for hours at a time. Truth to tell, I wondered if maybe that's what you were doing out there tonight. Picking up where he left off."

"Your father wants me to."

"Oh?"

The fingers on her neck paused, or that might have been Kira's imagination.

"I didn't say yes."

His hands moved down to the hollows under her collarbones. Kira winced when he touched the slash under its coat of liquid stitches, but the rest of it felt good. She let her head fall back against his lap.

"Hap?"

"Hm?"

"I think Jack might've been your half-brother."

"Daddy tell you that, too?"

"Not exactly, no. Just… things he said. The way he said them, like he was maybe counting Jack as one of his sons." And before she could stop herself, "And I guess he and my mother were… close."

Hap's hands came away from her. She heard his voice laughing softly in the darkness.

"I tell you what, Kee, you have got to have the strangest idea of foreplay I ever did hear."

Kira turned on the floor to face him. His lap smelled like denim, sweat and semen.

"Foreplay's what you do *before*," she said. "That part you didn't do at all?"

He lifted her. His arms were smooth and strong. Traded places, her on the couch, him on the floor.

His stubble brushed the soft flesh inside her hip. His lips planted a tender kiss on the top of her pubic mound.

"Hap?"

"Hush."

KIRA SAT PROPPED against the headboard, awake. Hap lay on his stomach beside her. His head curled in against her hip, and one arm was thrown heavy across her lap. His back rose and fell in time with his snores.

They were in her parents' bedroom. No way the two of them would have fit in her childhood bed— the suggestion itself was too embarrassing.

So they lay together on dusty sheets, in a room where her father once laid with her mother, and later with her stepmother, the woman who actually raised her. It was a strange feeling, to hold this strange new man in this room.

She wondered if, in his time, her father had felt the same way.

The house was a hundred years old. Generations of Stones had slept in this master bedroom, in this bed. Not the same mattress: she remembered the fire, out in the yard. It had been shortly before her stepmother moved in. A winter day, her cheeks and nose cold, the feathers from the mattress drifting in the air like a rain of burning stars.

Hap stirred. His body was soft in sleep, his mouth like that of a child.

Kira's eyes felt like they'd been attacked with rusty spoons, chipping right back to the bone. Whatever jelly was left in the sockets ached. She couldn't remember her last good night's sleep.

Last week. Another lifetime.

She lay awake and thought of Europe. Of Jean-Michele and the others, her friends and their constant rolling house party.

One season blurred into the next. Beaches in the summer, Skiing in the winter. Round after round of parties and playboys.

She thought of Marie and the little fat man with his own private island off the coast of Spain.

If she left tomorrow she'd be back with them in two days. Maybe less.

Hap reached, blind and unconscious. She dropped his hand back in her lap.

The moon shifted. Kira rubbed at her eyes.

She had a lot to think about.

THE SUN WAS STILL A red threat behind the trees when Deputy Graham navigated the twisting maze of backcountry roads out to the old Stone place. Other days, it was an hour when the day still held promise. Shreds of mist clung in the deepest parts of the ditches either side of the clay roads, not yet burned away by the touch of the sun.

Talk of rain, but same as always, it was just talk.

He was in full uniform behind the wheel of the county cruiser. Mouth dry, head pounding. A feeling in his chest like somebody had just cracked open his ribs and dumped in a bagful of snakes.

Bix rode shotgun. Behind his sunglasses, his eyes were unreadable, bloodshot and grim.

"We really going to do this?" Graham said. Just thinking about it set the snakes to roiling in his chest.

"Soon as the sun goes down, partner. By the time anybody figures out what's what, we'll have it all sewn up. You want to turn here."

Bix took the corner too fast. The back end slewed. The rear tires clawed for traction. Powdered Georgia clay flew high in the air.

"Hell, you trying to kill us?" Bix's grip was tight on the dash.

Graham swallowed and said nothing. His mouth felt like it was stuffed with cotton and the back of his throat tasted of bile.

A break in the weeds and he pulled in. Across the ditch and up the drive, tires going from gravel crunch to the tense hum of hard-packed earth. The house was on the left. Like Graham's place and most others around here, it was on piles to make up for the slope of the land, and to keep things cool in the summer. To the left, the barn and outbuildings, their entrances like black and open mouths. Anything could be hiding in those buildings, or in the shadows under that house.

He made a slow turn in the wide flat area between house and barn. Saw nothing. He tapped the brakes and dropped the engine into Park.

The two men looked at each other and stepped out of the car. Just like that, the cruiser's A/C was a distant memory and his uniform shirt stuck to his arms and neck and shoulders. Even this early in the morning, the air was already like an oven. Another couple hours, being outdoors would be like roasting in Hell itself.

They went ahead with this thing tonight, he reckoned he and Hell would have plenty of time to get acquainted.

Graham threaded the nightstick into the ring on his belt and dipped the brim of his hat against the worst of the glare. He resisted the urge to unsnap the holster on his personal duty weapon. Stones had a reputation.

"Was it their grandaddy, or great-grandaddy, machine-gunned all those revenuers?" he said.

"Just go knock on the damn door."

"No need."

The voice came from right behind them. Graham's only consolation was that he wasn't the only one who jumped.

The Stone girl stood, hipshot and defiant. A white hickory axe handle rested on her shoulder. She had to have come around the barn or down the hill through the tall grass, but the two deputies had heard no rustle or sound of movement.

"Gentlemen."

She wore men's cargo shorts low on her hips, and her nipples were shadowed behind the fabric of her thin cotton tee. Graham stammered and felt the heat rise in his face. In the end it was Bix who spoke.

"She wants to see you," he said.

"I get a choice?"

Her tone was icy and calm, a little eager even. Facing two armed male cops. Graham found himself believing every fool story he'd ever heard about the Stone clan.

His equipment belt was hung with a PR-24 baton and Mace, a Taser and a Glock 19. He held his hands up, palms out, and cleared his throat.

"Come on, miss," Graham said. "Please?"

THE SHERIFF WAS in her office. The blinds were drawn against the sun's heat and glare. The room, like her thoughts, was a dusty brown murk.

Light blasted in when Kira threw open the door. The Sheriff surged out of her chair, a prizefighter at the bell.

Kira's eyes were bright, challenging. Same defiant smirk she used to wear when she'd get caught sneaking back in before dawn.

"What've you done with my deputies?" the Sheriff said. "They were supposed to bring you."

"Last I saw they were fine,"Kira said. "Shit drivers, but fine. I imagine they'll be along shortly."

The Sheriff stood straighter and lifted her jaw. Sometimes it was hard to see the grown woman in front of her, not the little girl who'd loved her or the snotty teen who'd hated her.

"You drove Taylor's car over here to see me."

"Consider it a compromise. I'm here."

"What are you trying to do, Kira?"

"I'm not sitting in the backs of any more squad cars. Those days are over."

"For once, I agree with you."

Kira stared in disbelief. A silver star clattered onto the desk.

"Just put that on, raise your right hand and repeat after—"

"You've got to be kidding."

"There's a storm coming, Kira. You need to be on the right side when it hits."

"I'm only here a couple more days."

"Everything's up in the air right now, people looking to see which way the wind's blowing and who's gonna get swept off the board," the Sheriff said. "You stand with me, folks'll know."

"Ever think I might side with Taylor?"

"Kira Leigh Harrow Stone, I know your daddy and I raised you better than that. Now you put that on and let's get you sworn in."

The two women faced off across the desk. The Sheriff looked at her stepdaughter. Kira looked at the silver star.

She picked the badge up, held it with the tips of her fingers.

"You were right, you know. Old Man Taylor does want me to take over for him when he's gone."

The Sheriff stood in silence. Kira studied the badge in her hands. With her head lowered, the fall of her hair hid her eyes.

"He said Jack already agreed to be next in line."

"Why would you believe anything that old devil says?"

Kira looked up through her hair, blue eyes bright and piercing.

The Sheriff blew air through her nose and dropped back into her chair. The closed blinds threw stripes of muddy light onto the desktop between them.

"Truth is, I don't rightly know what your brother was up to when he— you know. I wish I did, but I don't."

Her fingers found the personnel folder out on her desk, pushed it at the corners until it was square with the edges of her blotter.

"Time I met your daddy, Jack was fourteen years old. Near enough a man, and not long before he was out on his own. Me and him, we never had the chance to get all that close."

"Not like you and me, you mean?"

The skin tightened around the Sheriff's eyes. Her mouth made a hard pained shape.

Kira rubbed one thumb across the words engraved in the face of the silver star. The click it made on the desk was the same sound as a small bone snapping.

"KIRA?"

Hap sat beside the hospital bed, a paperback novel open in his lap. He immediately tucked the book behind him, a man caught in a shameful act.

Kira stood in the doorway, hesitant. That strange awkward moment— someone you'd seen naked the night before, now with all their clothes and masks and armor back on. Wondering how much of what you were in the dark will survive back in the light.

The machines at the head of the bed chuffed, hissed and beeped. A fist closed around Hap's heart. This wasn't the right time, or the right place.

Kira looked everywhere but at Hap, or at the hunched shape under the sheets.

Hap came up out of his chair and crossed over to her. He took her hand in both of his own. His thumbs were large and brown on the small white back of her palm.

"I didn't think I'd come," she said.

"Ain't much. I mean, I gotta warn you, it ain't pretty."

"I thought…" Kira's voice trailed off. Her eyes dropped to the scuffed linoleum. Darker at the corners, where the mop didn't reach.

"I had to see."

Hap made a sound, short and bitter. The sound of it made him feel ashamed.

"You never were able to stay away."

The shape under the sheets twitched. Or it might have been his imagination.

Either way, Kira snatched her hand back. It came away slick and wet.

She stepped to the foot of the bed. Her spine was straight, her shoulders rigid. Her bearing was that of a condemned prisoner stepping onto the scaffold.

Hap was left standing in the doorway, unsure whose sweat was drying on his palms.

"YOU WANTED TO see us, ma'am?"

The Sheriff looked up at her two deputies. Graham and Bix stood like a couple of schoolboys called into the principal's office. She reached into the bottom drawer of her desk and pulled out a bubble light. The magnets on its base made a soft sound on the wood desktop.

"One of you put this on your personal vehicle," she said. "We don't have another cruiser, and I want the two of you patrolling separately. This here's the best I could do."

"Ma'am?" Graham and Bix shared a single guilty look. "Have we done something wrong?"

She looked at them a long moment.

"Just want y'all covering more ground is all."

"All due respect ma'am, that Stone girl—"

"Is gone in two days. Don't worry about her," the Sheriff said. "Not more than you have to, at any rate."

"But—"

"All three of us are going to be rotating heel-and-toe, one on patrol, the other two on call. Until this town quiets down again, you two are all I've got."

She looked down at her hands, spread on the desktop. In her mind's eye she saw four bodies, lying in the woods, surrounded by flies, bloating in the sun.

"That old bull gator's two best hatchet men are out of action," she said at last. "It'd be a mistake to underestimate him, we need to be ready once the other fish smell blood in the water."

Again that shared look.

Long after they left, she thought about that look. Thought about what it meant for her, and for her deputies.

About what it meant for her town.

KIRA DIDN'T THINK she could find the meadow now, even if she tried. She must have driven past it in the last few days, never once recognizing it. Everything had just gone to seed.

Ten years ago, the farmer still mowed for hay. Still used the land for pasture.

Even then the meadow was secluded. It was a popular spot for the older kids to park.

Bobby Taylor was nineteen years old. He was six feet tall, with hair a little too long and a bad look in his eye. He had broad shoulders and cords of muscle in his forearms and a way of winking at you when he smiled.

Kira would look down at her fourteen year old body and hate that the older girls had so much more.

Bobby was popular. Other kids sought him out, and he went with all the prettiest girls. He always had money in his pocket, always had access to liquor and pot, and he had the kind of charm made people forget his father.

Kira chased him. Trying to look older, she did clumsy things with makeup, made foolish mistakes with her hair and clothes.

Strangely, it was a day she hadn't been trying that he noticed. She'd been walking a fence rail, hair in pigtails. No makeup and a plain dress that she'd almost outgrown. Bobby had pulled up and asked if she wanted a ride.

They'd parked in that meadow.

It hadn't hurt as much as Kira expected. She might have been too scared and excited to notice. It never did quite feel good, not back then. But there was that dark rush of belonging. Of entering a secret world. Adult pleasure. Adult knowledge. For a time, Kira lost herself.

They were like Romeo and Juliet, from two warring families. She only saw him on his breaks from college. To keep their love a secret, Bobby continued to go around with other girls. Older girls. But he got mad as hell any time he thought she was out with another guy. Said he loved her too much.

Loving her didn't stop him with those older girls. Hearing those girls talk, their knowing gossip, Kira burned with anger.

There were fights, more than a few. Bobby had twice her mass and a mean streak. Kira had a bad temper and no hesitation. She had the speed, the moves and the savagery.

Sheriff Patterson became a frequent visitor out to the house. Her stepmother was his chief deputy, but Bobby's father owned him. There were nights in the cells. Talk of reform school.

It all came apart one hot July night. They were back in that same meadow. Four cars, a dozen kids, some music. An informal party. There was a little pot and a lot of beer. Too much beer.

Bobby had his hand up Cindy Nixon's skirt. A fight: Cindy on the ground, crying. Both hands pressed to her eye. Kira on fire, violence singing in her blood.

Hateful words, back and forth. Bobby's fist: solid bone, and fast.

Kira came up swinging, went down bleeding. Up, again, this time two guys from the football team trying to hold her.

Frozen looks on the ring of faces. Shame. Anticipation. Sick Excitement.

The fourteen year old was an outsider in their tribe. She would be punished.

Bobby tore the front of her dress. He grabbed her face and bit her lips. She spat blood in his eyes.

He laughed.

Kira pulled her head back.

Swung it forward, from deep in her spine.

Aimed square for the center of Bobby's face.

Bone snapped.

Bobby fell.

Her life changed forever.

Ten years later, Kira became conscious of antiseptic smells and machine sounds. She felt the cool metal of the bedrail in her palms and against her forehead, the hot salt on her cheeks and the tears beading her lashes. She was aware that she was no longer alone in the room.

"I'm sorry," a voice said from behind her, rich and mellow. "Unless you're immediate family, you can't be in here."

"I"m his fiance. I mean, I was. Me and Bobby here were going to be married."

The man in the bed was shrunken and twisted, wasted and curled. Skin so pale it was translucent. Blue veins branching and threading beneath the surface. He wore a diaper and a stomach tube, and his jaw was shaved smooth.

At the head of the bed a machine the color of eggshells thumped and hissed, cycling air through a hole in his throat.

Kira pushed a lock of hair from his forehead. The way they cut his hair wasn't quite right. Tears fell on his skin in soft wet pats.

"I bet he was real handsome," the nurse said. "You can tell."

"Like to break your heart."

VIRGIL HATED THE pig farm. He was a country boy, born and bred, used to farms, and bugs, and being where the nearest people were a long way off. But the pig farm always had a smell like old bandages, the flies and roaches were all bleached and washed out, and just pulling in to the main yard felt like the last place on earth.

He got out of his truck, made a little jump the minute his door thunked shut. Like he'd just closed himself off from the last piece of the modern world. Of his own life. He moved off between two mold-blackened outbuildings, following the sound of grunting beasts.

He found the man named Big Tom leaning over a fence rail, watching his pigs fight and jostle and tear at something in the mud in front of his boots.

Virgil didn't alter his pace. He didn't reach back and touch the gun stuck down the belt at the back of his pants.

There was blood on the pigs' muzzles.

He stopped a few feet from Big Tom. The other man was bigger, thick and wide, and he kept a punch-knife in the back of his belt buckle. None of that'd help him much in a gunfight. Not unless Virgil did something stupid.

Big Tom nodded. His face stayed slow and sleepy, but his eyes were bright and sharp. Those eyes took the situation in, seemed to make their peace with the way things were. The big man spit, tobacco juice turning the dry red dust into a wet constellation the color of human viscera.

"Way I figure it," he said, "ain't neither of us got enough to pay Temple on our own, and I damn sure know ain't neither of us wants that psycho son of a bitch mad at us."

The skin around Virgil's eyes tightened.

Big Tom spat again. The constellation turned into a shape that might have been a rope of intestine, or a gobbet of meat.

"I figure that makes us both safe. For now, anyways."

Virgil didn't step closer, but he did lean against the fence rail. His posture mirrored the man beside him.

The pigs squealed and fought. The meat and bone in the mud around them could have been anything. Virgil picked out the shape of a human wrist. It was covered in jailhouse tattoos.

"Jimmy?"

The thick-built man's mouth pulled sideways.

"He was there. He knew."

"Said he didn't give a damn who he worked for, I remember."

"You trust him?"

Virgil looked down at the pigs. Small chunks of bone crunched in their jaws and the mud was littered with scraps of tattooed flesh.

"Nah, reckon you done right."

Big Tom grunted. The two men fell silent.

The sun was brutal overhead, the heat punishing. The pigs made their feeding noises, Hell's own chorus.

"You got hold of Temple?"

"His handler, yeah."

"He taking the job?"

"Gets in tonight."

Virgil looked down at his own shadow.

"So Temple gets here," he said. "Then what?"

Big Tom squinted into the distance. Fat rolls shifted at the back of his neck.

"Temple gets here, and this time tomorrow you and me are kings."

He turned and spat. The pig whose eyes he hit reared and screamed, a horrible sound. Its tongue and teeth and snout were slimed with blood.

IN SILENCE KIRA followed the colored line painted on the floor. People in scrubs moved past, bustling. Others rolled beds or chairs, no hurry at all. The line on the floor was chipped in places, scuffed by so many feet.

At the edges, not moving, people clustered in twos and threes. Families. The worry and pain in their faces made her look away.

A lobby like only Americans could do them: televisions everywhere. Wheelchairs, plastic bracelets, brave smiles, a hospital not a hotel. Glass walls tinted the color of aquarium glass slid apart, and the full force of the summer heat blasted her chest, scorched her cheeks and throat.

She raised a sheltering hand, squinted into the sunflash patterns of distant windshields. She didn't know why.

"Back here."

Bobby leaned against a column, thumbs hooked in the loops of his jeans.

Except she was looking at Bobby years ago, not Bobby now.

This was Hap.

Hap.

Memories of the night before flashed through her, and and her face burned.

His smile was glassy, his expression pained.

"I didn't think you'd still be here," she told him.

"Me neither."

They stood in front of each other, just out of reach. Kira didn't know what to do with her hands.

A minivan with taxi decals pulled up. The driver and an orderly worked together to wheel a frail and bewildered old man into the back. An old woman hovered around them, hands shaking, face blazing with a fierce and protective love.

Kira moved off out of the way, blinking and wiping her eyes.

"That headbutt busted him up good," Hap said. "Bobby never did regain consciousness."

They had stopped under a magnolia at the edge of the parking lot. A splinter of shade before the heat and dazzle of all that asphalt and chrome.

"Is there even anything of him still in there?"

"Little flutters here and there. Doctors say it'd be a mercy to let him go."

"Then why—"

"When have you ever known Daddy to show mercy? Or to let go?"

"Good point."

The magnolia's curves echoed those of the human body, and its leaves were waxy and dark. Flowers the size of her head surrounded Kira with a funereal perfume.

"Last night was a mistake," she said.

"A *good* mistake."

"It can't happen again."

A man walked up, cigarette halfway to his mouth, lighter out and ready. He looked at them and moved off and away.

"So what are you going to do now?"

"Really? All I want is to bury my brother, his ashes I guess, get back to the Riviera and pretend none of this ever happened."

"Why do I feel like I hear a 'but' in there?"

Kira didn't answer. Not at first. The heat shimmering off the pavement around her seemed to reflect the fires burning under her own skin.

"Want to take a ride?"

KIRA DROVE LIKE a woman possessed. The trip from the hospital in Griffin back across the county line usually took Hap anywhere between an hour and an hour and a half.

She made the run in under forty minutes.

She slotted herself into gaps in traffic that were just about to open and slid away as they were about to close. She threaded her way between massive eighteen-wheel tractor trailers and blew past slower vehicles as though they were standing still.

Hap rode with one hand white-knuckled on the dash and the other clawed into the black vinyl upholstery. Every fresh burst of speed pressed him deeper into his seat. The muscle car's engine growled and roared, a beast off its chain.

"Growing up in that house like you did, you might not have heard all the stories about my father John Lee."

"Everybody knows about your daddy's driving, Kee. Please, watch the road."

An elderly pickup with a camper shell appeared in front of them, slid back behind them inches from the mirror on Hap's side.

"You know I asked my father once why he didn't race NASCAR, something like that?"

The back end of a UPS truck flew at the Charger's front grill. They passed with at least a coat of paint to spare.

"You know what my father said?"

"Kira, please."

"He said back when he was young enough to race, he never did see much point driving in circles. My father always said he liked a challenge."

"Looks like we've got company."

Kira flicked a glance at the flashing lights in her rearview. Annoyance showed on her face. She didn't touch the brake.

"Seriously, Kee, you need to pull over."

"Something I want you to see."

"He's a Smokey, GHP. Those boys don't play."

"I see what the old man meant about you."

They reached the far edge of Cunningham County. The shopping center blew past, Walmart and Goodyear and McDonalds and Ingles, all one long blur as they charged over the line into Harrow.

They grabbed air at the crest of the hill near the burned-out diner. The Dodge's shocks took the impact when they landed, and the flashing lights disappeared from Hap's side mirror.

"I would've been five, maybe six years old when my father set me on his lap and put my hands on the wheel."

Kira turned, a four-wheel drift. Dust and gravel flew.

"I wasn't driving, of course, but I sure thought I was. Even though my father was on the straight and narrow by then, he couldn't help sharing. By the time I was old enough to reach the pedals, I already knew more about driving than most people ever learn."

The back roads were unpaved, twisting back on each other at odd and unpredictable angles. The big-block Dodge flew over the red clay. Kira took one high speed turn after another.

The sound of the trooper's siren grew closer, then suddenly more distant. The cop had missed a turn.

"Thing you need to remember is, I haven't driven these roads since I was fifteen years old."

They whipped through a hairpin turn. Brush and rock flashed past the windshield before the Charger was lined back up with the road.

"It all comes back," Kira said, "but these old roads still throw up plenty of surprises."

They powered through a long downhill curve, and the Stone farm's mailbox lay ahead on the right. Hap gestured and tried to speak. Kira hit the gas. The engine roared and the farm sailed past.

Hap snuck a glance at the dash. Immediately wished he hadn't.

The red clay road was a rushing tunnel. That tunnel ended in broken brush and hard blue sky.

He grabbed the dash with both hands and shut his eyes.

Tires shouted over clay and gravel. Hap was thrown back and forth against his seatbelt. Dust and burning rubber stung his nostrils.

When he finally opened his eyes, the car was still.

Kira sat half-turned on the seat, one elbow propped on the steering wheel. Her hair was a wild black halo around her face.

Dust settled. Crickets resumed their chirping.

The state trooper's siren was faint. It shut off.

The spot where Jack Stone had died was right outside Hap's window.

"Now if I can do this, on roads I haven't driven since I was a kid and can barely remember, how am I supposed to believe my brother's death was an accident?"

THEY SAT OUT ON the front porch with a couple of beers.

Kira still had trouble thinking of it as her front porch. Her house. The boards behind her, weathered and gray, had been notched and pegged by her great grandfather sometime around the turn of the last century.

Hap pressed the cold can against his forehead, rolled it across one cheek. He drank from it and made a face, pulled a flask from his hip pocket and raised it to his lips.

His throat worked as he swallowed. Muscles moved under tanned flesh. Memory rose unbidden behind Kira's eyes. His flesh in moonlight, Bobby's under hospital fluorescents.

Hap drank fast. The can was more than half empty by the time his hands stopped shaking.

"I thought for sure back there, you were going to kill us both."

"Possible, I suppose." She rested her can on one thigh without drinking. Her eyes tracked a hawk turning slow hanging circles over some distant field.

"You really think someone killed your brother?"

"My only question is who."

Hap tipped the flask upside down, held it over his mouth until the last drops had fallen. He chased it with a mouthful of beer. Points of color rose in his cheeks, and his mouth was wet and red.

"Not much of a question, is it?" he said.

"I'm not sure I understand you."

"Well, this town just ain't all that big. If Jack was killed, odds are it was Daddy. Him, or somebody acting on his orders."

That distant hawk hung in the air, riding the thermals. Black feathers riffled at the tips of its wings.

"This is your father you're talking about."

"The old man's never been much of a father," he said. "And I think we can both agree he's a world-class son of a bitch."

Kira shook her head and set her untouched beer off to one side. She rubbed one palm across the ring of water it left on the skin of her thigh.

"It's not that he's not capable," she said. "I just don't see a reason."

"Since when does the old man need a reason?"

"He's cold-blooded, not crazy."

Hap rattled his empty beer can and looked past Kira into the house. She passed her full can over. Off in the distance, the black hawk hung almost still.

"I don't know," he said. "I mean, who else is there?"

"If your father really did mean to hand his little empire here over to Jack, just about anyone wants a piece of this place had a motive. Even you."

"Yeah, right. I've always seen myself as more the city type. Preferably a *distant* city."

"And what I hear, pretty much everyone agrees you're not cut out for a life of crime."

"There's that, too."

Hap drank and wiped his mouth with the back of one wrist. Crickets chirped in grass the bleached color and brittle texture of straw.

"I got another idea, but you're not going to like it."

"Tell me."

"How'd your stepmother feel about your brother becoming Crime King of Dogpatch?"

"You're not serious?"

"Well, everyone knows she ran into some trouble up in those hills yesterday. Scooter Wilkes was leading her up to where some of his kin were laying for her is what I heard." He raised the can and lowered it without drinking.

"Now, maybe something happened, and maybe it didn't. All anyone knows for sure is, our Sheriff came back alone, and nobody's seen hide nor hair of Scooter Wilkes since. So you ask if I'm serious, it's certainly worth thinking about."

Hap drank deep this time. Kira stared into the silent distance.

"Ask you one thing?" he said. "You figure out who killed your brother, what's your plan after that?"

Kira turned her face to Hap. Her eyes reflected the hawk's sudden drop. Going for the kill.

THE HEAT WAS merciless, the dust choking. The shack's boards were weathered and warped and split. Its roof was a bright piece of tin that stung the eye.

From the sides of that shack, a fence topped with spools of razor wire ran out in either direction. Behind that fence, junked cars rusted.

Kira stepped inside that shack and left the sunlight behind. The place smelled of dust, grease and oil, and something sour she could not define.

Shelves along the walls pressed the small space closer. Faded cardboard boxes on those shelves, filters for oil and air, many of them for cars that had been out of production before she had been born.

At the end of the room a man sat at a counter. He had a pornographic magazine open in front of him and a nickel-plated revolver on his hip.

"You Kimball?" she said.

The man looked her up and down. He flipped a page of his magazine, silicone breasts flashing on the page.

"Who wants to know?"

"I hear you've got a Charger out there. A '69, same as mine."

"Might. Might not." Again he flipped a page. "Hard to say."

Kira flexed her hands and fought the urge to reach across the counter. This man might have talked to Hap, if Hap had been willing to 'play amateur detective' instead of getting his car back from the hospital lot.

"You've got the towing contract for the county, right?"

"That we do." He smiled, three teeth missing.

"Then you'll remember that bad wreck last week. That Charger missed a curve, hit a tree."

The man who might have been Junior laid both palms flat on the pages of his magazine. He squinted at Kira, one eye brighter than the other, wary as any reptile.

"Could be…" He licked his lips. "Who's asking?"

"Look at me. That Dodge you pulled out of the ravine was John Lee Stone's."

The man's eyes widened. His jaw dropped.

"That was my father's car, and that was my brother behind the wheel."

"I'm sorry," he said. "I didn't mean nothing."

"The car."

"I THINK SHE knows."

"She doesn't know."

"Then why'd she put us in separate cars?"

"I'm telling you, she doesn't know."

The two cars sat at angles to each other, nose to nose. The department's cruiser and Bix's pickup with the bubble light mounted to the roof and a black wire trailing down through the window to the cigarette lighter. They were parked behind the burned out diner, on the four-lane at the county line. The sun threw shadows of the pine-tops like spear points at the deputies' feet.

Graham scuffed the dirt in front of his feet. When the dust settled, the shadow was unchanged.

"You seem awful sure..." he said.

Bix turned his face. Graham saw himself doubled, fishbowl-reflected in his partner's mirrored lenses.

"The boss had any idea, any damn idea at all what we're up to, you and me wouldn't be having this conversation."

JUNKED CARS SAT on cinder blocks and stacks of tires. The more thoroughly scavenged shells stood one on top of the other, their roofs smashed flat.

The cars looked like they had been dropped and stacked in no particular order. The open spaces between them formed a maze like the medieval quarter of a European city or a souk in North Africa.

Weeds and grass grew at the base of every car. The weeds were tall and dark, with a poisonous look. The grass was long and dry, burnt the color of a healing bruise. The open spaces between were baked to a hard red clay, dry and cracked. Kira's feet raised puffs of dust with every step.

The cars were a jumble of makes and models. There were oversized 70's gas guzzlers and boxy 80's sedans. There were a few more modern cars that, stripped down the way they were, could have been Fords or Toyotas or Nissans or Chevys. Many wore the scars of wrecks, silent testament to this county's roads.

Kira wandered the maze looking for her father's car. Crumpled panels and broken glass. Hoods and trunks and doors taken off haphazard. Engines stripped down or ripped out altogether. Seats missing or torn or left to rot.

Last year she had gone to a dance party in the catacombs under Paris. Now, with so many missing headlights, radiators and front grills, she felt she was once again walking past row after row of empty socketed skulls.

At the center of the maze, the junked cars had been made to form a rough open area. The earth in that square was grassless and hard, trampled flat. Strange dark stains spattered the center of the square, and something small winked there in the sunlight.

She prodded it with the toe of her shoe. A gold tooth, driven into the hard-packed earth. Despite the heat, she shuddered.

Her father's car lay at the far end of an obscure side alley. It was dumped between a Chrysler K car and a twenty year old Ford Taurus. Nowhere near the more recent wrecks, and nowhere near the larger cluster of vehicles from the 60s and 70s.

She might have wandered all day without finding it if she hadn't spotted the tire tracks. The forklift had been struggling under its heavy load, and the diagonal pattern of its treads pushed deep into the dusty clay.

The Dodge had hit head on. Its front end was notched into a deep vee from the impact, the hood folded into a hard geometric shape. The quarterpanels were crumpled, the windshield a sunburst of cracks centered around a ragged hole the exact size and shape of the top of a human skull.

The glass was still dark with blood.

The sight was like a fist around Kira's heart. She coughed and choked and put her fists against her mouth.

After a time, she unclenched her fists and lowered her hands. Her face felt prickly and cold, and her tears had left dark spots on the hard barren clay.

She went over the car with an icy eye.

The safety belt was still locked, its catch solid and firm. The belt itself was in good shape, the black nylon unfrayed. The places where the belt had been cut to remove Jack's body were single slices, no signs of tampering.

She bent down into the driver's side, put the transmission in neutral. With a little effort, the steering wheel moved smoothly, and the front wheels turned with it. Red prisms floated on her hand and arm, sunlight shining through her brother's dying blood.

She dropped and checked under the car.

Four tiny notches cut into the brake lines, one at each wheel. Sticky red fluid spattered and dried inside the wheel wells like arterial spray.

THE SHERIFF LIVED in a small place at the edge of the town center, where the last of the paved streets gave way to the wild dirt roads. Her house was small, its paint faded but not peeling.

She came to the door the third time Kira knocked. Her hair was down, her eyes puffy. A threadbare Atlanta Falcons jersey fell halfway down her thighs.

Kira stood with a storm in her chest, unable to speak.

The Sheriff studied her face. She closed her eyes and pulled air through her nose.

"All right then, come on in. Just let me put on a pot of coffee and change into something decent."

Watching her walk away into the back of the house, Kira was less surprised by the black pistol the Sheriff had been holding behind the door than by the sight of her stepmother's bare legs.

THE SHERIFF'S PARLOR was dark and cramped. A wall unit A/C fought a losing battle against the August heat. The furniture was arranged for a single woman, living alone.

Photos of John Lee dominated the room. Snapshots mostly, in store-bought frames. On the wall next to a prayer sampler, Kira's father stood out by the barn, shirtless, a bottle of Dr Pepper held loose in one hand.

From the look on his face, it was clear her stepmother had taken the picture.

Looking at the photo made Kira feel intrusive and voyeuristic, uncomfortable.

An 8x10 studio portrait stood on the table beside the couch. The three of them arranged just so, stiff and uncomfortable the way people always were, assuming the ritual postures of family love.

The department store they'd gone to was long-vanished now. Devoured by a larger chain that itself died from the debt of eating so much. Kira remembered the day — not the trip to the store itself, but the day. The way her special Easter dress felt, hot and scratchy. The strange and slightly alarming sense of occasion, seeing her stepmother dressed for church on a Wednesday and her father in a suit she didn't know he owned.

She tried to think if Europeans did the same thing, family portraits. She supposed they must, but for the life of her she couldn't remember any. The circles she moved in, children simply didn't figure.

The thought brought a strange lump to her throat. Tears pricked her eyes.

The Sheriff emerged from the back of the house, pants on and a different shirt, hair combed and pulled back. A white bandage stood out bright against the flesh of her bicep.

"Sorry bout that," she said. "Figure it'll be a long night on duty, so I went 10-7B for a—"

She took one look at Kira's face and moved to the kitchen in silence.

Sounds from that room. Pouring liquid, rattling spoons. They took their coffee on the small patio. A striped canvas awning shielded it from the sun, and the picnic table there had space enough for two people to sit.

The two women perched a hip each on the table top. Ready for fight or flight.

"So," the Sheriff said, "you given some more thought to taking that deputy's star?"

"My brother was murdered."

"Beg your pardon?"

"You knew. You did, didn't you? You knew somebody cut Jack's brake lines."

The Sheriff pressed the heel of her palm against her forehead.

"You and I are not going to have this discussion."

"Course not. Why should this be any different?"

"You going to put on that star?"

"I'm not staying."

"You were law enforcement personnel, that'd be one thing, but there is no way I'm discussing an ongoing investigation with a civilian."

"So there is an investigation? That's what you're saying?"

"Subject's closed, Kira. Wear the badge or leave it be."

"Everything's always the hard line with you…"

"Like you're any different."

Kira's coffee mug hit the picnic table with a sound like a slap. The lines hardened on the Sheriff's face.

"You've got a hell of a nerve," Kira said. "You left a crime scene rusting in a junkyard lot. You haven't taken any evidence, haven't interviewed any witnesses, haven't even dusted for a single damn fingerprint— but the minute I ask a single question, *that's* when you're worried about being unprofessional."

"And you haven't grown up one damn bit. Still nothing more than a reckless, angry kid."

Kira's hand flashed out. The Sheriff palm-blocked the shot an inch from her cheek and drove her stepdaughter's wrist into the rough wood planks of the table.

"My department's compromised, Kira. When that asshole Parker was Sheriff we still had a few honest men. Soon as I took over, I junked the bad ones and Taylor scared off the good ones. Now all I got is two deputies and that Cindi for dispatcher, and leaks so bad I might as well tell the old man everything I do myself."

Kira tried to pull her hand back. It stayed pinned.

"And how about that Kimball, down at the junkyard? You think I drape your daddy's car all over in crime scene tape and Taylor won't know all about it before I'm halfway around the front bumper?"

The Sheriff sat back. Kira rubbed her wrist and glared.

Her stepmother stared at her fists for a long time before speaking.

"This isn't working out anything like I wanted."

"Being Sheriff?"

"This. Us." She kept her head down as she spoke. "I just don't know what's wrong. Or how to stop it."

"Nothing's ever the way we want," Kira said.

"I keep remembering that little girl, couldn't hardly make a fist, kept bending her wrist when she punched. And I keep wondering what the hell happened."

Kira couldn't take the pain in the other woman's face. She had to look away.

"You can't investigate Jack's death yourself," She retreated to safer ground. "There's always the state police, or federal?"

"Admit I can't keep order in my own damn town?"

"If that's what it takes."

"Believe me, I'd do it if I thought it'd work." She rubbed the corner of her mouth with her thumb. "I can't say for sure the old man's got anyone in state CID, but everyone knows he's got judges and state senators in his pocket. In over forty years, not a single state investigation has gone further than he allowed it."

"The FBI then."

"Couldn't give less of a damn. Twenty, thirty years ago maybe, but nowadays it's terrorism or nothing for those boys."

Below the sleeve of the Sheriff's tee shirt, the white bandage showed a spreading red stain.

"I will get Jack's killers, Kira. I'll find them and make them pay," she said. "You don't have to worry about it."

Kira's hair fell over her eyes. She made no move to push it away.

"I heard something," she said. "About you and some brothers named Wilkes."

"Cousins. The Wilkes boys were cousins, fair few of them around here." Almost as an afterthought she said, "Less now, I guess."

"So it's true."

The Sheriff reached for her coffee, now gone cold.

"Question I keep asking myself is, why now? The old man hasn't tried to kill me since my first year in office, settled for hamstringing my department instead. So why now?"

"Ever think it's not Taylor?"

"Put on the star, Kira."

The two women faced each other across the table. The day's heat was a physical presence around them, hard and unrelenting.

THE GLARE AND FURY of the summer heat died slowly. By the time Kira made the turn to the house of her childhood, the sun was a dull orange torch burning in the tops of the tallest trees.

The red clay drive was covered in looping scars: she liked to come in fast and hot. Today she rolled up slowly, all the way into the open barn.

It was hot there, and close. Tools hung above a workbench in back, auto parts and paint cans and three generations of debris on the shelves.

She stood with her hip pressed against the flank of the Charger, warm as any living beast. As long as she could remember, this car's twin sat in this spot. Beside it, her grandfather's legendary Nash pickup.

The shell of the truck sagged on rotted wooden blocks. Rust had spread across the body, thinning the metal until the holes resembled patches of fine brown lace.

The windshield was made for two flat pieces of glass. One piece, the piece on the driver's side, was missing. The other wore a spiderweb of cracks, a small round chunk missing from its upper corner. Easy to imagine the roadblock, the orders, the stuttered bark of the tommy gun. The blood stains on the seat were faded, almost too faint to see.

Kira wondered if anyone in her family died of old age.

She touched her palm to the high strong curve of the Nash's hood, felt the rough texture of weathered brown steel and shuddered.

THE SHERIFF BUCKLED her gunbelt. Her shirt was starched and crisp and clean, and so was the bandage on her right bicep. She wondered if she should get stitches. Wondered if it was already too late. The ends of her hair were still wet from the shower.

After a moment's hesitation, she grabbed two spare clips and a box of ammunition. She stood in her kitchen// at her kitchen counter drinking one last cup of coffee and thumbing round after round into the large-capacity clips.

When she had loaded seventeen rounds into each, she slotted the clips into pouches on her belt and snapped the buckles closed.

It was the first time she felt like she needed extra ammo.

That damn Kira. The girl was young and headstrong and too damn cocky for her own good. She had the Stone temper, the Stone impulsiveness, and that godawful unshakable Stone conviction that they were a match for any challenge.

Worst part was, they usually were.

Everybody knew about John Lee's granddaddy gunning down those Revenue men in the 30's, and large and violent men crossed the street to avoid John Lee's daddy. There was no shortage of stories about her husband, either. Before he straightened out for her, John Lee was famous for raising hell, risking everything and staying just a gnat's whisker ahead of the law.

Now here was his daughter back again and twice as wild. Ready to ruin everything.

The Stones were throwbacks to a wilder and, simpler age. Kira was no exception.

The Sheriff threw the last of her coffee down the sink and rinsed the grounds down the drain. Her husband's old Falcons jersey was back in the top drawer of her dresser. The house was neat, ready for her to leave.

The last time, she had all she could do to make sure her stepdaughter got away in one piece. Now, everything was different.

Lines were being drawn, battle coming. This time, Kira Stone was no out of control teen but a young woman with more guts than sense. If she wouldn't accept the protection of the law, there was nothing the Sheriff could do to keep her from being caught in the crossfire.

Out front, she settled the crown of her hat on her head and adjusted the brim. A faint lick of air threw dust against her cheeks and throat.

The Sheriff turned her face into that faint breeze. The scent of trouble was on the wind.

THE WATER HEATER wasn't a big one. It didn't take long for the shower to go from hot to tepid, and then to cold.

Her black Givenchy hung on a hook by her towel. The dress was strappy and bare-shouldered. Its skirt was girlish and made Kira look like she had hips. She'd found it in a secondhand shop in the Marais, loved the contrast between the summery cut and the somber formal color. It had been her favorite all summer.

She hadn't planned on actually wearing it to a funeral.

She pressed the dress flat against the front of her body with her palm. She'd worn it to cocktails and dances, and endless parties. She tried to imagine ever dancing in this dress again.

Most likely she'd burn it when she was done.

The grief came again. The pain was physical, a phantom blow to the center of her chest that threatened to core out her heart.

Kira gripped the sides of the sink and focused on her breathing.

That horrible hollow pain abated, and she was whole again. Less than she had been a week ago, but still in one piece.

She rubbed the bathroom mirror with one fist, used the clear space to put on a quick dab of dark lipstick, a little something around the eyes.

She didn't feel ready. She never would.

Kira squared her shoulders, raised her head and opened the bathroom door.

THAT NIGHT, VIRGIL had supper with his family. He couldn't remember the last time he'd done that, just sat down with them and ate a meal.

About five minutes in, he remembered why. The kids were little monsters and his wife had a voice like a garden rake dragged down a picture window.

All the same, pushed the food in front of him around with his fork and didn't smack anyone. He smiled at the kids and nodded at the wife and breathed one great big damn sigh of relief when it was time to go meet Big Tom.

"Everything all right?" His wife caught him at the door, out of earshot of the kids.

"Course it is," he said. "Why wouldn't it be?"

He gave her his old confident smile. It didn't feel right on his face and he had to let it drop.

She saw— wives always saw too much— and looked away.

"Just work is all."

She still wouldn't look at him.

She'd been a pretty little thing, once. Skinny as a rail, with tits like you wouldn't believe. Hard to imagine it, now. Three kids had wrecked the hell out of that body, and it had been a long time since he'd seen any trace of the girl who'd reached up under her skirt and shucked her panties, handed them to him right there in the booth at the McDonald's.

"Hey. Hey now, c'mon, don't cry."

But cry she did. Real quiet, like she didn't want him to hear, when he could see her right there, tears rolling down her goddamn face.

He stuck his arms out, and she came into them. Held him.

"Come on back to me, Virge." Her tears wet the side of his face. Her mouth brushed his neck above the line of his tee shirt. "Come on back to me, okay?"

"It's just work."

But his thoughts were of pigs with black bristles and bloody snouts.

KIRA TOOK THE URN to the top of the hill. Too late, she'd realized her heels weren't in her bag. Lent to one of the other girls, or lost under a bed back in Malfi.

She picked her way up the hill barefoot. Dried grass scratched her ankles, and red dust clung to her feet. This country was no place for heels anyway.

As she reached the family plot, thousands of tiny tree frogs rose in invisible alarm. No breeze lightened her skin, but something moved in the upper branches of the trees with a sound like the ocean.

She moved among the headstones. Simple blocks of stone, dates going back over a hundred years. There were a few wooden ones too, whatever had been carved into them now little more than shadowed ghosts. A few sunken places had no marker at all.

A fresh grave sat at the edge of the clearing. The piled earth was bright and raw, glowing in the light of the dying sun.

Jack's grave.

That piled earth cast a long shadow. The hole beside it was lost in darkness.

Kira pulled the lid from the urn. It made a small coppery sound.

A thin gray wisp curled from the box. It hung in the air for a heartbeat and was gone.

Her brother.

"I wish I'd known you better," she said out loud.

The ash was coarse between her fingers. She scooped a small pile in her palm, tilted her hand slowly over the open grave.

After that, she did not touch the ash directly.

He'd had a whole life away from this place. Away from her, too. Friends. Career. Love, perhaps— some girl who missed him.

"And you came back here and lost it all."

What did Kira have to lose? Close friends who wouldn't remember her name in three weeks. Romances that rarely lasted a full season. One long endless party that would happily roll on without her.

It wasn't much, but it was hard to let go.

The sky in the west was transformed into a tunnel of light. In the east, darkness.

She stood between the two, the empty urn between her palms.

She imagined herself in the hole. Dead. Forever, dead.

She asked herself what, if anything, Jack would have sacrificed to avenge her death.

She asked herself what she owed the dead.

The light turned delicate, the color of rosebuds.

Kira stood before her brother's grave as darkness claimed the earth.

THE HOUSE WAS SMALL, and high on the hill. From where the two deputies stood, it showed black against the deepening sky, and orange lights glowed in its windows. It looked homey, like something out of a fairy tale.

"Goddammit, Nat, quit your woolgathering." Bix turned his head and spat. "I need to know you're gonna have my back."

"Fuck you."

"I mean it. You been a weak sister all day, and this here's where the rubber meets the road."

"That's what you said at the last house."

"Not my goddamn fault they weren't home, now was it?"

Deputy Graham straightened and looked around. At the bottom of the hill, the county's cruiser and Bix's pickup boxed in a brand-spanking-new Dodge Viper. Taylor's men, the higher-ups anyway, didn't even bother hiding their wealth.

All three vehicles were dark presences against the white gravel, and the dark woods pressed in. The trail was narrow. One man could damn near hold off an army in that spot.

That house didn't look half so welcoming now.

Graham pulled his weapon, racked a round into the chamber.

"Let's get this done."

THE TWO DEPUTIES made their way up the narrow trail. No shots. No movement. Not even a barking dog.

Bix and Graham shared a look. These guys, they kept watchdogs.

The house was small. A shack, really. Not much space under that roof for more than a single room. Two at the most.

That orange light glowed from every window. Not flickering, the way a candle would.

The deputies made those last few yards quick, a sudden burst of jingling harness and rattling equipment.

Graham stood against one wall, next to the window. His partner was out of sight, on the other side. His heart was racing, and like some kid playing hide and seek, he felt just about ready to jump out of his skin.

Like some kid playing hide and seek, the wall of the shack felt safe. The wall was base.

At least, until the adult part of his brain pointed out that the wall he was leaning against wasn't much tougher than cardboard. All that noise he'd made, and anyone inside could shoot right through.

The Glock was sweaty between his palms. He tightened his grip and grabbed a quick peek.

Bix and Graham called each other's names at the same time.

A brief confused moment where they were both trying to talk at the same time. Graham gave up on that, moved around to the door and gave it a good kick.

Not that it needed it — the door was already open— but his blood was up and kicking something just felt right.

"Jimmy had a watchdog, alright." Bix, coming around from his side. "Somebody blew a hole in that dog big enough to…"

Bix's words faded out. What they were looking at, neither man much wanted to speak.

The house was a single room after all. Not even a curtain to try to divide it up a little— last thing that place needed was to feel any smaller.

Bed, table, just the one chair. Small set of shelves looked handmade. In the open space on the floor, a fair-sized pile made up of sheets from the bed and a handful of automotive magazines all torn up, couple of Zane Gray westerns. In the middle of that pile sat a hurricane lamp, burning.

Graham looked at that lamp. Looked at the covers on those westerns. Looked at the torn pages from the magazines.

Looked at pretty much anything except that big splash of blood and brain all over the one wall.

Bix reached for the lantern. Pulled his fingers back real quick, shaking them in the air to cool them off. Grabbed a handkerchief out of his own pocket and used it like a potholder to lift the lantern up out of that pile and onto the table.

There was even splatter on the ceiling.

Graham licked the tips of his fingers, turned down the wick on the hurricane lamp. Shadows moved in closer around them, made it easier to ignore that wall.

"Could've burned this whole place down," Bix said.

"Reckon that was the idea."

"Then why not just burn it? Been long enough since we had any rain."

"Same reason he didn't leave the body. Figure our killer wanted some distance, maybe wanted to say old Jimmy just run off."

"Taylor's boys don't just run off. People talk like they do, but everybody knows the truth."

"Everybody knows, but nobody says."

"No sign of Big Tom Parkis out at his place, Virgil's woman is crying up a storm." Bix kicked the debris at his feet. "Now this..."

Graham looked down at the gun in his hand. Black metal. Black plastic. Holding it like that, he felt suddenly foolish. He jammed it back into its holster.

"It occur to you maybe we're not the only ones had this idea?"

NOTHING WAS RIGHT.

The Sheriff palmed the wheel. Her vehicle cruised through the place where the road made a crescent shape around a granite hillside, the type of turn they called a dead man's curve.

She knew this county. Her people had never been as rich as the Harrows, or as lawless as the Stones, but their roots went just as deep. This place was her home, and right now, tonight, something was wrong.

People weren't where they were supposed to be. Junior's was dark and shuttered. The corner store down at the crossroads that sold wine and beer after hours was locked up tight. A sign, handwritten in ballpoint pen on cardboard, said the owner had gone fishing.

She drove past the homes of Taylor's men. Every one, no matter how high or low on the food chain, showed dark windows and no lights.

It was like the whole town was holding its breath.

TEMPLE CAME FOR THEM at midnight. One minute Virgil was pacing the busted asphalt behind the old diner, traffic sounds from the highway bypass out front scraping his nerves raw. Next minute, there he was.

Temple.

At the far corner of the lot, where the shadows were deep and the trees encroached. Roots broke through the edges of the lot in that corner, and leaves moved, high in the trees, their sound the rattle of old bones.

A figure crouched. Something grown in a part of the forest where light never touched.

Virgil jumped. His hand fumbled at the gun in the back of his jeans. Beside him, Big Tom made a frightened noise.

Moonlight gleamed on a hard-boned skull, haystack shoulders. Everything else was lost in shadow.

"Temple?" Virgil hated the sound of his own voice in that moment.

The creature lifted its head. Face like a chunk of weathered rock. Thick beard hid the bottom half. Deep sockets hid the eyes.

That head lowered, raised. A nod. Points of light gleamed in those black sockets when Temple fixed his gaze on Virgil.

Virgil remembered his own hand. The one still held behind his back.

The gun's grip was comforting. That weapon was his only defense. It was hard to let go.

With an effort of will, he brought his hand away. Slowly.

Those points of light flared and turned away.

"Gentlemen."

It was a voice like somebody chain-dragging a tombstone.

"You're late." Big Tom's voice. Cranky, like a little kid. He didn't like that the man in front of them made him scared.

"Nice night," Temple said. "I had a look around."

So deep in shadow it was impossible to tell where the darkness stopped and Temple began. The air around him smelled like sulfur.

"I wanted to get the lay of the land."

Tom and Virgil eyed each other, wary in the moonlight.

"Pretty simple, really." Virgil swallowed and kept talking. It felt better to be talking. "I don't know how much Tom here told you, told your handler I mean. We just need your help with a little, whatchacallit, restructuring."

"You want me to kill an old man."

"Not just kill him," Tom said. "Make a real example out of that sumbitch, kind of thing'll give hardened cons and tough-ass peckerwoods nightmares for weeks."

"An old man."

That voice, something scraping at the bottom of an old well. Virgil shivered.

"Not just any old man," Virgil said. In spite of the heat, he shivered.

"We need you to stick around after, too." Tom, still cranky. "Give us a week or two to get bedded down solid. Anyone challenges our authority, you're right there."

A sound from the shadows. Rocks falling down the sides of an open grave.

It was laughter.

"It's your money."

THIS WASN'T GOING the way it was supposed to.

Bix and Graham finally found one of Taylor's hoods, a meth cook name of Arnie Slocum. Graham remembered him from when they were kids, Arnie always in trouble. His brothers and cousins were like a pack of wild dogs, and Arnie was the runt of the litter. Always game to get in trouble, always too dumb to run when they got caught.

He'd been a soft-hearted kid without a lick of sense. Now, a grown-ass man, he still didn't have the sense God gave monkeys. Caught red-handed using an old deer cooler for a meth lab— if a sorry collection of old buckets and bottles, aquarium tubing and duct tape counted as a lab— he greeted Graham by name and offered the two deputies a beer.

That was the scene gone wrong, right there from the kickoff. Bix tried to rescue it, acting tough. Graham wondered which guy in the movie he was imitating.

Took Bix a minute to get to the part about 'you're working for us now'.

Arnie just smiled and said, "Sure you won't have a beer?"

Graham grabbed Bix's arm, the bicep swollen with violent energy. Pulled that arm in close to his chest, pitched his voice low so the skeletal meth cook wouldn't hear.

"Look at him," he said. "Look around you, man." Over his shoulder, he called back louder, "Arnie, this where you make all that meth for Taylor?"

"I do all right."

Graham made eye contact with his partner— a look that said 'let me handle it'.

"Y'all gonna arrest me again?"

"Wasn't planning on it. How much'd you say you cook here? Like in a batch or whatever."

"Got four ounces one time. That was pretty good."

"Use any yourself?"

"Not while I'm cooking, no sir. Used to do, but I started a fire in the big lab, and my brothers like to beat my ass. Now all I got's this here, and I can't lose it, so nothing for me til the ice is out, no sir."

"Arnie…"

"Which is why I don't know if I can work for you gentlemen. Mister Virgil, he already buys a lot of what this little lab makes, and I just don't know if I can afford to sell more. Really y'all ought to pull up a seat and open up a beer."

"Arnie, you said the big lab."

"I don't know if my brothers got any to spare either. They surely make enough, real pure too, real good, but I'm pretty sure Mister Virgil buys up all they got too. Sells it all the way out from DC to West Texas is what I heard."

That got Bix's attention.

"This lab of theirs," he said, "where's that at?"

Like turning off a tap, the flow of words stopped. Arnie sat himself up a little straighter, made his mouth a flat line and pulled his thumb and forefinger across it like a zip.

Bix surged forward. Graham stopped him with hand on his chest, wondering to himself how much of this good cop-bad cop was an act.

"Arnie, I really do think we need to know where your brothers' lab is," he said.

"Can't do it," the little cook said. "I wish I could, but I can't."

Bix looking seriously pissed now. A point of light swam in his left eye, like a small imperfection in a piece of colored glass.

"The location of that lab is a secret location," Arnie said. "If I went and told y'all, I do believe my brothers'd kill me, sure as shit they'd kill you. That big old barn's got a dang minefield around it, I kid you not."

The air in the cooler was an eye-watering mix of chemicals and solvents and decades-old layers of hanging deer carcass. Added in with the testosterone smell of Bix's growing rage, and it was near enough to make Graham's head spin.

"Look—"

But it was too late. Bix surged forward, grabbed the front of Arnie's clothing. The bundle of sticks and cloth in his fists yelled and flailed.

"Tell me!" Bix roared. The small man made a thin high sound, a child's wordless scream.

They crashed and stomped around the inside of the cooler. Glass broke and bottles tipped. A great goddamn whoosh and the place was on fire.

TEMPLE PROWLED the darkness. Harkness, Georgia had a bare handful of streetlights just outside the courthouse in the town center. The rest of the town, and the county, was the domain of night.

He stood just outside one of those streetlights, his feet inches away from the outer edge of its glow. The town was like many other small towns he'd known. Georgia seemed to stamp them out like they were building from a kit, but Alabama and Mississippi had their share too.

For the most part, those towns were all much of a much. Grand old buildings and shabby new ones, businesses boarded up and businesses still hanging on, one side of the tracks and the other. Those making shady deals and the ones found out their deals had already been made.

Harkness was different. The drought had been hard all over, but here it was like the land itself was dying. Withered plants, brittle grasses, sick and dying livestock, everywhere dust and ashes— it was easy to imagine Hell like this. That the night sky overhead was the top of some stalactite-hung chamber, deep beneath the earth.

Temple felt this place. It spoke to him.

He checked out all four sides of the courthouse, from a safe distance and careful not to pick up either of the security cameras. The things were antiques looked like they'd record to an old VHS tape— if this place even had it in their budget. Not much risk, but Temple didn't take on any more risk than necessary.

He squatted on his haunches, became just another night shape in the dark. The courthouse was one of those sturdy old red brick and white granite piles. The Sheriff's office was on the east side of the building, ground level. From the rest of the town, security looked like it would be a joke, but after 9/11, you never could tell.

It was something to think about.

He looked up at the moon. Time he got to the old man, set eyes for himself on the senior citizen had his clients shitting in their britches.

A sound somewhere off in the night. Growing louder, a big engine but one of the new ones, sounded like a weed whacker on steroids. Rising in pitch, falling again with every change in gear.

Temple moved quickly up one of the twisted old magnolias in the square.

A glow in the north that had to be headlights. He watched it come, sweeping through switchbacks and hairpins. When it was close enough to see the actual beam of its lights, Temple steadied himself on the tree limb and drew a hatchet.

A few more tire-shredding turns and he was finally able to see the car.

It was a yellow Corvette.

Temple's lips pulled back from his teeth. He stroked the hatchet's blade, from thick iron spine to deadly sharp edge.

The land felt him too.

It had just offered him a welcome gift.

THE SHERIFF DROVE her county. She drove the twisting old bootlegger roads, dirt and dust and gravel, and she drove the crumbling pavement of the farm roads, from back in the days when folks around here still farmed.

Over six hundred square miles with fewer than four hundred people still living here. So many houses abandoned, deserted, collapsing in place. So few still inhabited.

She drove the night alone, feeling like the last person left on earth.

At the multi-lane bypass she stopped. Down the hill, on the other side of the county line, the shape of the native earth showed in a blaze of electric light over acres-wide parking lots. Like a woman's flesh showing through a torn garment, the sight made her feel prurient and ashamed.

There was traffic here. Enough that she had to wait to pull out and make her turn.

Everyone drove too fast. But then, the highway was built for it, engineered so the posted limits felt like crawling and their proper speeds made tickets a good source of income.

The Sheriff thought about pulling over a speeder or two. She thought about the lights across the county line. She turned her vehicle back towards her own town.

She rolled down her window as she drove. Full dark yet, but the smell of dawn was in the air. She flicked off the A/C and breathed deep. She had always loved the country air— rich earth, dew, night-blooming flowers.

At the memory, her heart surged with love.

Now the land was dust. Fruit withered on the vine, and livestock died in the fields. All those riches, wasted.

For reasons she didn't care to examine, her thoughts turned to her stepdaughter.

Light glowed at the center of her town. The dirty orange smudge was visible from a couple of miles away. There weren't enough working streetlights to produce that glow..

She hit the flashers and punched the gas.

"Bix. Graham. Get on in here, town square. You copy?"

Dead air on the mike.

She double-clicked. Waited. Double-clicked again.

Those two were supposed to have their radios on. She threw down the handset in disgust.

Hit the town square, tires squealing, an ominous knocking coming from under the hood of her vehicle. Soon as she got there, she dropped her speed down to a crawl.

One of the oak trees was on fire. And her brain had trouble processing what she saw beneath.

The sports car was gleaming new. The flames and her emergency flashers threw candy-colored lights in its jeweled surface.

It was also lying on its side. The marble plinth for the Civil War memorial leaned away from its crumpled hood, as though trying to escape. The statue of Colonel Harrow lay beyond, shattered into big ugly pieces.

The Corvette's top was down, and a great vertical hole had been punched in the windshield. It looked like a slit pupil in an eye the color of burst crystal.

Hap Taylor's car. And a body on the ground.

THE SHERIFF CLIMBED down from her vehicle. One hand was one the holster at her hip.

The body on the ground did not move.

The burning tree cast a hellish glow over the scene. Her emergency flashers painted it in bursts of red and blue. Her truck's headlights dazzled off paint and chrome and granite, and the air was thick with the smells of motor oil and fire.

She played her Maglite over the body. Broken glass like diamonds in the light. Wet gleam in the hair, the grass beneath.

The body lay face down, and maybe she was grateful for that, but he was the right height and build for Hap Taylor.

She knew she should speak. Ascertain injury, give first aid or phone across the county line for paramedics. She looked at the body again. More likely the coroner.

A shadow moved. She swung her light. A smell like burnt matches stung her nose and her gun hand cleared leather.

Too late. Pain jolted up her arm. The gun flew.

The Sheriff spun with the impact, brought the barrel of the flashlight down, fast and savage. The lens cracked, the bulb broke, and a deep male voice roared.

She drove a kick at the source of that sound, center mass. Like kicking the tough and fibrous mass of an old tree.

Movement flashed at the edge of her vision. She ducked, felt cool air on her scalp as the hatchet swept the Stetson from her head.

A hatchet? Part of her brain wanted to know who the hell brought a hatchet to a gunfight.

Except it wasn't a gunfight. Not anymore.

She brought her Maglite up. Across. Back up on the other side.

Sparks flew and steel sang with every blow.

The flashlight was heavier and slower than the hatchet, but its steel barrel and five D batteries kept the black iron blade from splitting her skull, opening her guts, slashing her throat.

Every impact sent a ringing jolt up her arm. One caught the flat of the blade against the back of her hand and sent the Maglite flying.

The blade flashed again. Three harsh swipes ripped the air.

The Sheriff was driven back. Her truck's door mirror smacked the back of her head.

Her attacker laughed.

THE SHERIFF SQUARED off against her attacker. The man was bare to the waist, muscle moving like a nest of ropes beneath his skin.

Red and blue light strobed off the top of his bald head, lit his skin the colors of danger. Colored sparks reflected deep in the sockets of his eyes.

The fist that held the hatchet looked like a bag of walnuts.

No light glinted from the black iron blade.

"Say, you're pretty good." He wiped blood from his mouth with the back of one wrist. "This is going to be all right. Yeah, all right."

He kept his stance low, a shadow in the dark, a haystack doing ballet. The black blade skimmed over the grass, weaving slow circles.

The Sheriff's PR-24 rasped out of its ring. He gave her time for that. She held the baton against her forearm, tonfa handle thick and comforting in her fist.

Grass blades whickered. The hatchet came up fast, whanged against the baton. A blow like a boxer's jab, light and quick, feeling her out.

If a boxer's jab could chop through bone.

"Yeah, this is gonna be great."

The man's reach was murderous. And whatever most folks thought, big men didn't have to be slow. This one certainly wasn't. This one was fast, horribly fast. Every blow was like the strike of a venomous adder.

She kept her weight light on the balls of her feet. Her left fist was ready on the handle of her baton. Her right hand was in a world of hurt. Swollen and stiff already, bruised deep in the bone.

"You want to tell me what this is about, partner?"

"Name's Temple, babe. Maybe you heard of me."

Temple. She had heard the name. Everyone heard the name, right along with Candyman and The Hook. Same as kids made up stories about those bogeymen to scare each other, thugs and lowlifes made up stories about Temple.

"Temple ain't real," she said.

That earned her an overhead chop aimed at the crown of her skull. Her baton rang, a single clear note. He danced away from her counterstrike like he had all the time in the world.

"Real enough, I figure."

Playing with her. This sonofabitch was *playing* with her.

Then and there, the Sheriff decided to make this smug bastard pay.

"Taylor tell you why he wants me dead?" She padded to her left, her right hand hot and throbbing now. No bone bruise, the back of that ax head had broken a bone.

A sound like rats moving behind walls, or leather dragged across a basement floor.

It was Temple's laughter.

The smell of burning matches intensified.

He was on her in a flurry of blows. The black iron blade seemed to be everywhere in the air at once.

She gave ground, away from the SUV, away from the wrecked Corvette. Temple crowded her flank, never letting her get too far.

"Why?" More of that horrible laughter, another swipe with the hatchet. "Why don't really matter now, does it? Not the ride you're about to take."

Another crashing blow, this one aimed at the juncture of neck and shoulder. Her right hand was a hot balloon swollen with pain, all but useless.

"Might be money," Temple said. "Reason most folks want each other dead— money or love."

He feinted right, swung left. The Sheriff slid under, cracked the baton backhanded across his knee.

Temple grunted. The black blade faltered. The Sheriff, out of position with all but her right hand, followed through.

The rising palm strike caught the bony shelf under his beard. The impact sent a queasy jolt of pain up her arm. Bile flooded her mouth.

Temple rocked back on his heels, dazed. The Sheriff spat stomach acid and aimed for the solar plexus. It was her best kick. She'd see he got medical attention once she had him locked up.

At least, that was the plan.

Aiming for that intersection of fragile bone and vital nerve centers, the Sheriff struck nothing but air. Temple twisted away from the blow— he was just that fast.

He was also off balance.

She came at him with the nightstick. Twenty-four inches of rock hard polycarbonate sliced the air, a three-blow pattern that didn't care what it hit.

A jolt of impact, and Temple was gone. Whatever he was wearing below the waist flapped and snapped as he rolled away.

The Sheriff snarled in frustration.

Temple came out of his roll three yards away, agile and expert. Dead grass caked the shoulders and knees of his clothes. The smell of dust flooded the air. He favored his right knee, and he still had the hatchet.

"You're not half bad, babe." He coughed, spat. "Not half bad at all."

"Surrender now, and I'll go easy on you."

Again that sound, his laughter. What on earth was wrong with that man's throat?

"You got spunk, I like that," he said. "Gotta tell ya, this has been fun."

"Just getting started old man. You ain't seen nothing yet."

Temple's smile was wolfen in the darkness.

He charged. The hatchet wove slashing black patterns in the red and blue light. He used his size and his strength to overwhelm her.

The Sheriff danced back, her weight poised, her nightstick a blur in motion.

The air rang every time hatchet struck baton. One on top of the other, a trash can drumroll, a fire alarm.

Her right hand was a throbbing mess. Her lungs were on fire. Every blow she blocked felt like it was going to tear her arm out of the socket.

She caught the rhythm of his attack, drove a punishing shot into the nerve cluster on his right bicep.

The attack faltered, but he still held onto his weapon.

She planted her feet and smashed her baton down across the wrist. The hatchet chunked into the turf.

Her blood soared.

Too late, she realized she'd left herself open.

She saw the fist, a brief flash. A bag of walnuts. A brown brick.

Her vision flared, and her ears rang. Her body seemed far away, unimportant.

Time jumped.

The Sheriff was still on her feet, slumped against the overturned pickup. One shoulder against the hood, the other against the windshield. Emergency flashers hurt her eyes, and there was broken glass in her hair.

The nightstick was still in her hand. A foreign artifact, alien, puzzling.

Darkness moved across her vision. Something large. Something looming.

"You sure are something, you know that?" the darkness said. "Fought like a goddamned bobcat."

A massive hand held her chin between thumb and forefinger. His skin smelled of charred wood and stagnant water.

"Now, I won't kid you. This is gonna hurt a little, but the hard part'll be over quick."

She spat blood and spoke the name.

"Temple."

"For what it's worth, darlin', wasn't the old man hired me. Come morning, he'll be just as dead as you."

KIRA WANDERED the house. Her house, she supposed, though it didn't feel that way. This was her father's house, and her grandfather's. Jack's maybe. But not hers.

This was the house where she'd found her mother's body, and held her father's dying hand. This house, this town, this land was history and death. And if she let it, this place would tie her down and swallow her whole.

It would be so easy. Revenge and blood feuds had once been a way of life here. Everything she'd been taught as a child told her to stay, to find out who cut Jack's brakes and make them pay. To do that, she'd end up wearing a badge for her stepmother. Or taking over for Taylor.

And of course, there would be retribution. Whoever did it, they'd have somebody to avenge them. And so on. And so on. It would be a loose thread: every time it was plucked a little more of the garment would be destroyed.

Eventually, there'd be nothing left.

She stepped into her parents' bedroom. The master bedroom. Easier to think of it as the master bedroom, to make it neutral that way, when the sheets were stained with sweat and the air still smelled of last night's sex.

Sex.

She'd had sex with Hap. Now he'd follow her around for the rest of the week, worse than he had the last few days. Or, seeing as he'd snuck out sometime before dawn, maybe he wouldn't. She wasn't sure how she felt, either way.

She sat down heavily on the bed. It was all so much. Just overwhelming.

Her mother and Taylor.

Her and Hap.

The old man and her stepmother, a devil and an angel on each shoulder, trying to force her to choose sides.

And someone had cut her brother's brakes. Some underling of Taylor's, trying to keep Jack from taking over. Maybe even her stepmother. Try as she might, Kira couldn't discount the idea that the woman would go that far to keep John Lee's son from falling into Taylor's hands.

If Jack even was John Lee's son. The thoughts circled back on each other until Kira thought her head would explode.

At some point she fell asleep. Her dreams were of blue green water and private islands, the movable feast of her friends' lives, Marie and her funny little fat man.

"I WONDERED when you would come."

The intruder stalked the darkened gallery. Taylor was able to see him overhead, black on black, moving like smoke.

"Come down if you wish." Taylor was not so old that he was unable to put a little iron in his voice.

The intruder came over the side of the railing— shapeless black garment flapping like bat wings.

The man landed lightly, rose to a crouch. Bare to the waist, the garment wrapped around his lower torso made him seem like something extruded from the floor itself.

The air around him filled with sweat, testosterone and the unmistakable stink of sulfur.

"Very theatrical," Taylor said. "Would you like to sit?"

Candlelight glittered in the stranger's eyes. His bare shoulders and bald head gleamed, oily with sweat. His face was a mask of grim and stone-faced intent, but Taylor hadn't lived this long without learning to see through masks.

"You seem confused," he said.

"Wanted to see this old man everyone's so damned afraid of." The intruder's voice was a deep rasp. Something out of childhood nightmare.

"So you're him," the man said. "You're Taylor."

Taylor said nothing to that. There was nothing to say.

Eventually, the other man broke the silence.

"I'm Temple."

"Is something wrong with your throat? Some childhood damage?"

The man flinched, but did not move. Taylor had the pistol-grip shotgun cocked, his finger on the triggers. The remark had been a goad, but not enough to spur the intruder around the table.

"Mouthy," Temple said, "for a dead man."

Again that urge to counter, to match attack for attack. Taylor could use that. He simply had to find the proper hook.

"Your handler reached out to me many times over the years," he said. "Are you curious why I never wanted you?"

A muscle jumped at the corner of Temple's eye.

"You're unpredictable. That makes you useless to me."

"I've never once missed a target," Temple rasped. "Never once."

Pride. That was the hook Taylor needed.

"You're sloppy. There's nothing you do I couldn't get from a bunch of bikers or convicts for a tenth of the price. And with less collateral damage. You're a sloppy, overpaid amateur."

Again, that muscle jumped in Temple's face. This time the corner of his mouth moved with it.

"I will tear the living heart from your chest, old man."

The shotgun in Taylor's hand was a weapon for close quarters. The short barrels that made it so devastating also meant that a blast would be little more than an inconvenience at this range. Taylor needed the man closer.

"And kill me slowly, no doubt. Your threats, sir, are unimaginative and predictable."

To Taylor's surprise, Temple laughed.

"Think I'm beginning to see what your boys are so afraid of," he said. "You just don't rattle."

The way he said it, the words were a compliment.

"Care to tell me which of 'my boys' you're referring to?" Taylor noted the man's expression, carried on. "It hardly matters. Tomorrow one or the other of us will kill them."

"How you figure?"

"You were paid in full before you started?"

"Don't work like that," Temple said. "Half up front, half when it's done."

Now it was Taylor's turn to laugh. For a moment the act threatened to overwhelm him, to kill him then and there.

Temple didn't come around the table to help. After what felt like forever, Taylor got his laughter— and the coughing fit— back under control.

"I know what my men make. And what they keep. I doubt two, even three, of them together could come up with your retainer."

"Two of em did."

"That half up front is the last money you'll ever see. But not bad, I suppose, for one old man…"

That provoked him. Temple's fist rose and fell with his wordless yell. A black iron hatchet with a bloodstained blade quivered in the oak tabletop.

"So," Taylor said. "Not just one old man."

"You're my third. They want a clean sweep. No one who might get in their way."

"You'll have a job of it then."

"Already got the Sheriff."

Taylor's eyebrows rose. If he hadn't needed one hand on the gun, he might have clapped.

Then a thought followed. Winged fear brushing across his heart.

"Kira Stone…"

"She's next."

"Leave town now. She's out of your league."

"That so?"

"The Sheriff was her stepmother."

"Aren't you going to ask who else I took tonight?"

"Hardly matters," Taylor said. "You have well and truly kicked a hornet's nest."

"Then who?"

"Tell me something," Temple said. "Your boy, he drives a yellow Corvette don't he?"

The distance was wrong. The time was wrong. Taylor didn't care. He brought the shotgun level with his shoulder and fired both barrels.

The last thing he saw was black iron coming at him, spinning end over end.

THE CRASH WOKE Kira. It was less a sound than a physical presence that rushed through her bones and lungs, lingered vibrating in her blood.

Thrown from sleep, still clinging to threads of dream, she wrestled with the tangle of bedsheets. She was fully dressed, half-sitting and half-lying on top of the bed, wondering what the hell had happened.

Her mother's jewelry box was on the floor along with several photos knocked from the wall. The rocking chair was moving back and forth and clouds of dust hung in the air. It hadn't been a dream.

She stumbled over unfamiliar furniture between the bed and the door. In the living room she picked up speed. The floor here was all wrong, running at a downhill angle. Furniture was tipped and scattered, and moonlight streamed through open window, glittered on broken glass.

She hit the front door moving fast, only to pull up short. Her front porch was gone. Whatever had crashed into the front of her house was half-buried in the wreckage. Now a splintered pile of kindling and eight feet of empty space were all she had between her front door and the ground.

Out the back door. Around the side. The truck sat wedged into the front corner of the house. The support beam there was splintered, and the wall above leaned out at a crazy angle. Big square headlights shone over cobwebs and floor joists.

A figure knelt on the ground outside the vehicle. Kira broke into a run.

As in a nightmare, she ran as hard as she could and never seemed to move. Details jumped out, crisp and jagged and all too real. The county decals on the 4x4. The open driver's door and bloodstained seat. The single light on the roof rack bathing the scene in on-again off-again red.

Time seemed to jump and cut. One second she was running without movement. The next she was almost on top of the kneeling figure.

The Sheriff stopped her with one upraised palm.

The woman who raised her, the woman who stood for law in a town run by outlaws, pushed at the dry red clay beneath her palms. She pushed and grunted and pushed until her feet were underneath her. A single painful inch at a time, one hand held tight against her waist, the Sheriff pushed herself to a standing position.

One side of her face was swollen. Her uniform was covered in blood. She kept that hand hard against her waist, but her eyes burned with fierce determination.

She straightened her spine.

Lifted her chin.

Looked Kira straight in the eye.

Took two steps, and collapsed.

Kira rushed to the crumpled heap, gathered her stepmother into her arms.

"You're okay." The older woman spat blood. "I'm—"

"What happened? Who did this?"

"—here in time."

"We gotta get you to a hospital."

Even as she said it, she realized that the nearest emergency room was two towns over, that any ambulance would be at least an hour away.

"You're in danger, Kir- Ki-" The effort of saying her stepdaughter's name started a coughing fit. Blood sprayed, a fine mist. Her muscles were iron bands, burning hot from some unseen forge.

"Danger," she finally said. "Danger."

This was the woman who had stood, hard and strong and tough as nails, over the whole of Kira's life. The woman who had taught her everything. The woman whose only fault was that she wanted her stepdaughter to live up to her own example.

"Temple," the Sheriff said. "Danger."

"I'm gonna put you in the back seat of my car, get you some help. Won't be the easiest ride you ever had, but I guarantee it'll be the fastest."

"Listen to me." Her one good eye blazed and her free hand clamped on Kira's bicep like a metal hook. "Temple... Coming here. You need to run."

"Look, how bad is it? We get you to a doctor..."

"I'm fine."

"Taylor's going to pay for this."

"Temple... wants... him too. Already got... Hap."

"But... who?"

"Kira, stop."

"I'm not leaving you."

"Forget me. Go back... Paris." The iron hook tightened. "Be safe."

"I—"

"For once. Be safe."

The hand fell away. The iron-banded muscles went slack.

"I love you," Kira whispered.

Too late, she saw. Without the hand held tight around the Sheriff's middle, there was nothing to seal the wide deep cut, to hold in the woman's intestines.

HAP FOUND HER sat at the kitchen table, crying. Her stepmother's body lay stretched out on the table in front of her, and the woman was a godawful mess.

It was a macabre sight. Damn macabre.

Kira didn't hear him come in. She didn't hear the couple times he called her name.

He touched her shoulder. A whoosh and a clatter and the floorboard banged his knees. His arm felt like it was being ripped out of the socket and one small hard-boned fist hovered in front of his face.

"Whoa! Whoa! Kee, it's me!" The only things he could think of to say.

"Hap?"

She let him up one little piece at a time. Like maybe she wasn't quite sure.

"What the hell happened here?"

"She said you're dead. Someone named Temple got you."

"Well I ain't dead. Just in Macon, which ain't that far off I guess." He risked a glance at the body on the table. "Did you say Temple?"

"You heard of him?"

"Shit, everybody's heard of him. Like, turn out the bathroom light and look in the mirror, say his name three times and Temple will appear."

"Whoever killed my mother was real."

He noticed that she'd said 'mother' instead of 'stepmother', but let it go without comment.

"She looks kind of peaceful, don't you think?"

'Hap, don't."

She shrugged away from his touch in a way that made it clear reaching out his hand again might not be the healthiest thing he could ever do.

They stood a little distance apart from each other, looking down at the body on the table.

Waxy skin, splashes of blood. Hap had seen worse on TV. The Sheriff almost could have been a Hollywood special effect, except for the smells, drying blood and punctured bowel.

It was real. It was all too real.

"Come away with me, Kee."

She looked up at him, blue eyes bright under that black hair.

"Seriously," he said, "we leave right now, drive straight to Atlanta airport and get on the first fucking plane out of here."

He had her attention now.

"There's nothing here for you anymore, Kira. Just a place where you don't want to stay and a killer my daddy always said was too dangerous to hire."

"Oh god, your father... Hap, we've got to warn him."

"Have you seen that army he's got up to the house? Daddy's gonna be fine."

He stepped in, touched her upper arm without suffering bodily injury. He built on it, pulled her in and stroked her back in that way she liked.

"Kira, I ain't worried about him. I'm worried about us. Let's get away from all this blood and death, show me round Paris or Barcelona or one of those other places you talked about. What do you say?"

"I want that, really I do."

"Great, grab your bag and let's go."

"But there's a couple of things I gotta do first."

Hap knew the way he held her changed. It was just as well she couldn't see his face.

FOR SUCH A SMALL woman, Kira's stepmother was certainly hard to carry. Even with Hap helping out, it was hard work.

They'd wrapped her in a bedsheet, and each had an end. The trip up the hill was short enough, but it had never seemed so long.

"I still say old Bill Rhineland's got people for this."

"Keep your end up. I don't want her dragging on the ground."

"But if we just let Rhineland—"

"You don't want to help, you can leave right now."

"I just don't see…"

It was like that, all the way up the path. Slow going, the moon behind the trees, rocks and roots and plain stubborn ground hiding in the darkness underfoot, and Hap's mouth running in the background.

And her stepmother's body, a dead weight bumping against her with every step.

Kira felt numb. Actually numb. Her lips, her fingers, the backs of her arms were pins and needles, as though they'd gone to sleep. Her mind was white noise, an old TV displaying a signal no longer broadcast.

The woman she carried had made her oatmeal with raisins on rainy mornings. Had taught her how to tie her own shoes, and how to make a proper fist.

The white noise in her thoughts, the numbness in her body, these were blessings.

They were all that allowed her to carry her burden up the hill to the family plot.

"Gentle now," she said. "Gentle. You drop her in there like a sack of potatoes and so help me…"

"Jesus, Kee."

"I can't give her flowers or her pastor, bring out a bunch of people from her church, but we can damn sure treat her with proper respect."

They got the body lowered. The white bedsheet that served as her shroud was a gray smudge at the bottom of the grave.

The red clay Kira had dug out just two days ago stood piled to one side. Rich and dark when she'd lifted it from the earth, two days in the sun had dried it to so much iron powder. Hap reached for the shovel.

"Hang on," she said. "We need some words. She at least deserves that."

"Temple catches us out here, you think he'll say a few words over us?"

"*Putain*, I said I'd go with you."

"Then let's fill in this hole and get going."

"This man scares you that much?"

"Word is, he uses a hatchet. Keeps it sharp enough to shave."

Kira shuddered, remembering her stepmother's wounds.

From that knob of hill she could follow the rise and fall of the land around her, as sensual as the curves of a woman's body. The tops of the trees were black beneath the wild starry sky, and the house and barns below were moonwashed toys, small and insignificant.

"Hap?"

"What now?"

"Where's your Stingray?"

"Back up at the house, least by now I hope so. You made me leave it at the hospital, remember?"

"Oh."

She looked back at him, standing between the open grave and the pile of dirt, looking like his bladder was twenty minutes past full.

"Do you know any words?" she asked.

"My family never was the churchgoing type…"

"I haven't been since I was little. Now I wish I'd paid more attention."

A few scraps of poetry came to mind. A little Rimbaud, some Baudelaire. A piece of a Shakespeare sonnet. Nothing complete. And nothing right for the moment.

In its own way, that was how it had always been between them.

Kira stepped up the the edge of the grave.

"I wish I had the right words," she said, "but I don't know if any words ever could be right. So much about tonight ain't right, what's one more thing? You're buried next to Papa at least, so that's something you would have wanted."

She blinked away tears. Hap shifted behind her, his nerves and fear like a smell on the air.

"You and I didn't always see eye to eye, but…"

She stopped a moment, trying to swallow around the knot in her throat.

"But you always looked out for me. You taught me to be brave. To be tough. To be strong. To be like you."

A shadow passed over the gray smudge of the shroud. Kira looked up: a cloud, passing over the moon.

"Now, me and Hap here, we're going to honor your final request. We're going to turn tail and run. We're gonna get out of here and go someplace safe, forget all about the danger to his daddy, and what's already been done to you and Jack. We're gonna be good little cowards and…"

She straightened. Another cloud passed across the moon. She could feel it cool on her cheeks, a definite breeze.

"Hap, I can't."

"I know."

She turned in time to see the broad flat blade of the shovel rising at her face.

GOD DAMN KIRA. God damn her.

She looked so small down there, lying in the bottom of the grave. Curled up, like a child sleeping.

He couldn't believe he'd killed her.

The minute Hap hit her, he regretted it. But dammit, it wasn't like she didn't deserve it.

Temple was after them. Death himself was coming their way, they needed to escape, to get out right fucking *now*, and she just kept on totting up a list of errands to do on the way.

God damned ridiculous, is what it was.

Minute she'd starting talking about staying, actually goddamn *staying*, he'd snapped. Just like that, snapped. Same as that guard out on the porch a couple days ago. Hap, who always kept his temper down and his smile up, had lashed out.

And this time, he'd killed the woman he loved.

He could see the top of her house from here. The Sheriff's truck crashed into the side, the one he came in parked in the dirt out front. He actually got two-three steps down the trail before he pulled up short.

Hap saw what Kira meant now. He would've got in the wind, left the Sheriff lying on that goddamn table instead of dragging her up here and dropping her in a hole. Death looking over their shoulder, breathing down their necks the entire goddamn time, filling the hole in seemed just about as dumb as it got.

This was different. When it was someone you cared about, it was different.

No way Hap was going to talk himself into staying behind. He wasn't that stupid.

But neither could he bear the thought of Kira's body in that hole, open to the sky. Picked at by birds. Just the thought made him want to throw up.

A few extra minutes to fill in her grave… Was he that stupid?

Temple was coming. Nothing short of a miracle he wasn't here yet. Kira was dead. She wouldn't even know if she was buried or not.

Hap took a step down the hill, took another back up. The kind of jerky dance he used to do years ago, a little boy with a full bladder.

Something banged his leg. He looked down at his hand.

He was still holding the shovel.

KIRA HEARD A MOAN.

It happened again before she realized the sound came from her.

She tried to lift her head, decided to lay where she was.

It must have been a killer night: she had the mother of all hangovers, her mouth tasted foul, and someone had wrapped her up in this heavy blanket.

She wondered where she lay. Not a bed. Beds weren't this lumpy, and they never had metal and things under the sheets digging into her.

Had there been something with a shovel?

She was curled on her side, her head in the crook of her arm. The air under that blanket was starting to go warm and stale.

She couldn't move under that blanket. Mentally, she cursed Jean-Michele and whoever else thought this was funny.

One shift, one small shift, and a thin stream of dirt poured over her cheek. She knew that dirt, rough and granular. That smell, like no other place in the world.

Kira was back in Georgia.

Memory came back in pieces, broken shards in random order.

The shovel. Her stepmother. Hap's voice. The grave. Trying to roll with the blow, landing in the grave.

Lying dazed as dirt peppered her skin.

Parts of the picture were still missing. Her memory jumped, and skipped, and circled back to strange small details.

Kira was too busy pumping and kicking with her legs to care.

Knees in toward her chest, feet back out. Knees in, feet out.

That was the idea, anyway. Under that blanket of dirt, her legs barely moved.

Knees in, feet out.

The hot dry horrible summer was on her side: she never could have shifted the wet red clay that had been in the grave when she dug it out days ago.

Pump in with the knees, kick out with the feet.

Knees, feet.

Knees. Feet.

She kept her arms strong around her head, her shoulders high. Dirt fell through anyway. She could hear it rattling down around her, taste it in her mouth.

Knees. Feet.

Pump. Kick.

Knees. Feet.

The dirt above her was shifting. The more her legs moved, the harder she pumped and kicked.

Her breath became ragged. Her lungs kept sucking in the same air, each time with less and less oxygen.

She kept pumping and kicking.

It was black in that hole. Her eyes were shut tight. Bursts of light swam across her vision.

Knees.

Feet.

Pump.

Kick.

The earth shifted loose with a surprising suddenness. Like a stubborn wine cork, her legs popped loose, leaping into her pocket of air.. Her knees damn near hit her in the chin.

Kira moved fast.

Light-headed.

Dizzy.

She moved fast.

With her knees free, she had the leverage to turn face down.

Turned face down, she was able to push with her legs.

Dirt filled the little pocket of air where her face had been. It streamed down around her on every side.

It gave her more to push against.

Kira thrust her face into fresh clean air. She spat Georgia clay from her mouth and blew it from her nose and wiped it away from her face.

She opened her eyes to a sky the color of gunmetal, threw back her head and laughed.

That son of a bitch was going to pay.

WEDNESDAY

KIRA PULLED HERSELF up to the lip of the grave. That bastard Hap had only filled it halfway in.

She supposed she should be grateful. Instead she couldn't help thinking of him as lazy and sloppy.

Or maybe just in one hell of a hurry.

She spit again, more grit, for what felt like the thousandth time. The taste of that dry Georgia clay would be with her forever.

She raised her fingers to her forehead. The bump made her queasy when she touched it, but balance and vision were fine. She'd taken worse.

The world was bright and still, lit by that gray glow of the hours before sunrise. Mist clung in the tree roots, and the planet Venus, the morning star, was visible overhead.

Clouds gathered on the horizon, a storm front marching in from out over the Atlantic.

Kira stared into that eastern sky. Thunderheads reflected in her eyes.

SHE DIDN'T STOP to rebury her stepmother. Three feet of dirt would do. At least for now.

She didn't try to fight the fire that son of a bitch had set. All that hot dry weather, by the time she came down the hill from her own grave, the house her great grandfather had built a hundred years ago had gone from smoky to an outright blaze.

Staggering down that trail, she could feel the heat on her face. As she got closer, her skin prickled and tightened, and her hair floated on the fire's unseen currents.

In that house were her clothes, her passport, her phone. Her plane ticket.

Her whole life was in that house.

Kira let it burn.

The barns were untouched. No time, or he just hadn't thought of it. She wondered if it said more about Hap or her that he'd whacked her in the face with a shovel and buried her alive, and *still* ran like a jackrabbit to get his ass out and gone.

Turned out, he was right to run.

The Charger crouched, a black and silent beast. Waiting.

Kira ran one palm over its curves, glad for the support. Reflected flames danced in its polished surfaces. She walked all the way around the car. No brake fluid darkened the sawdust.

Too much of a hurry, or no point cutting brake lines when you've already buried the body.

The car door opened with a heavy thunk, deep in the metal. She knelt beside the open door, leaned in. Her fingers found what they sought.

Tooled leather. Walnut. Oiled steel.

FIRST LIGHT FOUND Virgil and Big Tom at the pig farm. It wasn't a place where people came. First sound of a car, they'd have time enough to get ready.

Virgil stretched and yawned and scratched his hairy belly. A second later, Tom's eyes closed and his big jowls opened too, the man's mouth a wide dark hole.

Little bit of meth would have kept them up just fine. Would've also keyed them up even worse than they already were— they'd be wide awake and jumping at phantom noises, shooting out the windows. Instead they had a cracked bowl full of cigarette butts, an inch or so left of what had been perfectly good bottles of Jack and Beam, a deck of cards gone dogeared and sticky, and a stack of wooden kitchen matches neither cared to win any more.

"Think he's done it?" Virgil said.

"What, all of it?"

"Yeah. No." Virgil's hand brushed the table near his Ruger. Both men had their guns out on the table. He also had a .38 in his boot, and a knife on his belt.

"The old man," he said. "You think Temple's done the old man yet?"

"Old man ain't come for us. Not yet, anyway."

Tom tried to sound casual, but the man was listening even as he talked. It'd been a tense night- this point he was like a guitar string tightened until it was about ready to pop off its fret.

Virgil pushed himself away from the table.

"I can't wait no more. I gotta see."

THE OLD PLANTATION house stood silent. The sun was a bloody smear at the edge of a deep bruise. Those thunderheads in the east were gathering higher, and darker. The shapes of the oak and pecan trees in the dirt yard stood out against the predawn sky. Their shadowed canopies were black and menacing.

Not a single guard in sight.

Paint blistered and peeled from the front columns. The wood beneath was the gray of a corpse's skin. The front steps and much of the porch were sagging and rotten.

The wide oak door stood open. The dark mouth of the hallway beyond was still, waiting. A chorus of crickets rose in full voice around her, and whippoorwills shouted in the trees above.

The house itself was silent.

Some sensible part of Kira's mind told her to circle around the back of the house, find a way in there.

Her palm found the walnut grips of her grandfather's Colt. Scrape of leather and the weapon stood free in the air. It felt good.

She told the sensible part of her mind to go hide in fucking Europe.

Shoulders squared, back straight, she marched straight through that open door.

No trap or ambush waited inside. Only Taylor.

The old man sat at the head of the long table, in the room full of dust and shadows and cobwebs. The front of his once-white suit was dark and wet.

Kira moved closer.

The room smelled like an abattoir. There was blood, a lot of blood. And heat. And flies.

Taylor had died hard.

His chest cavity gaped, raw and horrible. Broken sticks of rib flexed outward at the edges, and there was a hole the size of a man's fist where the heart should be.

The pistol-grip shotgun was in his hand. No way Kira was getting close enough to find out if it had been fired.

This was her second dead body of the night. She was becoming something of an expert on hatchet wounds.

The body rumbled and shifted. Some trick of decomposition no doubt. An unnerving one.

The head toppled off the neck and rolled onto the table.

Kira jumped, and let out a small cry. She leveled the gun at it but managed not to fire.

The head landed on the flat shelf of chin and jaw. Without a neck the face was upturned. It fell by chance in her general direction.

No way to explain the eyes. They seemed to stare into her own.

The house was empty. Kira was sure of it. She explored the rest of it anyway.

Anything to get away from that room.

Maybe Hap had been right to want to run.

In his sick room, the photograph of her mother was gone from the dresser. It was the only one missing.

On impulse, she twirled the knob on the old fashioned safe. Stopped the numbers on the month, day and year of her mother's birth.

The latch clicked open.

The only thing inside was a small notebook. Red leather cover worn to a sheen in places, stained in others. The edges were foxed, the binding splayed to the point a thick rubber band held the whole thing closed.

Tucked under the rubber band, a card. One word, handwritten, in a tight slanted font:

Kira.

She took it from the safe, thumbed the corner of the pages. Edgewise glimpse of more tight slanted writing. A lot more. Names, dates, instructions. She stuck it in her back pocket and looked around the room one last time.

No sign of that photo.

Upstairs, space for twelve men, iron cots and foot lockers. She had never met her grandfather Harrow. He hadn't approved of his daughter's wild ways, hadn't approved of her marriage to a Stone. And that disapproval had extended to his only grandchild.

She wondered how the stuck-up bastard felt having his family home turned into a barracks.

The thought made her lips curl up at the corners.

The master bedroom had once and for many years been Taylor's. The old man's presence, his personality, were soaked into the walls and floor, imprinted on the furniture. Signs of Hap's habitation— rumpled sheets and a full ashtray, a random jumble of hair products on the dresser, the ghost of his aftershave— lay like a thin skim on the surface of his father's life.

The smell of his aftershave brought a whipsaw of memory: the flash of his smile and his cowardice, the feel and taste of his skin and his arms swinging that damn shovel.

She holstered the gun.

"Shit."

It was the only thing she could think of to say.

Back downstairs, the house was as empty as she had first believed. A smell of matches in the back hall, but no signs of life.

Out back, she found out why.

Corpses, piled and scattered.

Blood, dripping and pooling. Great puddles of red, soaking the cracked dry earth.

Birds, a brave few feasting unconcerned. Others fluttering up into the trees, onto the roof of the house, to watch. Still more, circling overhead.

Weapons, a separate pile.

Taylor's entire bodyguard.

Kira's pulse beat in her throat. Her dirty tee shirt did a quick faint jump over her heart.

Temple was real.

And he was a monster.

THE TWO DEPUTIES rolled through town on their way to headquarters. Both were due on shift in half an hour anyway. Their clothes were soiled and the air inside the car filled with chemical smoke and the sour odor of their bodies.

Arnie Slocum never had told them where to find his brothers' meth lab. He hadn't made it out of the burning deer cooler.

Graham still wasn't sure what happened. Bix and Arnie were wrestling back and forth, equipment spilling and breaking everywhere. Next minute the room's on fire and Graham can't see a thing, not a single damn thing. Door behind him, fire in front of him, it doesn't take much to get outside. That much he knew.

What Graham had struggled all night with, what he was still struggling with now, was what had happened in the room behind him. The deer cooler was just a little bitty space, maybe ten by ten. Not exactly the kind of space you got lost in. Bix had made it out just fine.

So what the heck happened to Arnie Slocum?

By the time Graham's flash-blinded eyes cleared, there was nothing for it. The cooler was a torch, a bonfire, a damned conflagration. All they could do was watch it burn.

Bullshitting on the porch over a few beers, taking over the local crime empire seemed like a fine idea. Burning a man to death changed all that.

Graham looked over at his partner. Bix drove with white knuckles on the wheel, eyes locked straight ahead behind his mirrored shades. Knots of muscle bunched at the corner of his jaw and a large twisted vein stood out on the side of his skull.

The man had gone harder behind the things they'd done. He seemed grimmer than ever.

Graham just wanted not to throw up.

The screech of brakes and squeal of tires broke his thoughts. His partner's car door was already open, some scrap of profanity lost in the open air. He followed, hands shaking as he threaded his baton into its ring.

The air was flat and oppressive the way it got before a big storm, a giant hand smothering. The old men who sat their mornings out front of the Bluebird were standing in the town square.

Graham's tired mind struggled to play 'what was wrong with this picture'.

Not that it wasn't obvious. An overturned car and a toppled statue weren't exactly things you'd miss. More like the enormity of what he was seeing refused to register.

"That's Hap Taylor's Vette," he said.

"Yup." The knot of muscle at the corner of Bix's jaw looked like two halves of a walnut.

"Lot of blood, too."

"Yup." The walnut halves ground against each other, locked in combat.

"Figure that's him? Hap, I mean?"

"Nope."

Bix gestured to the scorpion tattoo on the side of the victim's neck. One of Taylor's latest crop of thugs.

The two deputies stood, hands on their belts, looking around at the whips and splashes. Somebody out there was an enthusiastic painter. And he liked the color red.

"Still think we're the only ones want to take over?"

Bix turned his face to the dark clouds massed in the east. The front coming in off the Atlantic was gonna be a doozy. Right now the whole world felt like it was holding its breath.

Images of the screaming meth cook jumped up every time Graham shut his eyes. He could smell the burning flesh.

"Sorry, what?"

One of the old men had been talking to him. They were milling around like extras in a zombie movie, messing up his crime scene.

"Said, my daddy remembered when they put that statue up." One liver-spotted hand fluttered in the general direction of old Bo Harrow, busted up all over the red clay and dead grass. Old fellah looked like he just might cry.

Now another old guy was waving a pistol around. He wasn't exactly pointing it anywhere, but the way his hands were shaking wasn't exactly a comfort.

It was a pearl-handled black Sig Sauer.

THEY TOOK SEPARATE cars. Tom swore the seats in his Hummer were the only ones did any good for his back. Virgil swore his Escalade was the only choice for those roads.

In truth, neither wanted to let the other drive.

Back behind the wheel, Virgil started to relax. That big Cadillac power plant and sweet suspension had him feeling like he wasn't so much driving those dirt roads as flying softly over them.

He drove under a great red tunnel of light, sunrise bouncing off the undersides of clouds in the east. He tried to remember something his mother used to say about shepherd's delights and sailor's warnings.

His phone lit up in its console. A picture of a mud-smeared pig, and the sound of grunting. He tapped the screen to take the call and his new partner's voice filled the Escalade's stereo speakers.

"You thought any about what you're gonna say?"

"What?"

"If the old man ain't dead yet. How do we explain being out his place at the crack of fucking dawn?"

Virgil scratched at his beard and slowed through a curve.

"We don't."

"Come again?"

"That old man's still alive, I'm gonna shoot him myself. And Temple can fucking whistle for his money."

Silence on the line.

"I think…" Tom said. "I vote we pay Temple anyway."

Virgil didn't want to admit it, but he'd been thinking the same thing. He'd dealt with killers before. Hell, he'd killed men himself. But Temple was different.

Just thinking of the man turned his guts to ice water.

"Holy—"

A black shape rocketed through its turn in front of him. A thick cloud of red dust roiled from under its wheels, a devil car spitting an early taste of the waiting flames.

Virgil jerked the wheel, sent the Escalade skidding toward the ditch. It was a sophisticated and expensive piece of machinery, full of computers and such. The brakes didn't lock, and the truck didn't go out of control, but it did kick up one hell of a lot of rocks and dirt getting out of the way.

His rearview showed nothing but dust. He could only hear that engine's throaty roar fading away.

"You see that?" He caught the sound of his own voice, all but yelling.

"Least we know one thing," Tom's voice said from the high-end speakers around him.

"That the Stone girl's still alive?"

"That Temple's work ain't done."

THE DEPUTIES STOOD together, kept their voices low. The old guys were half deaf, most of them, but this still wasn't a conversation they wanted overheard.

Deputy Graham held the Sheriff's pearl-handled Sig the way, back when he was an altar boy, he used to hold the communion plate.

"You know she'd never—"

"Nope. She wouldn't." Bix tilted his head and spit.

"Either way, we got competition."

"Yup."

Graham rubbed his thumbs over the blue-black surface of the slide. Small halos appeared and faded. He knew they should be cordoning off the scene, bagging and tagging evidence, calling in the state CID.

Instead he stood holding that custom pistol cradled in his hands. He felt empty, and lost.

"You realize," Bix said, "whoever this is, they did us a favor."

He leaned in, his gaze as sharp and bright as any predator.

"She was a good woman, a good cop. I hate to think she's gone. But you know we'd have had no mercy and no quarter so long as Grace Roberts was alive."

"True."

"So we got another player. So what? Let them do some of the hard work for us before we take them off the board."

"They'll be thinking the same thing…"

"So watch your six. We do this right, we can win this thing."

Graham could smell his partner's aftershave and the doublemint gum he chewed. He could smell the blood at their feet roasting in the summer heat.

He looked down at the gun in his hands. The grips were almost small enough to fit a child's hand.

"If she is gone…"

"She is. Bet on it."

"Reckon that makes one of us the new Sheriff."

"Makes you the new Sheriff."

"She never did name a Chief Deputy."

"Which case it's seniority, least til the next election. And if we're still alive by then, we'll have this thing sewed up tight."

Bix stuck out his hand.

"Congratulations, Mister Sheriff."

Graham shook, but his heart wasn't in it.

"Seems to me," Bix said, "we don't want to find ourselves hip deep in some blue ribbon federal task force, we need to get us a suspect in custody, and quick."

A fly rose from that butcher's ground to circle the two men. It landed on the back of Bix's hand and flew away, staining his skin with a small fleck of blood.

"Anyone in particular?" Graham said.

A grim smile rose in Bix's face.

"THAT BITCH." Big Tom turned his head and spat. "That tin-plated one hundred percent certified fourteen carat solid gold BITCH."

Virgil stared at the flames. Even this far back, the heat was warm and tight on his face.

"It's just a house."

"That was not just a house, and you damn well know it. That bitch burned down our center of goddamn operations. She took out the one place everyone knows where to come. We'd be sitting right there in that goddamn house showing the others they didn't have a single goddamn thing to worry about if it weren't for THAT BITCH."

For a minute the big man looked about to burst a blood vessel. Virgil wondered if that would be such a bad thing.

"Could have been Temple," he said.

"Temple?"

"Think about it— I didn't see who was driving that car, did you? Her and Taylor both could be in there right now."

"We told him to make an example, not to burn the place down."

"You get the feeling that fellah maybe isn't all that much for following orders?"

They were silent a moment, watching the flames. Sweat gathered in Virgil's armpits and ran down his back. That fire was hot.

Big Tom looked like he was trying to do math in his head, or maybe keep from farting in church.

"Nah," he said at last. "Nobody else drives like a Stone. It was her."

He was right enough. No need to say it.

The first of the pecan trees burst into flame. Soon they were all burning, on both sides of the house.

"Supposed to be a fortune in that house."

"I heard the rumors."

"Cash. Gold. Jewels. You seen that big safe."

"You're welcome to go on in and get them."

"Just a low down dirty shame is all."

Virgil thought about killing his partner then and there, but Tom still had people loyal to him, people Virgil was going to need.

He kicked at a rock in the drive. It went skittering off toward the fire. He got to wondering about the barns, about the things they'd stored there off and on over the years.

He got to wondering what might be of value in there now. Tom didn't seem to notice him wander off.

The big man did come running when Virgil shouted for him, though. Like something off that TV show, all that fat bouncing and jostling when he ran.

He stopped when he saw the writing on the wall. Spraypainted in that enamel the boys used to repaint the cars.

Tom turned a deep red color, like something inside him was coming to a boil. Virgil spat.

"Get your best men," he said. "Tell them to dress for hunting."

The burning house crackled and roared, a voice they could hear but whose words they couldn't make out. Pecans popped and snapped in the heat, and burning leaves rose in bright spirals.

KIRA SAT IN HER stepmother's office. The room smelled of pine cleaner and lemon furniture oil. Her clothes smelled of blood and smoke and grave dirt.

The chair behind the desk was a creaking old thing. The leather was cracked, the back and seat permanently hollowed to the more ample dimensions of old Sheriff Patterson.

The chair was unfamiliar, intimidating, uncomfortable. She sat in that chair and stared at the big Colt revolver on the desk and the manila folder open beside it.

Grace Roberts was dead.

Her brother Jack was dead.

Her father, gone when she was twelve. Waved goodbye to her school bus and fell over dead in the yard an hour later.

Old Man Taylor had used his connection to her family as a lure, and now he was gone too.

That last of Kira's blood was gone from this earth. Every last connection to them lost.

Now the only mother she'd ever truly known had been taken from her.

Not every last connection, she thought. Her grandfather's Colt lay before her, oiled and lethal.

Ironic: all she'd wanted since she got here was to escape these ties of blood and obligation. Now she couldn't imagine returning to her old life, couldn't imagine ever again using the name Harrow. She was a Stone, through and through.

All she wanted now was that gun on the table in her hand, her enemies in her sights.

And the keys to the department's weapons room. That thumbuster Colt might punch a hole in the side of the world, but after what she saw at Taylor's, she'd feel better with automatic weapons and body armor.

Thing was, she couldn't find that key anywhere.

She drummed her fingers on the desktop. Her hand brushed the edge of the manila folder and she pulled back as though bitten.

The folder was poison. Pure poison.

The form naming Kira a new hire carried a date four days old. Her first day here. Every line was neatly typed. The sunken gray impressions on the page were strangely old fashioned, sign of a department so strangled for funding it couldn't print out a PDF. There were forms for taxes and insurance, forms requisitioning equipment and forms releasing the county from liability. More forms than she had ever seen in her life. She didn't even know she had a social security number until she saw the places where her stepmother had typed it.

A Stone with a badge. The whole idea of it was crazy.

Only one box was left blank on each form.

The space for Kira's signature.

THE DISPATCHER burst out of the courthouse, flapping and squawking. She kept it up all the way across the lawn.

She wasn't making a whole lot of sense by the time she reached the deputies, but the odd word here and there was enough to give them the gist of it.

They followed her back inside, equipment rattling on their belts. Cyndi hustled along in a quick little waddle, the back of her skirt smacking around, just the way Graham liked. Other days, he'd always enjoyed that view.

Today just wasn't one of those days.

Everything was happening, all too fast.

The Stone girl was a pain in the ass. She had a mouth on her and drove like a goddamn lunatic, but that was it. She had no part in this, no interest in staying around. Her only danger was that some of the others might use her family name to rally around her.

Bix's plan for a jailhouse suicide was too much.

Cyndi's heels made a click-and-clatter through the courthouse foyer and into the office. The leathery slap of the deputies' steps was close behind. The three of them stormed through the gate of the bullpen. Bix's fingers beat a quick little rhythm against the butt of his gun.

Cyndi stopped. She threw one arm dramatically in the direction of the closed door to the Sheriff's office.

Graham was ready for a young girl, crying and distraught. He was ready for a bad attitude and possible violence. He was ready for tears, anger, denial or confusion. He followed his partner into the office with one hand on his cuffs and the other on the snap to his pepper spray.

Bix stopped, so sudden that Graham ran right into the man's back.

The Stone girl stood behind the Sheriff's desk. A big goddamn revolver like something out of the Old West lay on the scarred wood in front of her.

Her posture was straight, her stance firm. She was scuffed and dirty, with what looked like dried blood on her face. The room around her was a murk of brown shadows, and the air smelled like fire and death.

The star pinned to Kira's chest shone, a point of golden flame.

"Hold it right there," Bix said. "You're under—"

"You sure about that?"

Bix stiffened as though struck.

"Your hand moves any closer to that gun, deputy, and you *will* regret it."

She didn't move. She didn't have to. That thumbuster Colt was right there on the desk, inches from her hand.

Everything Graham had ever heard about her family, every legend, every crazy story, it all took on a different light looking down at the barrel of that gun.

"I didn't kill Grace Roberts, and the both of you know it. Now, I don't know how these rumors get started…" Her eyes seemed to dwell on Graham's a moment too long. "But we're going to nip this one in the bud."

Bix seemed to swell up in the chest.

"We—"

"Probably didn't realize that Sheriff Roberts hired me on days ago. Paperwork was sitting right out on her desk."

Graham's thumb came away from the cuffs in a greasy slide. He wondered at what point he'd let go of the pepper spray.

Kira shifted. One hand stayed near the Colt. The other gestured at the front corner of the desk.

A neat stack of papers glowed crisp and white in the gloom.

He snatched up the forms, read with a feeling like an elevator falling out of control.

He looked over at Bix. A tight web of lines pinched the skin around the man's eyes.

Graham had to swallow twice before he found his voice.

"Sheriff Roberts brought her on as Chief Deputy."

"But that means—"

"That's right..."

Kira looked from one to the other, her eyes bright and hard and fierce.

"You're looking at your new boss."

KIRA DIDN'T TRUST her deputies.

The two men, Graham and Bix, were jumpy and on edge. Graham was sweaty, his color bad. Even in the stony brown cool of the office, dark circles spread from the armpits of his uniform and the collar of his neck. Bix's eyes kept jumping side to side, searching the room like an animal in a trap.

Worse, the man's hand kept drifting down to his holster. His palm would touch the butt of his pistol. He'd look at her and pull it away as though burnt.

For the first time she knew what her stepmother must have felt, her own first day as Sheriff. She didn't have to deal with a full staff of Taylor's men. She also wasn't stepping into the job after years as Chief Deputy. She didn't have a day of training, and the town was in the middle of a disaster.

Kira closed her eyes and conjured Grace Roberts in her head. The woman she'd known, not the one she'd buried.

Small. Hard. Leather and iron and fires burning deep.

When she opened them, Kira's spine was straight, her eyes level and steady.

"I know you boys meant to lock me up," she said. "You got troubles right now, and that'd be one way to wrap them up fast."

Graham flinched like he'd been slapped.

"I won't say there's no hard feelings, but I am going to give you boys a choice."

Information passed on a look, so fast it hummed.

Bix's right hand moved. Kira's moved faster. His was still a flutter, a blur at the edge of her vision, while her grandfather's Colt was leveled at the center of the deputy's forehead.

"Long as I wear this star, you're my men or you're nobody's. You follow my orders or you can give me your badges right now."

Silence. Stillness.

Kira thumbed back the hammer on the revolver.

A bead of sweat rolled down the side of the man's face.

"Do you understand me, Deputy Bixby?"

"Yeah."

A pause, too long for Kira's liking.

Then, "Yes... ma'am."

THE DOOR TO THE Sheriff's office swung open, loud. Deputies Bix and Graham came busting out, not with that awful Stone girl in cuffs like Cyndi expected, but moving like their tails were on fire.

The office door was left open. She heard the phone lifted from its cradle, clatter of buttons dialing.

Cyndi pushed her chair out from her station. Usually, leaning out that little bit extra that way, she could catch at least the drift of what was being said, if not the whole conversation.

Usually, she was happy enough with the drift of what was said. Or more like, Taylor seemed happy enough with her reporting back the general drift.

This morning was different. Here it was, gone half seven already, and Sheriff Roberts still hadn't reported in. That *bitch* Kira Stone sat in the office and wouldn't leave.

This was one morning the old man was going to want to hear every word.

Leaning wasn't going to cut it. Cyndi rose to her feet, quiet as she could, tiptoed over to the corner near the door. When the office door was closed, she could get right up to it with a glass. Hanging open the way it was, she had to stay out of sight.

Life would be simpler if she could just listen in on calls through the switchboard, but the system they had didn't work that way.

Murmured voice on the other line. Cyndi could almost make out the words.

She leaned in closer.

And a little closer. Balancing on her tiptoes, she cocked one ear, concentrating.

And damn near jumped out of her skin when the Stone girl caught her.

"I— You— I—"

"Cyndi, go home."

"You can't…"

Her voice trailed off as she saw the gold star.

"That's not— You can't— You're—"

The Stone girl spun Cyndi around, got her moving toward her station. No, not her station, the gate to the bullpen.

"You can't—"

"You can clean out your desk tomorrow," Kira said. "You're fired."

THE TWO DEPUTIES were back in one car now, the county cruiser they usually shared. Graham was at the wheel. Strictly speaking, it was Bix's day to drive, but the fact was Graham did not want to be stuck in the passenger seat right now, with nothing to do but fret.

He was bad enough as it was.

"This is it. We're dead."

"Quit talking crazy," Bix said.

"Stones and Taylor go back a long way. What's the bet she's lined up with the old man?" He banged his palm three times on the wheel. "She knows what we did last night and she's sending us out there to die."

"You don't watch your driving, we're dead before we get there."

"Look, I'm just saying—"

"I know what what you're 'just saying', and *I'm* saying I don't want to hear it. We got the guns, and the badges, and all that good shit. Taylor and his boys need to be afraid of *us*."

The road topped a small rise and dipped down, quick and sharp. Graham grabbed tight on the steering wheel with both hands, and both deputies fought to hang onto their lunch.

A couple of quick turns, and Bix shifted again in the passenger seat.

"And if the girl *is* in this with the old man, we'll sort her bacon too."

This, from the guy who'd called her 'ma'am'.

"Tell me something..." Graham said.

"What."

"Where was all that tough talk back at the station?"

Bix opened his mouth, some snappy comeback no doubt. Thought better and shut it.

Graham guessed his partner was the same as him: neither wanted to admit it, but the Stone girl scared the crap out of them.

They knew what they'd find at the house a fair while before they got there. The pillar of smoke had to be visible for miles, and the same wind blowing in that storm front was raining ash down all over the west side of the county.

It was all too much like last night.

Except for the spectators. The fire in the meth lab had to have been visible for miles around, but they had watched it burn alone. Daylight at Taylor's mansion, though, that was another story.

Fire like that, in that place, folks came out to see. The road up to the house was choked with cars and pickups. Lights and sirens weren't much use when no one was there to move out the way.

The deputies ended up doing like everyone else, parking on the road and walking up the drive. At least when they got to the small crowd rubbernecking in the middle of the drive they were able to push and shove and call out 'police business'.

The house had burned down to the ground. Long hot summer, dry old timber, the place had gone up like a tinderbox. Graham didn't want to say it, but he'd had visions of himself living in that house. Doing it up real nice, everybody calling him sir.

The place where the house had been was roiling flame. A few sticks still stood, and the front columns had fallen in and were taking their own sweet time burning.

It was a hell of a fire, and a hard thing to see.

He looked back at the crowd. He'd grown up two towns over in the next county, but he still knew pretty much everyone standing there. Place was too small for it to be any other way.

They stood like sleepwalkers, kinda swaying. Firelight danced on their bodies, and their faces were what he'd imagined people looked like back in the days of public executions.

"Sir?"

"You reckon this is what the girl sent us out here to see?" he asked his partner.

Bix turned his head and spat. "Oh, she wanted us to see this all right. Only question is, why."

"Sir?"

It was an old man. Another one. The morning was full of them. Peterson, Peters, something like that. Spent most of his days sat on the chairs outside the Bluebird. Shirt sleeves buttoned down to the wrist even in this weather, gimme cap telling the world it was Miller Time.

"Yes sir?" Graham might, or might not, have burned a man to death last night, but he still had his manners. "Help you?"

"Something you should see." He raised one bony hand and beckoned.

They followed him around the east side of the house. Far around, the heat was blistering. It was the strangest sensation, that godawful heat on one side like to roast you in your skin, on the other the cool breeze that ran ahead of the coming storm.

They came around the back of the house and stopped dead in their tracks.

"That," Bix said, "is one hell of a lot of dead men."

The pile of corpses blazed as bright as any torch. The kerosene or gas or whatever had been used to set fire to the Taylor house had also been doused over the pile. That sharp petroleum stink mingled with the smells of burning in a way that sent Graham's stomach sideways.

"I do believe we're looking at Taylor's personal guard," Bix said. The smell seemed not to bother him. "Think that one over there might be Joe Bob Gaiter."

"Smells like they barbecued a hog with the hair still on." This from the old man, a note of glee in his voice.

Graham leaned down between his feet and threw up.

It seemed to take forever. No food — he hadn't been able to eat since Arnie Slocum. Just streams of bile and spasms that felt like they were breaking his ribs from the inside. When he finally looked up, Bix and the old man both stood with their backs to him, ignoring him, and he felt ashamed.

"Reckon we know what she wanted us to see," Bix said. "Big question now is, why."

Graham wiped at his chin and looked away from that hideous bonfire. Hearing that crackle and roar, and smelling that awful stink was bad enough. Not looking was his only hope of hanging onto what little stomach he had left.

Almost by accident his gaze settled on the barns and outbuildings.

"Bix."

"Hey, wash that hand before you go tapping me with it. I don't want to get your—"

"Bix."

Spraypainted across the side of the barn, gleaming enamel, the letters a good three feet high.

"I reckon *that's* what she wanted us to see."

STONE HOLLOW. 12 NOON

"ANYTHING?"

Big Tom looked up at the question. His phone sat on the table, black and inert. A cigarette burned down between his fingers. He stared at Virgil for a moment before retreating into his own private space.

"You're right," Virgil said. "Too soon."

"Too soon for a while yet. They won't even be out there yet."

"I guess." Virgil flexed his hands and paced the scrap of open floor.

"Hell's got into you, anyway?" Tom said. The ash on his cigarette was over an inch long.

"Same thing's got into you. We spent all night cooped up in this shithole, ain't like I want to be back."

"Just a few more hours."

"Last night was bad enough."

The air was stifling. And foul. Full ashtrays, empty liquor bottles, body odor heavy with testosterone and fear. The shack smelled exactly like two men had spent the night in it waiting to find out if they lived or died.

And they still didn't know.

"Jesus," Virgil said, "can't you at least open a window or something?"

"Be my guest." Big Tom lifted the cigarette to his mouth. The ash collapsed across his knuckles. He dragged on the burnt filter and threw it on the floor.

"Just so happens it's the maid's day off." He went to fish out a fresh one, crushed the empty pack in his fist.

Virgil did think about opening a window. But the only thing smelled worse than this goddamn room were the goddamn pigs.

"Fuck it." He reached for the Beam. No more than a mouthful at the bottom of the bottle. "Fuck."

"You're so goddamn restless, go on down to Stone Hollow. Bet you got time to catch up with the rest of them."

"Fuck you." Wasn't much left in the bottle of Jack, either. He took it anyway.

"Or, sit back and let the boys take care of it the way we agreed. They're armed for fucking bear. Let them work."

They were silent for a time. Tom lit another cigarette. Virgil swigged from the bottle.

He thought about going outside, get some air. But the air out there was full of Tom's pigs, and they'd been enough to make him come back inside the first two times.

"Think he'll show?" Tom asked. His big arms were folded like stacked hams and the fresh cigarette had burned halfway down.

"I think that's what she was hoping for. You sure you can't call him?"

"Ain't exactly the kind of guy carries a phone." He stubbed out the half-smoked cigarette and reached for another.

"How'd you get ahold of him before?"

"That last jolt at Raiford, I met his handler." The wheel of his lighter scraped. Flame rose. "And before you ask, no I don't know how his handler gets hold of him neither. For all I know he sticks pins in a voodoo doll."

"Shit." Virgil took a pull from the bottle, wiped his mouth with the back of one hand. "He'll show. Just be good if we could make sure he did, is all."

"That money we were gonna pay him, you got your half?"

"Took some doing, but yeah."

"I don't," Big Tom said. "Front money to get him down here was damn near all the cash I had."

"You ain't serious."

"Got a few things cooking. Be fine when they pay off..." He seemed to remember the cigarette in his hand. Tapped the long ash, took a hit. More nicotine filled the hot still air.

"I gotta ask, are you out your damn fool mind?" Virgil pinched the flesh and bone between his eyes. "You brought the most dangerous killer anybody's ever heard of to our doorstep, and lied about being able to pay him?"

"Didn't lie, exactly. All that money up at the Taylor place, gold and jewels and whatnot, I figured there'd be plenty there."

The two men had known each other for decades. In better days they might have said they knew each other better than their mothers ever did, and it would have been true.

Virgil understood two things in that moment: Tom was in bad shape, desperate. And Tom planned to kill him.

He put the bottle down on the table. Within reach of the nearest pistol, a Browning Hi-Power. Within reach, but not too close.

"And now you got just as much from Taylor's place as what's in your pocket?"

"Temple's a scary motherfucker, I'll give you that…"

Tom didn't stub out his smoke on the tabletop or floor. This time he reached for the ashtray. Six, eight inches from a battered . 357.

"…but at the end of the day, he's just a man."

"Sure about that?"

From the kitchen, a voice like something chained at the bottom of a well.

Tom dove for the gun on the table.

A black hatchet seemed to sprout from his chest.

Virgil's hand closed on the Browning.

The world went dark.

THE DEPUTIES DID not go back to work. Without a word spoken, they drove to Graham's house because it was closest.

His dog barked and hid under the porch. Poor animal didn't like the smell of all that blood and smoke and death any more than his master did.

The two men clumped up the steps. Bix stayed outside while Graham grabbed the last few beers from the icebox. Back out on the porch, his butt hovered over the seat of the rocker and dropped. He was just too damn tired to lower himself down gently.

Bix said, "It's eight-thirty in the morning." Like the time was what bothered him.

Graham snapped the top and lifted the can to his lips.

The beer was so cold it hurt. After the day and night they'd had, it was just right.

The two men drank in silence. A few times, Graham felt words rise up inside him. Arnie Slocum. Sheriff Grace. The slaughter at the Taylor place. The sights and sounds and smells of the last twelve hours would come slamming into him, and whatever words rose up would sink right back down to the bottom.

To his surprise, Bix spoke first.

"I—"

The sound was a rusty bark. The groan of a hand pump that hadn't been used in far too long.

"I—" He tried again. And like an old pump, that dry bark gave way to another, and another, and then a wet torrent. Bix's shoulders shook, and his hands covered his face and the sobs rose and broke in his chest, blubbered across his lips.

Graham reached out a hand to Bix's shoulder. Let it drop without touching.

He drank his beer and tried not to listen and stared out into a sky without color.

For months, Graham had hungered for a cool breeze. Now, chill air skirled around the corners of his porch, and he shivered. Birds and insects had gone quiet, the whole world hunkered down, silent except for his partner's sobs.

"I just can't." Bix's eyes were red and bleak. Every word was a raw strip of flesh peeled off his hide.

"I thought, hell I don't know what I thought. I can't do this. That woman… Temple…"

"Something tells me ain't neither of them's taking prisoners."

"I damn near put us in the middle of those two."

Graham used the back of his left hand to wipe beer from his lower lip and chin. The skin was rough and smelled of smoke.

"I'm sorry, partner," Bix said.

Graham wanted to say 'it's nothing', or 'forget it'. He couldn't force himself to make polite words.

"I thought it'd be easy," Bix went on. "The old man made it look, I don't know."

"Taylor and Sheriff Stone got something in common—" Graham's thoughts went to the bodies piled behind the old plantation house. "Something we don't."

"You just called her sheriff."

"Guess I did."

"What are we gonna do?"

The beer in Graham's hand was warm now. He drank the last of it anyway, sour and bitter.

"Keep our heads down," he said. "See who walks out of them woods. Take it from there."

VIRGIL WOKE SPITTING blood and straining at his bonds.

He couldn't see, but he could feel cool air on his face and neck, the backs of his hands. He could hear thunder rumble in the distance.

And everywhere, everywhere he turned, he could smell the disgusting odor of Tom's pigs.

He was tied to a chair of some kind, ankles and wrists. He thought about trying to tip it, thought about ways he might get out of the ties. He swallowed blood and pushed his tongue in the space where teeth had been.

He could hear the pigs, snorting and grunting, squealing and crunching. They were close. Against his will he smelled them. He smelled pig, and blood, and shit, and a whole bunch of other things he didn't want to think about. A whole bunch of sounds and smells that brought back one single image— a scrap of meat and bone covered in jailhouse tattoos.

"Good…" A voice like black leather wings.

Flat metal, cold against his cheek. Virgil flinched. The blade moved, and the blindfold fell away.

"You took so long," Temple said, "I started without you."

The chair was out at the edge of the feeding pen. Big Tom, what was left of him, lay in the mud. All of his pigs had blood-slicked snouts.

"You heard," Virgil said. "About the money."

"I heard about the money."

Broad daylight and open air didn't make that voice any less creepy.

"Then you heard I got mine. I wasn't the one planning to cheat you."

No answer. Two pigs the size of small tractors fought over the same chunk of flesh.

"I don't have it here, but I'll tell you where it is."

Temple leaned in from behind. His beard tickled Virgil's ear.

"Tell me about Stone Hollow."

"I'm, I'm sorry, what?" Virgil couldn't take his eyes off the pigs.

"Stone Hollow. Where you two sent your men."

"We—"

"That girl called me out. Why there?"

"Don't you want the money?"

"I wouldn't go that far," Temple said in that tombstone voice. "Half a payday is better than none. And then you're going in the pen there with your friend."

A hard and callused hand gripped Virgil's face, forced it to look at the pigs.

"Only question is, will you be alive or dead at the time."

The big and bristled shapes jostled around what was left of Big Tom. One pig raised its head and met Virgil's gaze. Its eyes were small and sharp, and strings of red slime drooled from its jaws.

"Now," Temple said, "tell me about Stone Hollow."

THE STORM WAS coming. The wind was picking up, the first breeze Kira had felt since she'd come back. It was cool on the back of her neck and blew her hair around her face in a dark halo.

Behind her, black clouds roiled, piling higher and higher, a fist raising to strike.

The town fathers stood on the front steps of the church. Where last time they'd been united in their disapproval, this time their body language was like a clutch of old hens who'd seen the farmer sharpen an axe.

The star on her chest got them talking. Hissing little whispers, snatches of *'see I told you —'* and *'who does she think —'* and *'she's got no right —'*.

The gun on her hip kept any of them from speaking up too loudly.

She locked eyes with each and every one of those *capons* until they fell silent.

"It's true what you've heard," she said. "Grace Roberts is dead."

Lots of wide eyes and side-to-side looks at that. Before the whispers could start up again, she started back in.

"And yes, she's gone and now I'm wearing her star. Papers showing it all nice and legal are back in her office, but I don't reckon you care too much about that. This town never did give a tinker's damn for the law."

The mayor— shabby brown suit and a face like a boiled ham— turned a deep red. He tilted his head a little to one side and opened his mouth but Kira stared him down.

"No, you bunch have real problems this morning. Last night, the same man killed my stepmother also killed Old Man Taylor."

Every face on those steps, from the reverend to the mayor, was lost in private calculation. Figuring angles, figuring risks.

Just the way Taylor had said they would.

"You all may not know this, but the old man wanted me to take over for him. Now, I hadn't given my answer yet, but he did give me what he had on every single one of you."

Well that set them going, clucking and squawking and flapping. She gave it a moment to die down before starting in again.

"Whoever brought in that enforcer wants the old man's operation. They want this town. You *putains* have some choices to make."

Kira raised one hand, ticked the points off on her fingers.

"You can give up the town. You never really had it anyway, what do you care who runs it? Your new bosses might even pay you a little something. But they don't have all your dirty little secrets."

She raised a second finger. "You can call in outsiders. GSP. FBI. Bring them in to clean house. Do that and I promise you, those of you who survive *will* go to prison."

A third.

"You might be tempted to harm me." She turned her head and spat, blood and grave dirt. "Others have, and the day ain't through."

She closed the hand into a fist.

"Do that and I won't bother with blackmail. I will shoot you dead where you stand."

The mayor was staring blue murder. A knotted vein stood out on his forehead.

"You think you have choices, but you don't," she said. "The only choice you've got, the only way any of you come through this in one piece…"

The reverend looked like he might faint.

"Stay out of my way."

THE SHERIFF'S DEPARTMENT had showers. Just like a gym, six of them in a single tiled room, lockers just outside. They were a holdover from more prosperous days.

Kira didn't trust them.

Folks too cowardly to face her head-on might just be tempted to shoot her in the back. That shower room would be an ideal place to do it.

Instead, she drove the black Charger to a place she knew. She left the car at the side of the road and walked into the woods. Wandered around a bit before she found the place she remembered.

It was different, of course. The world always was, remembered through a child's eyes.

The clearing was smaller. The river neither deep nor wide, more a creek. The woods scrub oak and birch, not an enchanted forest.

Her hands reached for the buckle on her gunbelt. Leather and steel fell to the forest floor. A doe, hunkered down and hiding at Kira's approach, leapt from cover and crashed off into the trees. A flash of white and gone.

She stripped. Her tee shirt stuck to her skin. Her shoelaces were caked with dirt. Her home was a ruin, a few charred sticks and a chimney. All she had were the clothes on her back, and they were also destroyed.

The water was cold. Biting. Twenty years ago she and Hap Taylor stood at the edge and he let her look down the front of his swimsuit. A few years later, he took a beating when they froze their hands, punching through the winter ice to catch crawdads in a mason jar.

She pushed her face underwater. Came up gasping, heart hammering. That water really was cold. She forced herself under again. Fingertips scrubbed at her scalp, her skin. When she raised up again, a red clay halo floated on the water around her, slowly pulled away in the moving current.

It took time. Especially where blood had caked around the knot on her head.

She was lucky to be alive. Except she didn't feel lucky.

Or alive.

She slicked her wet hair back with her palms. The woman she had been had died back on that hill. Smacked with a shovel and planted in the ground, dead.

Whoever, whatever she was now just hadn't been buried yet.

When the last of the dried blood, the last of the dirt was gone from her skin, she stepped out of the creek. The wind out of the east pebbled her bare skin.

Her stepmother's clothes were a strange fit. Sheriff Roberts had kept a few things in a locker at the station: sports bra and briefs, spare uniform. Even shoes and socks. An orderly woman.

The two women were close in size, but there were differences: Kira was wider through the shoulders, enough that the uniform shirt didn't fit right at the arms. The pants were just the smallest bit loose, riding low on her hips. The Timberlands were an old pair, worn to her stepmother's stride.

Kira cinched the laces tight. Ditched the uniform shirt. She couldn't afford that pinched fit slowing her down.

It might get her killed.

Again.

She buckled the gunbelt to her hips and pinned the Sheriff's star to the gunbelt. She didn't wear the star for any great love of the law. Despite what she'd said back in town, she didn't even want the office.

She wore it to honor the woman who'd worn it before.

Kira drew her grandfather's .45 revolver. Opened the gate, spun the chamber. She knew it was loaded, but there was something comforting in the gesture. She flicked it closed and reholstered the weapon.

She was ready.

TEMPLE MADE HIS camp in an abandoned quarry. Equipment rusted in scattered piles-- iron and steel fused, transformed into strange reptilian orange shapes. Rain water had filled the vertical shafts. What had been a cliff face ringing with the sounds of blasted rock was a lake, silent and still.

And deep.

Blind fish swam in its black waters, white and diseased. Diving down, Temple had found a pickup truck in the murk. Sealed away from the fish, the three skeletons on the bench seat filled the cab with their own disintegrating remains. Only their skulls showed through the windshield, sightless eyes staring, heads moving in unseen currents.

Temple liked the quarry. It felt like home.

He squatted at the edge of the water. Dipped a hand in, let the liquid run over the top of his bald head. He thought about those three in the truck, and the view they shared. He thought about others down there with them.

He dripped more water over his bare scalp.

Reached for the long-bladed knife.

Scraped it over what little stubble grew.

Noon was a ways off yet. Time enough to get out to Stone Hollow and finish this business.

He reached for his hatchets.

He had a couple of things he wanted to do first.

TOM AND VIRGIL'S men were hoods, but they were country hoods. Hunters. Campers. Men who knew the lay of the land, and men who grew up killing.

Temple's favorite.

He let the every last one of them move past him on the trail. Close enough to touch. Single file in a ragged column, assault weapons in their hands. Trying to be silent, so no crosstalk.

Only the quiet slap and jingle of extra ammo. The rustle of camo-patterned cloth and the creak of boot leather. Fifteen sets of nervous breaths, wet lips, wheezing lungs.

The last one passed Temple. He stepped out, took him.

The nervous breath stopped. The wet lips dried. The wheezing lungs stilled.

He caught up with the next one further up the trail.

Showed him what real silence was.

Three more died that way, a third of them gone before they reached their place of ambush.

The killers stopped, gathered. Their leader used hand signals to point them to their positions. It took him longer than Temple liked to note the absence of his men.

First break in discipline: a murmured 'what the fuck'. Annoyed, not suspicious.

One of their number was sent off back up the trail to see what happened.

He never came back.

Temple watched as their unease grew. Crosstalk started. Discipline grew slack. One of the hunters even called a friend by name, a hoarse whisper released into the woods, lost in the trees. Temple was able to circle the clearing and take another.

The hunters were in a quandary: they needed to be in position for their ambush, but not one of them wanted to sit up in a blind and leave whatever was out there still at their backs.

All their lives, these men had used these woods for killing. Everything that flew, skittered, slithered or scurried learned to fear their deadly presence. Temple imagined a flight of ducks, lifting into the sky. A crack, and one of their number fell, victim of a predator none of the others ever saw, ever knew.

While he imagined, he circled the clearing and took another.

Lucky seven.

Temple timed his movements to the coming storm. The wind rose and fell, a steady presence growing stronger among the trees. It sang in a voice of dried leaves and fallen needles, and long howling moans.

That voice swallowed any whisper of his movement, every sound of his dying prey.

He pulled the body down and away as it fell, gently removed the long-bladed knife.

This part of the forest had never been logged, but it had known fire. A generation ago, maybe two. A few hardwoods survived, many of their trunks lost to runners of poison ivy. The pines had come along fast and reached a good height.

Tall trees, but not so many they blocked the light. Like everything else two steps off the path, the clearing where the hunters gripped their weapons and learned fear was a riot of ferns and shrubs and barely rooted saplings, small players reaching for their chance at the sun.

Temple left his victim on the forest floor. The soles of the man's boots were two feet from his nearest friend.

If they were fewer in number he'd end it now. All them focused back on the trail behind them, he'd be able to get three, four at least.

Eight remained. All armed and nervous. He eased back from the group and moved back down the trail.

The next phase was his favorite.

He threw a rock.

The hunters knew he, or something like him was out there. They knew the sound of the rock landing on the forest floor was a trap.

They also had to look. Half of them missing, their nerves unraveling, they could only stay so long in the clearing shouting into the trees.

Sooner or later, they had to send someone, to act as a scout.

Or a sacrifice.

Temple threw a second rock. This one struck the hollowed-out trunk of a dead tree. The sound was deep and booming and lingered in the air.

The leader grabbed a man by the collar, pushed him cursing out of the group and down the trail. Temple, little more than a shadow among the roots of an old oak, crouched and waited.

The unlucky man made his way deeper into the forest. Soon the group was lost to sight. He moved in slow shuffling steps, eyes darting, finger on the trigger.

Temple watched him come.

The man came closer. Close enough to hear the rattle and wheeze of his lungs. Close enough to smell his fear.

He passed within inches of Temple's position. The sole of the man's right boot was a hand's breadth from Temple's nose when he struck.

Temple rose from the forest floor, axe blade flashing. In less than a second the man was hamstrung and disarmed, on the ground and screaming.

Temple put the long knife through cheek and tongue before once again vanishing into the trees.

This was the fun part.

Seven men now, hunters, killers. Their friend, their drinking buddy, their partner in crime, somewhere back up the trail. Screaming, wordless and in pain.

The longer they listened, the worse it would get.

Two of the hunters must have been closer to his victim than the others. Or maybe just more foolish. They took off down the path at a dead run, calling the man's name.

Temple let them pass before he stepped out and threw his hatchets.

One blade chunked deep in the back of a hunter's head. The other in the spine, just below the skull.

His aim had never been as good with his left.

Small arms fire lit up the forest. The hunters had heard these two's voices suddenly stop.

Temple was already off and moving. Nowhere near the place they aimed. He still had one hatchet and his long-bladed knife.

More than enough.

The assault weapons rattled to a halt. Clack and clatter of five men reloading, all at once, shaking and clumsy.

If he'd been closer, he could have finished it then.

Just as well. This way was more fun.

The downed man was still screaming. The gobbling sounds could have been cries for help. They could have been anything.

The storm was closer now. The light filtering through the trees was muted, a cold twilight that made it easier to move unseen. Thunder rumbled in the distance.

The remaining hunters were losing it. Firing at random noises. Shouting at the trees. Cursing at their screaming friend to shut the fuck up.

Temple worked in closer.

They never had a chance.

STONE HOLLOW. KIRA had last seen it as a little girl. Her father John Lee had taken her and her brother. Showed them the old bootlegger road in and out. It hadn't been used much since Model T's jostled over ruts originally laid by stagecoach wheels.

The Charger was big for the narrow path. Brush was taking over on every side, but that hard clay had been too long packed, too hard-used over two centuries, to be anything but bare.

Kira took it slow going in. She told herself that way she'd know the curves and the dangers coming out.

She told herself she would be coming back out.

She said it, but she had a hard time believing it. In her mind there was the path in front of her and nothing but white space beyond.

The old coach road reached its end. There was space enough to back-and-fill a horse and wagon. Kira turned around, nose out. She was at a notch between two ridges, at the top of the hollow.

She opened her car door. Stepped out. She eased the door almost, but not quite, shut. Left the keys in the ignition.

She ran two fingers under the elastic on her sportsbra, wiped away the sweat collected there. The last echoes of her motor had faded away, but neither birdsong nor crickets rose to replace it. The only sound in the forest around her was the voice of the wind.

Kira adjusted her gunbelt and started down the path.

THE COMING STORM darkened the sun. Kira walked the rutted track in in twilight at noon. The wind hissed and moaned and howled in the trees, and the air seemed to prickle on her skin.

Halfway down, the path made a dogleg bend. Birds burst into flight in front of her, a great black fury of wings.

As they rose into the tree tops, Kira saw crows, buzzards, hawks.

Scavengers.

A few steps further, the smell of death. Whatever they were feasting on was just beyond those trees.

Her palm lingered on the butt of her gun. She pulled it away.

Whatever waited at the end of the trail, she was going to look it in the eye.

The Hollow was where her people had gotten their start. Legend had it Old Josiah Stone built his first still here in 1830. Certainly generations of Stones had made liquor here since. As she moved through the floor of the valley Kira saw rusted boilers, the tumbled down remains of stone fireboxes, half-buried spools of copper tubing gone green with verdigris.

Here and there, ribs of granite protruded up through the earth. Some of them still wore the scars of old explosions.

She wondered again at Hap Taylor's question: Did anyone in her family die of old age?

At the base of the hollow, a small fire burned.

Kira drew closer to the flame. On either side of it, assault rifles stood stacked into short towers. Bolts were open, magazines removed. The firelight gleamed on the weapons' metal surfaces.

In answer to her unspoken question, a voice spoke from beyond the flames.

"I didn't want us to be disturbed."

Crouched on a jagged piece of granite, at first, and second, glance he seemed to be one more shadow on the valley floor.

Kira looked him over. He was bald and bearded. His bare chest and shoulders were smeared with something dark, and the shapeless black garment over his legs melted into the storm-dark forest around him.

His voice was low and scraping, and his eyes gleamed with points of reflected fire.

"You must be Temple."

"NICE PLACE YOU got here." Temple gestured with one arm.

"Heart of this county," Kira said. "My stepmother always figured it was the courthouse, and Old Man Taylor thought it was that house he stole off my mother's father, but every bit of it started right here."

"Taylor spoke well of you."

"He wasn't a good man, but he was something."

"Why did you burn down his house?"

"Same reason you tore out his heart, I reckon."

Kira wondered at the calm she felt, like a sheet of ice between the world and her fear. She expected sweaty palms, a thumping heart. Not this sheet of ice between the world and her fear.

"And why is that?"

Damage to his vocal chords: Every word was the scrape of a shovel filling an unmarked grave.

"You wanted to send a message."

"And you wanted to erase it."

"Taylor's men used that house as a rallying point. As a symbol. You wanted to scare the crap out of those men. So did I."

"Mine was better."

"You paved the way for a new leader. They were gonna knuckle under and follow whoever hired you. I burned the whole mess to the ground."

"And writing on the side of the barn?"

"That," she said, "was for you."

Laughter, like scraps of tree bark torn away and thrown to the wind.

"You're something, you know that?"

"So I've been told."

"Not many talk to me like that," Temple said. "Not many talk to me at all, and those that do are mostly half pissing themselves when they do it. You, you're not afraid at all."

"Truth to tell, I figured by this point one of us would be dead."

"There's always time for dead." Something like a smile moved under his beard. "Right now I'm enjoying this."

"Ask you something?"

One hand moved in the shadows. *'By all means'*, the gesture said.

"Who hired you?"

"Two of Taylor's lieutenants. Men who wanted to move up by vivid example."

"And these?" She meant the guns stacked beside the fire.

"Same men. They thought maybe they wouldn't pay me."

"I see." Kira hated the next question, but she had to ask. "And Hap Taylor, he wasn't any part of this?"

"What, the son? The one in that ridiculous yellow Corvette?"

"He didn't hire you?"

Lightning flashed. A bright flicker.

Temple unfolded from his rock. One limb moved at a time, a strange insectile grace.

"That's enough," Kira said. Her palm hovered inches over the gun butt. Her entire body lived in that hand.

Temple stopped. Stood across from her, hands out at his sides.

Hard to tell, but he seemed amused.

"Was Hap Taylor one of the ones hired you?" she said. "It's a simple question."

"Didn't you hear? I left pieces of your sweetheart all over the town square."

Something in him coiled. Tensed. His shock at Kira's laughter was genuine.

"Hap's still alive, you dumb son of a bitch. Least he was last time I saw him. Swore up and down he didn't have anything to do with this, must have been the first time a Taylor actually told the truth."

"Son of a bitch." Temple shook his head. "He got away, huh?"

"Wasn't him in that car."

"Don't suppose you know where I can find him?"

"I find that out, I'll kill him myself."

"I thought you two were—"

"We were. Until he hit me with a shovel and buried me alive."

Temple's shoulders shook. That torn-bark laughter rose out of him again.

Somewhere behind Kira, thundered rolled.

"I like you," Temple said. "You've got grit."

Kira flexed the fingers of her right hand.

"I'm starting to wonder, do I even need to kill you."

"Pardon?"

"No money in it for me, no professional pride. All it'd be is a waste of a beautiful woman."

"I'm not beautiful."

"Strange time to argue the point." Temple's voice was layered with menace.

"A woman gets tired of just being looked at."

"I already said you got grit. Takes more balls than any man I've known to come out here alone, wearing a gun that's half as big as you and twice as old."

"My grandfather's," Kira admitted.

"And you'd have walked right into an ambush." He gestured at the stacked weapons. "Big brass balls and not a lick of sense."

"That's what you might call a family trait."

" You know how many like you I've killed over the years? It ain't even worth considering."

"Going soft in your old age?"

Temple snorted. The sound was warmly and distinctly human.

"I ain't getting paid, and you give me no personal reason to want you dead." One long fingered hand stroked the matted beard.

"You know how many have got to say they met Temple and lived? Count your blessings, girl. Go home. Have your babies. Tell your stories. Live your life."

He eased back. Shadow swallowed his figure, the welcome embrace of an old friend.

He was giving her a pass. The most dangerous killer in five states, the man whose name meant death, ugly death, all over the underworld, was letting Kira go.

Her palm found the butt of her gun.

"Think you forgot something."

He froze in place. Barely visible in the forest shadow, his eyes points of burning light.

"You killed my mom."

Kira raised the Colt and fired.

ONE SHOT.

The Colt revolver was a storm in Kira's hand: its muzzle flash was a sheet of lightning, its shot the sound of thunder. The kick of it, that jolting impact up her arm and through her body, left her in no doubt that she controlled elemental forces.

Temple was a blur of motion. His black garment fluttered and snapped, his charge tracing an unpredictable path for Kira's heart.

A flash of steel. Kira ducked, went over backwards. The thrown hatchet sliced air, a kiss on her forehead.

She held onto the gun as she fell, the barrel trained on the rushing black shape before her.

Everything happened so fast.

The palm of her left hand fanned the hammer back, shot after shot.

The forest floor smacked between her shoulder blades

Temple loomed above her, a darkness that threatened to swallow her whole.

A blade gleamed, long and wicked.

The Colt clicked down on an empty chamber.

The blade slashed. Kira clubbed at the wrist with the heavy gun barrel.

Bright pain, just below her chin. Blood poured, even as the blade tumbled away.

Bald head and burning eyes filled her vision. She clubbed again, willing the gun butt to break those features.

The blow was weak.

The blow was nothing.

His hands were slippery on her bleeding throat.

His fingers were strong.

Blackness.

KIRA WOKE TO RAIN on her face. The air above her head was shimmering and green. Points of light fell to burst, wet and cool and life-giving, against her skin.

She raised a hand to her aching throat. The enormous Colt revolver rose into her vision.

She used her other hand.

Sitting up brought dizziness and pain, and a fresh rush of blood from the knife wound. She clamped her hand tighter on the cut, and the blood slowed.

Temple knelt at the edge of the clearing. His back was covered in mud and stones. Kira followed the ragged dirty track his passage carved in the forest floor.

The rain ran in pink slicks down her legs. An awful lot of blood was being washed away.

A drift of leaves had blown up on one side of the killer. His hands lay in his lap, turned to the sky. Rainwater gathered in his palms.

He stared, sightless and blind, into the forest before him.

The forest he hadn't quite reached.

What Kira had taken for mud and stones were actually meat and bone.

Exit wounds.

All five of her bullets had carved great chunks from his torso. Still Temple had been able to cut her throat, to strangle her til she stopped moving.

To cut her throat.

She was sitting down. She hadn't been aware of it, but there she was, on her ass in the mud and the rain, Temple's blood washing away from her, her own blood oozing quietly between her fingers.

Easiest thing in the world to lie down. Just ease over onto her side and close her eyes.

She pushed with her legs. Put the hand holding the gun on Temple's shoulder to steady her.

He toppled. She stood.

She had a long walk ahead of her, back to the car.

Then, if she wanted to live, she had to drive like hell.

SIX MONTHS LATER

"ALRIGHT, BOYS. RIGHT there's fine."

Rough earth scraped his knees. The black hood was pulled from his head.

Even before they took off the hood, Hap Taylor knew where he was. The only place he could be. The only place he was ever going to end up.

Even so, part of him was glad: There was nothing in this world like the sounds and smells of Georgia in the spring.

He blinked in the sudden brightness. Light became shapes, became sight again.

An enormous round belly filled his vision. Somewhere beyond, a familiar face.

"Kira, you're looking good."

He tried the old smile, a sideways shake of the head.

To his surprise, she smiled back.

"Such a liar." For all the menace in the gun at her hip and the gold star pinned to the holster, the warmth in her voice seemed real.

"Truth."

"I'm fat and I'm scarred and you know it."

"Little extra looks good on you, and the scar," he lowered his voice. "Well, just between you and me and the fence post there, I always did think pirate chicks were sexy."

She blushed. Same as she had back when.

For the first time since he'd heard his name spoken in Juarez, Hap felt something that, if not hope, was certainly its kin.

He dared to look up, to look past her. The yard was a hive of activity. Folks going this way and that, everybody brisk about his business. Maybe half of those moving around the yard wore deputies' uniforms. The others were a type Hap remembered all too well— a lot of scars and prison tattoos.

"This place looks good in the spring," she said. "Can't remember a time I saw everything so green."

The land was indeed a green riot. Wildflowers Hap hadn't seen since he was a kid. Birds singing and chattering. He couldn't spot it, but the breeze definitely carried a faint trace of honeysuckle.

"Look, Kee, what I did—"

"Don't worry about it."

"I know it was wrong, I just—"

"I said don't worry." A flat edge of command in her voice now.

"All that's in the past," she said. "You were scared and you panicked and I don't hold it against you."

"Well then, you think you could untie me?"

"Boys." Rough hands on his arms and shoulders. A blade snicked the zip ties from his wrists, he fell forward when they let go.

"Let's walk."

She meant Hap. He pushed himself up from his knees.

Kira didn't look back. Like his father that way: used to being obeyed.

"They weren't too hard on you?"

Hap rubbed at his wrists and thought about the best way to answer.

"Nothing worth complaining about."

"Good. Some of these fellas get a little enthusiastic sometimes."

"I—" He was about to start back in on apologizing but caught the look on Kira's face.

"I see you did a bit of remodeling."

"Whole county. Your daddy left me everything I needed— we're fixing up town, extending some of the paved roads, next couple years building a school."

"I meant the house."

"Well, between a truck crashing into the side of the house and the place burning halfway down, it needed some work."

They were both silent a moment. Kira fierce, Hap watchful. They both knew who had set that fire.

"You seem different," Hap said at last.

"I am different."

He stepped in close. That old heat flared up between them.

"Not that different," he said.

Her mouth rose, softened. He kissed her, tender as the flowers budding around them.

His fingertips went to her waist. She stopped him with a palm flat on his chest.

"Maybe not that different," she said. "But different enough."

He touched the swell of her belly. Felt what the loose shirt had disguised.

"Is this why you brought me back?"

Wonder and terror fizzed in his blood.

"Kee, am I going to be a daddy?"

"Maybe." She stepped back, out of his reach. "Suppose that remains to be seen."

"But—"

"Sit down over here a minute. I'm carrying a bit of a load."

It was insane. She gestured at a patch of bare earth, small green shoots just poking up through, and Hap thought she meant sit on the ground. But before she'd taken three steps, hard men were running with furniture. There was a table, and two chairs. Iced tea and two glasses. A goddamned sun umbrella.

These convicts and killers set up an on-the-spot cafe, and Kira acted like it was the most normal thing in the world.

"I know you must have missed the tea," she said. "Nowhere else in the world does it quite right."

Hap rubbed at his wrists and stared at her belly. Sitting down, it was a lot easier to see. And her tits, how on earth had he missed those?

"You know, I do have a question or two about this." She rubbed her stomach and took another sip of tea. Ice cubes clinked in her glass, and the world around them smelled green and growing.

"For one thing," she said, "I've had a fair few months now to ask myself how it happened."

"I seem to remember a film strip in health class…"

"Not the time."

"Sorry."

"You surprised me that night at the house, but I got that Plan B — the morning after pill? An embarrassing experience, I can tell you. And then to have it not work…"

Her face changed as the penny dropped.

"It didn't work because I was already pregnant. You son of a bitch."

"You didn't remember?"

"Remember what?"

"That night, in the woods outside the juke joint. I thought you were—"

"Well I wasn't." Her hands went to her belly. "Oh, she just kicked." The smile she gave Hap was magic.

"Never trust a Taylor." But there was warmth and amusement when she said it.

"You said 'she'?"

"Yup, a little girl. I'm naming her Grace."

"For your step— for your mom."

Hap knew how a soldier felt, when his boot touched the edge of a mine. Or a camper bathing in a stream, seeing a cottonmouth swim past.

Kira set her half-finished tea on the table— Hap's was still untouched— and stood up. In seconds they once more stood in an empty field.

She ambled forward, her walk different now he noticed. Hap moved to catch up.

"You know, Kira, if I'd known..."

"That's not why I brought you back."

"Oh?"

"I know who killed my brother, Hap."

"Hey now, I don't know who's been—"

"When you cut his brake lines, you left your prints all over the wheel well."

He searched her eyes. They were blue and hard.

He looked down at his own hands, burning as the blood returned.

"Why'd you do it, Hap? Just because he was taking your daddy away?"

Hap's hands blurred. Tears smeared his vision, and his upper lip trembled out of control.

"You god damn fool," she said. "Sheriff Grace didn't get a print worth a damn, but your face just told it all. I can't believe I just out-bluffed a Taylor."

Hap was crying in earnest now.

"Are you going to kill me now?"

"I will admit the thought has crossed my mind."

Her hand rested on the butt of her gun. Fingertips stroked the leather just above the gold star. She didn't seem to notice she was doing it.

"Thing is, you've put me in a hard place, Hap. You killed my brother, my last kin, and that calls for blood. But you gave me my baby, this family's start, and that does deserve a certain amount of consideration."

"What, what are you gonna do?"

"Come on down here, out onto the road. And for god's sakes, clean your face."

He thought about running, but there were her men, here and there around the place, and that gun at her hip.

He followed her down the drive.

"The house isn't the only wreck I had fixed up. Cost a fair penny, but…"

The dirt road was a lane and a half of red Georgia clay. Wildflowers bloomed on either side, colors so bright they all but shouted.

Two vintage black Chargers crouched on that dirt road. Wheels almost in the gravel at the outside edges, door handles almost kissing in the center.

"I'm going to take the one your daddy gave me," Kira said. "I'm used to it and, if I'm being honest here, it always reminds me of that day in the barn."

"I remember."

"That means you've got Jack's car. My father's, but Jack was the last one to drive it, so you see what I mean."

Hap wiped at his lips with numb fingers. The last time he'd seen that car had been the middle of the night, crouched down beside the wheel well with his pocketknife.

"What are you doing, Kee?"

"Drag race. You and me, straight line all the way down to the curve at the end. There's room enough for one car to make that turn, that's how we'll know the winner."

"This isn't right."

"That's rich, coming for the guy who killed my brother, got me pregnant, hit me with a shovel and left me for dead."

"You said you didn't hold that against me."

"This is a fair chance. More than you gave me, or Jack."

"I can't race you, Kira."

"You might want to try."

Again, her fingers tapping that holster.

"But, you know what they say, nobody drives like a Stone."

"Nothing to it." Kira eased one hip over the doorsill, moving careful in her pregnancy.

"Just put the hammer down and don't look back."

ACKNOWLEDGMENTS

Many thanks to Iain Gammie, Karen Browning and Hazel Whiteman. The version of this story that they read was not the version in your hands, and I thank them for every bit of help along the way.

Hazel also deserves that extra bit of gratitude for putting up with me. Writers aren't easy to live with, but somehow she manages.

Apologies to the good people of the town that Harrow, Georgia is based on. We went back in 2014 to check details, to soak up the sights and sounds and smells, and to drive those roads-- including that hairpin turn at the end of the lane. An awful lot has changed since I used to visit my grandfather every summer (some of the roads are paved now!), and somehow you've managed to keep all the best of your community while leaving behind the worst of the parts I wrote about.

And of course, Charlie. I wrote that 'crazy surprise twist' at the end with no idea that you had been conceived a week earlier. As I write this now, you're one week old because yes, rewrites take me awhile. :)

I love you Charlotte Grace Malley.

ABOUT THE AUTHOR

Steve Malley is an American living in New Zealand. He tattoos from The Ink Spot in Christchurch, on the South Island. Because he travels all over the world and everybody knows writing and drawing aren't real careers, his mother has decided he must be a secret agent.

PREVIOUS TITLES

Poison Door
Crossroad Blues
Blood and Skin

Short Stories

Hayley
Emma